DARK WORKINGS OF
WILD WOMEN

DARK WORKINGS OF WILD WOMEN

DONNA J. W. MUNRO

Dragon's Roost Press

Dark Workings of Wild Women is published by Dragon's Roost Press.

This anthology is © 2025 Donna J.W. Munro and Dragon's Roost Press.

Artwork by Tara Gibbs-Tokarski

Printed in the United States of America

Ingram ISBN: 978-1-956824-62-9

Print ISBN: 978-1-956824-63-6

Digital ISBN: 978-1-956824-61-2

Dragon's Roost Press

2470 Hunter Rd.

Brighton, MI 48114

thedragonsroost.biz

PUBLICATION ACKNOWLEDMENTS

"A Rosie by Another Name" *Imps and Minions* From T-Dot, 2019

"After Saving Hansel, Gretel Found Herself " *Corvid Queen*, 2019

"Besties" *Blood and Ashes* from 13 O'Clock Press, 2018

"Bone Hives" *Earth: Elemental Series* from Eerie River Publishing, 2022

"Feeling Sorry for Assholes" *Blood and Ashes* from Hellbound 2040Books, 2019

"Flood and Melancholy" *Borderlands*, 2020 and *Monstrom* from Madness Heart Press, 2023

"Four Horsemen of the Happy Hour" *Penumbric Magazine*, 2021

"From Above" *Women Destroy Science Fiction* from Weretraveler, 2021

"Grandma Needs a Visit" *Branching Out* from International Tales of Brilliant Flash Fiction, 2021

"Hall of Windows, Hall of Lights" *The Gray Sisters V.2*, 2020

"Haunted Castle" *Mithilda*, 2020

"Hell is Other People" *Graveyard Girls* from Hellbound Books, 2018

"Her Teeth are Long and Full of Venom" *Electric Spec*, 2022 and *The Other Stories Podcast*, 2024

"It Rises from Between My Bones" *Pseudopod*, 2021

"Lady Lampshade" *Post-Roe Alternatives: Fighting Back* from B-Cubed Press, 2022.

"Lady Monstrosity" *Dark Descending* from Pixie Forrest, 2022

"Made of Crows" *365 Tomorrows*, 2022

"My Clay Head" *Jack O'Lantern* from Wicked Shadow, 2023

"Parade of the Loyal" *Immortal Works* from Flash Fiction Fridays, 2019

"Progress and the Shawnee Bend Witch" *Song for the Elephant Man* from Mantle Press, 2019

"Sink" *Water: Elemental Series* from Eerie River Publishing, 2023

"The Organ Trade" *Locked In* from 13 O'Clock, 2018

"Three Graces in Autumn" *The Gray Sisters V.1*, 2020

"What Happened to Heather After J. D. Exploded" *Creepy Pod* Patreon Feed, 2022

"Women of a Certain Age" *Blood and Ashes* from 13 O'Clock Press, 2018

*For all the women who taught me what being a woman was beyond
SUGAR AND SPICE.*

*There are too many great women to list, but Julia Fisch is my forever
bestie. More than one story in this collection is influenced by her
constant friendship and love.
Boop, Judy Fitch.*

*And as always, Matt Munro, who is my beloved. Thanks for
believing all the time.*

CONTENTS

MAIDEN

MOTHER

CRONE

BADASSES

MAD WOMEN

MONSTERS

MAIDEN

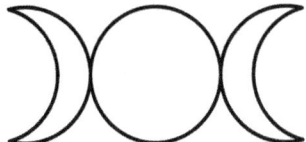

Women begin as girls. Innocent, malleable, angry.

A ROSIE BY ANY OTHER NAME

WHAT DID I EXPECT? Of all my children, only Grendella has a heart of gold.

The others are hell-spawn. Rightly so!

But Grendella finds beauty in the hideous and charm in the nasty. Her pug nose and ruddy cheeks shine with excitement when the sky lights up in the fire of a sunset, which is the work of our nemesis if ever I've seen it.

More than once, I've wanted to pitch her from the battlements. The sunshine that pours from her giggling mouth illuminates the corners where the damned hide. Her fingers trail along the spines of my *Necronomicon*s while she sings a song about daisies. Daisies! No flower is more repugnant to hell, with its cheery white petals bonneting a sun-yellow face.

My wife, Morguen, swore that Grendella would grow out of her goodness. A demonic responsibility might fix her, I thought. My intentions were bad. You know what they say about bad intentions.

I drew my pentacle and called up a lower demon, misshapen like a dog in a larger dog's skin. Lion's head without the fur crown. Teeth and horns, of course. What kind of demon would it be without those?

I called it forth, trapping it in the star.

"What do you wish, mortal?" The beastie grumbled. The pain of the containing fire burned blue across its body.

"You'll be servant to Grendella."

The demon licked his lips.

"I'm claimed, beast. I desire you for my child."

It cocked its head, listening to the voices of hell confirming all I'd said. "Fine. . .Master." The thing's pointed tongue lolled across the words as if they tasted sweet.

That evening, during dinner, my children reported their workings. The eldest caused a fire that burned the school to the ground. My middle boy pushed an old woman climbing a stairway. She won't be climbing ever again. Grendella picked at her plate of roasted entrails. She probably had nothing to report, of course. My heart quakes when I think of a child of mine being so damned good.

"Grendella, you know we all must work to uphold our vile reputation with the Lord of the Flies. What evil did you create today?"

She squirmed, avoiding the accusing glances of her siblings. Finally, she looked up and gave me her bravest face. "I tried, really. But whatever I do turns out . . ."

"Good?" Morguen asked.

"I have a solution." I nodded to our servant. He retrieved the beast I'd conjured and dumped it into Grendella's lap. The creature's teeth clacked as its pewter-skinned body sagged against her. Its head lolled, and saucer eyes shot with blood and yellow light fixed on hers. The demon sprayed stench, brimstone, and rot from its pores.

Morguen laughed, knowing that a demon would work against Grendella's goodness at every opportunity. Perhaps our youngest might be damned yet.

That night, Morguen came to our chamber shaking her head.

"What?" I peered over my studies for spellmaking and the many uses of flayed skin.

"Your plan isn't working. Go see Grendella's latest project." She huffed. "Deal with this mess before it becomes something we'll answer for."

My wife never minces words. Worshippers of Satan don't hide behind niceties and kindnesses that are a waste of time. We say truth because truth is the sharpest knife.

I made my way down the hall, ancestors grumbling from their stern portrait perches. Not for the first time, I wondered what they thought of my youngest daughter's purity.

I opened her door and stepped into a room we'd draped with black silks and hung with depictions of Dante's *Inferno*, a favorite nursery rhyme for damned children.

Grendella's creature sprawled out, swaddled in soft towels. The puddles on the floor from the bathroom and the wafting scent of lavender led me to believe she'd bathed the demon, perfumed it. And now sat on the floor scratching 'round the base of its horns. She crooned a song into the demon's ear holes with the name she'd chosen—Rosie—woven through the promises of love. It purred. Purred!

"Grendella," I roared. "What have you done?"

She jumped. Flowers tumbled from her hand and landed upon the demon's skin, puncturing it . . . though the creature seemed to enjoy the sensation.

"It felt like I should care for Rosie. It felt . . . right." She caught the problem in her words, and her face fell into a lovely pout. She bit her lip and distractedly placed a final flower upon the creature's head.

That final flower, a sweet kindness, created a cascade. The creature's skin split where the petals touched it and peeled away in clumps, turning first to ash and then to powder that lit the room with a white haze. Its teeth fell away, and the horns turned to ivory all in the space of a soul's fall.

Grendella laughed at the change, which would have been great had the transformation been painful, but the demon sang joy. From the ashes rose a phoenix bird. The soul of a fallen angel redeemed by my daughter's hand! How would I explain this to the bright lord?

"Thank you," Rosie said. Then, it rose on white wings through the peaked roof, gathering trapped souls to ferry away to the other place.

I was doomed!

"Father?" Grendella rose from the bed. "I didn't mean to—"

"Stop, child." I slid to the floor. What would the master say about my losses? About my girl and her abilities? What would the neighbors say?

Grendella sank down next to me as I worried. She put her plump hand on my cheek, cooling the embarrassment with a touch. She hugged me. Not something we encourage, but the warmth of her arms and the sigh of her lemony breath on my neck gave me such joy.

Joy.

I stood and pushed her away from me. "No more of this, child. You must find your evil."

She smiled that gentle grin and said, "I'll try, Father."

In my chest, something panged. Loosened.

Damn it!

PARADE OF THE LOYAL

THE LOYAL GATHERED in our yard.

"Get away from the window." Silent tears rolled down Mama's face as she gathered up the little-uns. "Gretta, take the babies down into the cellar. They won't leave until they get what they came for. I won't let them have you."

I nodded and gathered up the sniffling littles—Joey in his diaper, dirty-faced Judy, Lottie dragging her blankie behind, and the twins, Hope and Hazel, left to us by the neighbors when they went Loyal. We lined up, held hands, and walked quietly to the cellar door. I pecked Mama's cheek and drew the littles down into the basement. They whimpered but kept their sniffles in. We were trained to be quiet.

Mama shut the door and locked us in.

As we got to the bottom of the steps, I heard her through the floor. The Loyal came in, feet slapping on the oak. In my imagination, I saw them circle around Mama, their faces covered by the masks sewed to their skin, circle-glass eyepieces shaded red, and long elephantine nose-hoses to breathe through.

We might never see Mama again.

Dirty-faced Judy reached up and tugged on my sleeve. "I'm scared, Gretta. "

I hugged her up and listened to the shuffling from above.

The poor littles didn't understand the Loyal parades that came every week. They just knew people disappeared. Each of their mothers. Their fathers and grandmas. Now Mama.

"Me too, Judy. Want the story?"

They nodded and pressed in closer.

The shuffling above broke into unorganized thumps. Mama was fighting them.

"Once upon a time, we gave up our president."

Mama's singsong murmurs as she pleaded to be left intact.

"We gave up our old way because we were scared of people, violence, and evil. The blessed leader created the Loyal."

Silence upstairs. My stomach turned, but for the littles, I kept it to myself.

"So the bad guys got changed."

Hope tugged on me. "'Cause we wanted to make them stop, right?"

I nodded. They knew the story. It's the only story we were allowed anymore.

Upstairs, Mama gasped. Joey whimpered against my shoulder, poor baby.

"The Loyal get their brains scrambled so they won't hurt us. They wear the mask so we know them. Can't take it off."

"Mama's not bad, though," Hazel said. "Why are they getting her?"

I shook my head at her. Hazel's old enough to know better. Questions are illegal. She and Hope were the next oldest, and they couldn't be babies anymore after today.

"The Loyal work for the blessed leader, and now we are safe again. The more Loyal, the more safe."

Mama screamed, and I knew it was almost over upstairs. She'd be gone, then I'd be Mama. I wish I could run away or sneak the kids off into the woods. But the parades of the Loyal never stopped. There was no escape.

"Someday, we will all be Loyal." They all said with me, ending the story as it always did.

The thumping upstairs unified again as they marched Mama away. The marching never stopped.

"Gretta—"

"Mama, now," I said.

"Mama, when they come to get you, will they take us too?"

"Eventually."

Joey's thumb popped out of his mouth long enough to ask, "Why does the blessed leader need everyone?"

Lottie's wide brown eyes watched him and them me, shifting back and forth.

I shrugged and pulled Lottie into my lap, petting her soft yellow hair.

"I don't know."

I watched their sweet faces and understood their confusion. Sometimes I wondered if it wouldn't be better to let the Loyals get us all now. Get it over with. But then I remember what my real mother said before they took her.

"You children will fix our mess someday," she said when we hid together. "We gave him our freedoms to feel safe. You kids won't be as scared as us."

Her words seemed like a gift back then. Back when the world still had families, occupations, differences, and the blessed leader had a name. I believed her.

Now that I was Mama, looking into the eyes of my new babies as they watched me for rules and protections, I didn't see her words as a gift. They were chains.

I shook out of the memory and stood, pulling the kids up to their feet. We needed to eat and clean up and find things to burn for heat.

"What happens when we all are Loyal?" Hope dusted herself off.

I thought about it as I pulled Joey up onto my hip and stepped onto the stairs.

"I guess we'll finally be safe."

WHAT HAPPENED TO HEATHER MCNAMARA AFTER J. D. BLEW UP

ALL I ever wanted to be was Cyndi Lauper. Bright red hair shaved on the sides, bustier and tulle skirt, face like the happy mask from a theater, a voice that sang with the strangeness of the time. Big hair, lace gloves, shoulder pads.

But I was a Heather.

If you know anything about Heathers, there's a code.

No one gets to have red hair or shaved heads or strange voices.

I was blond, a cheerleader, and a follower.

A follower because Heather was insistent.

Any and every Heather.

I didn't really exist without them. Them and Veronica.

By the time I'd become the number three, I'd given up on my own thoughts, my own path.

Until Heather died.

And Ram and Chandler.

I thought about killing myself because everyone was doing it.

Because I heard the echoes of their voices in every song.

As people lied about knowing Heather or caring about Ram

and Chandler, I whirled through the hallway, as light as an autumn leaf and just as dead.

Veronica made them ghosts.

Made them gods.

Made them real.

No amount of Aqua-Net or neon yellow was going to do that for me.

"Poor Little Heather" was what they said when I reached out for help.

If everyone jumped off a bridge, would I? "Probably," I'd said to Veronica.

The thing is, her story went on. She and J. D. almost blew up the school. They overthrew the Heathers from within. Then Veronica saved us all.

Saint Veronica walks among the geeks and the freaks lifting them up.

No time for Tweety.

My story felt . . . unfinished.

I was the nice Heather.

The accepting Heather.

Dumb, weak, victim Heather.

I'd had enough.

When the bomb blew up outside the school while we cheered and chanted in the gym, something inside me exploded too.

Veronica had stopped me when I'd tried to end it in the second-floor girls' lav. She'd squeezed my cheeks and made me spit out all the pills. I could have been gone, floating on a cloud with Ram or—even better—without him.

I could have been . . . real.

Sometimes at night, I screamed with the pain.

Knowing she was in the world twisted like a knife in my head.

Veronica and J. D. had changed the whole world. Made it

over in their image. And when I asked for meaning, violence was the answer that they gave.

I had been Heather McNamara—cheerleader, quiet beauty, blond and blue-eyed. I shed her the way a snake sheds skin to grow.

I split open, and what came out was rougher. Meaner.

I found Veronica the night of prom in her room at home. She was watching VHS slasher movies with Martha and Betty, losers she'd lifted from the social swamp of Westerberg HS. I climbed up the same trellis J. D. had. I watched them fuss and fawn over Veronica. She smiled like Madonna . . . no. Like Cyndi in the "Girls Just Want to Have Fun" video. Damn it. She was Cyndi.

I could never be.

There wasn't room for me in her story.

I waited for Martha and Betty to leave.

I followed Betty to her car.

She was Veronica's memories because she knew her the longest, so I used a rock, and I cracked open Betty's head. I picked out the pieces of bone and scooped out the pinkish-white flesh inside. I didn't eat it because, ew. But I put it in my fanny pack for later. No need for a suicide note. I wanted people to know it was me. I wanted to be made real, and I wasn't sharing the credit with Betty's bluing corpse.

Martha had decided to walk home. Ever since the accident, she'd been different. Veronica had lifted her up, sat with her at lunch, called out to her in the hall. Martha smiled more. She slimmed down a bit . . . not like skinny or anything. Just healthier. And she reached out to others and lifted them up in kind.

The girl was all heart.

Veronica's heart.

I'd be sorry to kill her, but for me to be real, like Veronica and J. D. and Heather and . . . and . . . It didn't matter.

I caught up with her and fell into step next to her, but she didn't see me. I was covered in Betty's blood, and my mall bangs were flat from my sweat, but I was still invisible. I had been since Veronica saved me.

"You can't hear me, can you?" I asked.

No reaction.

She turned down Elm Drive and picked up her pace, walking out of Veronica's neighborhood and across the tracks into the trailer park. She whistled as she walked right through me. She felt like Cyndi sounded when she sang "Time After Time"—all wistful and sweet. She opened the door of a trailer and walked in. I watched her move from room to room through the windows, to the back of the trailer. She turned off her lights, and I saw the glow of a TV cast against her

I wanted to be real so bad. Like Kim Cattrell in *Mannequin* finally come to life, only with bigger hair.

I needed Martha's heart.

I slipped into the trailer where an old woman snored on the couch with a little rabbit-eared TV that hissed static to the darkened little room. There weren't any chef's knives out like you'd see in *Halloween* or some other slasher flick, but I found a sturdy knife in a drawer and headed for Martha's room.

She was curled up on a tiny bed watching MTV. The latest Big Fun video played bright with bold letters flashing the message of the song—*Teenage Suicide (Don't Do It)*.

I was way past that.

The knife slit her throat before her eyes even focused on me, but as she gurgled and bucked, I think she finally saw me. She even tried to say my name.

My hands were slick with her blood after I sawed open her ribs and cut away the lung and arteries that caged her heart in her chest. Once I had it in my hand, I marveled at how small it was. I'd expected something so much bigger.

I shoved it into my fanny pack, slipped out of the window, and hit the ground running.

At Veronica's house, I threw pebbles at her window and

waited for her to come down to the backyard. We'd always played croquet there, and it seemed like the best place for her to see me and remember me.

She stepped out of the house, still wearing the red scrunchy she'd taken from the other Heathers. Her crown. Maybe even her halo.

"Heather? Is that you?"

I stood in the shadowed pool of the elm tree, hoping the dark hid my sin.

"It's me."

"What are you doing?"

I took a deep breath and all the words rushed out. "You saved the other Heathers and made over Betty and Martha, but you forgot me. We were supposed to be best friends, remember? And you forgot me. You didn't come for me and I got lost, but . . . I . . ." The words were savage in my mouth.

And all she had in her eyes was pity.

I didn't say it right. I never did. Pretty, but just in the background. Useful, but only when something dumb needed doing. I was a victim.

"Make me real, Veronica. Make me real, because it would be so very."

And I took the bit of brain and the heart out of my pack and held them out for her to see.

"I brought these for you . . ."

Veronica didn't flinch. She'd seen death and gore before.

"Who are those from, Heather?"

And just then, I couldn't speak.

Sometimes I didn't know what to say. It was part of who I was.

I advanced into the moonlight, holding the bits of her out for her to see.

I found a word.

"Please."

I stood a head taller than her, but she seemed to loom up.

"Please, Veronica."

"You killed them, Heather. All Heathers are monsters. All of you." She took a step back and folded her arms, ignoring my gifts.

"Make me real, and I'll be better."

"You'll always be a Heather."

I crushed her memory and her heart in my fists.

She wasn't going to help me. I fell to my knees and screamed, but no one would hear me.

"Stop it, Heather. I can't make you real. You have to do that. You can't steal meaning. You can't take someone's brains or heart and expect to use them. You have to have your own."

But I don't.

How I wanted to kill her. What made her better than me? Her brown hair? Her edgy smile? Her fucking name?

I was on her in a second. She's no athlete, and I am. Good thing I'd kept the knife.

I peeled her like a banana.

It was a tight fit, but skin stretches. I made my way inside and found her stapler. I washed off and got dressed, pulling the red scrunchy onto my new brown hair.

I became Veronica.

They'd have to see me now.

And maybe, once they saw me, I'd dye my hair bright red.

Like Cyndi.

MY CLAY HEAD

I KEEP my thoughts in the clay head I fashioned after Daddy threw me down the stairs.

It's an ugly thing. Bulbous eyes and a nose so childish it looks drawn on. Lips puckered like flat worms perch over a pointed chin.

It's nicer than the head on my neck, though.

My attendant, Lissy, gently lifts me from my bed and puts me in the wheelchair in the morning. Even though I'm twenty-five, I'm small, and she says it's no trouble.

I still worry that I'm a burden to her, even as she shows me so much care.

Daddy doesn't look in my eyes when she wheels me up to the dining table. Her quiet spooning of soup and tutting as she wipes my lips exist in a different reality than where Mommy and Daddy sit at the other end of the table with Jacob and Rachel, whispering their lives between bites.

They never look at me. It's like they think their silence will erase me from their lives.

I can't speak through my shattered mouth. My tongue died the day I bit it off bouncing down the stairs. My windpipe crushed against my larynx on the last impact, robbing me forever of my voice.

But I listen.

The details of their lives go into my clay head when Lissy wheels me back up into my room.

At night, I pull myself into the chair and wheel down the hall to the elevator. The house is quiet. Only dust and moonlight pools interrupt the deep dark I swim in. Only my soft, whooshing wheels against the deep runners in the halls interrupt the studious silence. I stop in front of each of their bedrooms, pressing my hand to the doors to collect their dreams and thoughts.

The selfish wishes of a life when mine is so far from what I'd hoped for.

When I get back upstairs, they all go straight into my clay head.

The next morning, I make my way back to Daddy's office with Lissy trailing close behind. He's on the phone screaming at some client about their short-sighted reaction to the market. His anger soaks into me like heat from a blanket, warming my fingers and the palms of my hands. He looks up at me between calls, and his face crumples.

"What the fuck, Lissy? Take her ass out of my room before I fire you. Do you think I want to look at that mess?"

When she returns me to my room, I push my fingers into the ever-wet surface of my clay head, lacing all that I feel between the other thoughts I've put there. All the things I know are fibrous threads, weaving an image of the family's wants and needs.

I know what Mommy wants.

It would be easier for her if I wasn't here.

Secrets are easy to keep when they live in the attic behind heavy locked doors. They are hidden, and sometimes, they waste away. They'd like it if I wasted away. It would be a relief.

Then Jacob could win the cup for his debate skills.

Rachel could premier as the most eligible deb.

Mommy could have her parties.

Daddy could ignore the dent in the stair where my head smashed open.

He caused that dent because he didn't approve of my "lifestyle."

Lissy was . . .

Lissy went by Gloria then. We'd been together from the first day we met in the dorms at college. Love at first sight. Inseparable and hot in a way I'd never felt with the boys at the country club mixers who used to paw at me with entitled hands and highball breath. With Gloria, I was free and happy. I was myself.

Those memories swirl in the surface of my clay head, sweet and sour, sticky and prickly all at once.

After graduation, I wanted to introduce her to the family. We'd decided to move away to be who we are in the open, away from Mommy and Daddy. I thought maybe if we were far enough away, they'd let us be together. We never got that far.

Then . . . I fell.

Gloria became Lissy to care for me. It was the only way they'd ever let her near me again.

Sometimes, it's almost enough.

Now, Lissy and I spend every night together. Her sitting in the corner, singing me songs, telling me stories to bring me back to before.

How I love her.

She watches me press my fingers into the wet clay, teaching it about my family, implanting every slight. Molding in each hurt until the clay is hot and angry in my fingers. She must feel the things I give as it passes between. I give the clay my pain because there's nowhere else for it to go. I sag as the exhaustion takes me.

Filling my clay head takes something out of me.

Puts part of me into the soft red clay.

Then Lissy wraps around me, whispering into my torn ear about how she still loves me.

How she will never love again after me.

Daddy took her from me, as sure as he took all my dreams.

She stays. She takes care of me, and I love her.

But he took her just the same.

He thought I was done.

Smaller.

But I took the clay and pressed all of what I was into it.

Then, I pressed all of what they did into it.

As I did, it started to breathe.

Now, it growls.

Tonight, I wheeled out and caught my daddy.

He'd found Lissy in the hall bringing up some tea and had pressed her into the side of the hall, his fleshy mouth against her neck and his hand up her shirt. She struggled and shrieked, but he kept at her, his other hand covering her mouth.

My clay head is ready.

I press it to my neck, and the wet bits push into my skin, fusing with my spine. I stand once it laces in and feel all that hate. All that heat and power-flow I'd stored flow back into me.

He doesn't see me coming.

Thoughts are power.

Hate is fuel.

"Daddy," I say as I pull him off her and lift him above my head.

Lissy screams. I knew she would, since she couldn't know what to think about my new second head and my shambling gait.

"Daddy," I say as I carry him down the hall, whipping and flailing above my head. Mommy and Jacob and Rachel come out of their rooms screaming, but they can't get Daddy out of my hands. They don't follow when my head turns and growls.

"Daddy," I say through both mouths as I throw him down the stairs.

Then Mommy.

Then Jacob.

Then Rachel.

I turn to Lissy and try to kiss her, now that I have my mouth back. How long had it been since I'd been able to return her love? Since the accident, my mouth is a ruin, but my clay head lips work well enough. I press a kiss on her gaping mouth, but my clay head doesn't know how to do it. How to brush softly or to temper passion.

It smashes into her face with all the love I'd pressed into its reddish skin each day. The pent-up passion flows out, along with my rage.

The clay seals her lips so she can't breathe.

No matter how much I love her, my love can't help her breathe through the press of my clay tongue inside her throat.

Soon, she lays next to my family.

My clay head cries when we put them into the furnace.

My clay head weeps for each of them in turn.

They'd fed it from the first day it had ears.

They're all the clay head knows.

I cried only for Gloria, who'd never thought to take me away from here. To save us from them and from ourselves.

Me and my clay head.

HAUNTED CASTLE ON THE MIDWAY

LEANING against the arcade's coin machine, Molly watched summer people walking the midway and wished, like them, she could just leave. The knotted ties of her three-pocketed apron around her waist might as well have been chains. What had started as a summer job until she went to college turned into a sad little career after she flunked out. Too many nights of pot-smoking at the quarry instead of going to class. As she leaned, she hummed a song she couldn't quite remember, "Push, push, push."

"Miss? The Donkey Kong ate my quarter." A boy with more glasses than face looked up at her.

"Here." She gave him a quarter from her apron without a second glance.

The midway creaked with age. Gray boards rattled as people walked. But as old as the midway was, people still came, drawn to the charm of a bygone era, to ride the carousel's hand-painted horses, to snuggle in one of the Ferris wheel's tippy steel cages.

After three years at the arcade, she wasn't distracted by the summer folks. Flirty boys living on their parents' dime looking for kicks with trashy locals stopped being fun years before.

No, Molly's serious pursuit, besides babysitting video games, was being a scholar of the midway, watching the people filter through—observing their likes, what they spent money on, and what they avoided.

The haunted castle.

Perched near the end of the flickering neon strip past the Skee-Ball and the test-your-strength machine. Beyond it, the dark of the hills swallowed the buzzing light in gulps, leaving a blackness deeper than the night's violet sky. Molly watched the haunted castle with every spare second she had.

It was growing.

There's been three sets of blacked-out windows one day, and then five sets the next.

The haunted castle won't be photographed, she discovered. Molly tried for years, especially after the first time she'd noticed it stretch. She brought out her phone and pressed the button, but all that showed up was a screen black as pitch, even though she took the picture on a clear summer afternoon in full sun.

She tried again and again and finally gave up.

The library had scrapbooks back to the founding and the first days of cameras, showing the clearing of trees, the earliest facades on the midway, the valley stretched out next to the seaside in picturesque stereo cards. But not one picture of the haunted castle.

"Miss? Donkey Kong . . ."

"Nope. Sorry, guy. The machine ate it once. This one's on you."

The boy blocked her view of the castle.

"I'll tell my dad. He'll make you give me my money."

He bobbed there until she finally broke down and handed him another coin. "Try a different game, kid."

Then he left her alone.

No one ever went in the castle. No one talked about it.

Yet, the lit-up sign flicked with a sick yellow flood of light, red letters aflame in the center with a ghoulish white-skulled creature glaring over the top. The washed-out paint might have been yellow once. Two stories with a pitched roof and no particular style other than a squatting troll.

"Push, push, push." Molly murmured the lyric circling her brain and thought back to when she'd tried to get in a couple of years before.

She'd chickened out with her hand on the doorknob, but not because she was scared. Everyone and everything had ceased when she touched the knob. Summer people froze, and the carousel music's notes quieted. Nothing moved or breathed.

Standing there in the shadow of the building, with the entire town's held breath in her hand, she knew they'd suffer if she went through. That somehow, their lives were wrapped up in or . . . antithetical to the existence of the haunted castle.

To keep them alive, she stayed away.

In her mind, the haunted castle became . . . alive.

Since then, she'd watched it. Watched the tourists cross the street to get away from it. Watched birds fly in circular detours to avoid the airspace above it. Watched it grow.

And the locals didn't know what she was talking about when she mentioned it.

Jenks, the owner of the arcade, only ever said, "What haunted castle?" His gaze slid past the building every time Molly pointed at it.

It was like the building only existed for her.

And the urge to try to open that door writhed in her mind as she leaned every day, watching from the arcade.

It spoke to her.

"Push, push, push."

Made promises as it flexed there at the end of the midway.

She chewed on her thumbnail, considering it. "Should I go in?"

"Anything's better than this," was her answer to herself.

Every lunch break, she locked the arcade door and crossed the street, intending to open the door. She'd stare into its black windows. It beckoned, but she'd turn away, heading home to eat and rest before her second shift.

This time, her feet kept moving until she found herself a breath away from the door, hand hovering over the knob. Then, when she touched the metal, her ears felt stoppered and the stir of wind disappeared. She knew if she turned around, she'd see the whole town frozen mid-step, mid-bite, mid-laugh.

But she couldn't look back. Not if she wanted to finally know what it was.

She turned the knob and stepped into the dark hall. The passage before her narrowed from comfortable to a cramped crawlspace within feet.

She should go back, but if she went back, all she'd see was shadows and ashes of what had been. The world faded with each inch she crawled.

Her eyes stung with the bright heat that churned around her in the passage. The floor softened as she moved, humid and rubbery under her knees and palms. Fleshy.

Molly raised one hand and sniffed. The iron bitterness of blood. Her stomach lurched.

Then it spoke, screaming inside her head.

"MOLLY. MY MOLLY."

"DON'T TOUCH HER!"

The voices felt like something she knew but couldn't name.

She was only her hands and knees and mind inside the house of horror.

The floor dropped from under her, and she tumbled into a space so huge that the inky black swallowed her. She floated, wrapped in heat, sweat dripping from every patch of skin.

"Hello?" Her voice wavered with the trembling of her body. She was nothing. Nothing with thoughts. Nothing alone. And what she knew, floating there, was that the whole world, the midway, the town, and the dark hills weren't real. They were a memory. A cotton blanket muffling the pain of the heat burning her.

"Hello!" she screamed at the voices.

"DON'T TOUCH HER."

Heat exposed every nerve. Fire crackled along the length of her bones.

She was dying.

It all came back.

The stoned make-out session at the quarry with the cute summer boy. Driving home so wasted she'd covered one eye to see without a double. The ravine. Glass and blood and fire and a crunch that collapsed her head.

Someone laying her in an ambulance.

Then the midway.

Molly stretched, screaming. She swam in the hot river of air, deeper and deeper into the dark.

The voices were her mother and her sister.

"DON'T DO IT!" Their desperation a harmony.

The stench hit her. Burning hair, crisped meat. Molly pushed into it, following the scent through the ink. Before her, a pinprick of light appeared and grew. She followed it as it opened up like a window before her.

It bubbled out as she pressed, hanging over the other place.

A white room lit by florescent flickering bulbs, humming. Gray sheets that led to the darkened end of the hospital bed. And herself, in a yellow nightgown, face peeking out like a ghoul, red-webbed wires fanning out to machines filling all the space behind her like wings.

And there, on either side of the bed, her mother and sister wept.

"She's suffering," a doctor at the foot of the bed said. "We kept her alive so you could say your goodbyes, but she's withering. You wouldn't want to be kept—"

"She's in there! I know it." Mama's voice came out like a slap.

And then her sister, Mary, leaned in, whispering into her ear, "Come on, Molly. Push on through. Push, push, push!"

The doctor shook his head, staring at the chart. "She's gone, Alice. Braindead."

Molly pushed. She pressed her whole body against the blazing heat of the barrier between them, stretching it. Every place she touched fought back—stinging, blazing hotter, crisping her flesh into black char.

Push, push, push.

She opened an eye. Only one because the other felt like a rock inside her head.

"Oh my God, look, Mama!" Mary grabbed Molly's hand and squeezed, shifting bones long ago pinned but still a mess of fragments.

The pain rushed in, and Molly panted to get past it, but her lungs didn't work. A machine breathed for her. Five seconds in, five out. She tried to cough to dislodge it, but she was only bright pain and knotted scars.

"See, John?" her mother said, voice triumphant.

Only he'd been right about suffering.

Molly mumbled around the tube in her mouth. "Mrump murph."

"What, sweetie?" her mother asked.

The doctor hurried to her bedside and leaned in. "Say it slower, Molly."

"Urrrpllurr meeehh."

"What?" the doctor asked.

But Mary laid a hand on his shoulder. "I understood. She said, 'Unplug me.'"

Mama wailed, but Molly jerked her head in a nod. It hurt like lightning in her head, but she had to make them see.

Mary leaned in and whispered, "I love you, Molly girl."

Back on the midway, Molly walked out of the haunted castle, where everything stood frozen, just as she'd left it. She spun, enjoying her painless body. Down the midway, the neon lights flickered out in her wake. The song came to her as she walked away, and she mumbled, "I love you, Molly girl."

MOTHER

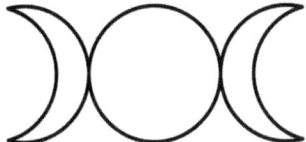

Women create while suffering, fighting, and gutting threats.

SINK

Lia's face reflects the blue of the water as she sinks into it, the little skirt on her suit ruffling up in the water. Her hands reach for me as she slips into the azure water. I scream for her and see every bubble that slips from between her slackening lips as it trails up and pops against the side of the boat.

The others on the boat just keep fishing.

I reach down, even though I know the boat's too tall and the water's too deep.

Why didn't I just jump in after her?

I scream her name and stretch, but my legs are anchors on the deck of the boat. There are fins darting through the chum at the front of the boat. Fins that dart toward her splashes.

And the water goes from bright turquoise to a velvety red.

"Marla, you're dreaming!"

Warm hands shook me out of the nightmare.

Tommy wrapped me up in his arms and rocked me against his chest as I wept and moaned.

"Lia," I cried, though it muffled into his shirt.

He sighed and pulled me into the bathroom. He started a shower and stepped in with me, humming and soaping my hair as the hot water pattered on my face and mixed with my tears.

After a few minutes, he pulled me out and wrapped me in a towel, hugging me to him.

"I'm sorry," he whispered. "I should have . . ."

I shook my head and stumbled away.

I couldn't hear him say the words he always said. Not on that day. "Don't, Tommy. Let's just . . ." I took a deep, shaky breath. "I'll make coffee."

He nodded, turned from me, and sank into his thoughts— not much better than my nightmares, I'm sure. For me, putting one foot in front of the other, boiling coffee water, and sprinkling in some tasteless creamer was enough to banish the dream to the back of my mind.

It's fine.

It's over, and no one blames me.

At least not out loud.

And Tommy has his own well of guilt to deal with for being drunk that day, for being below deck puking, for bringing us out with his buddies, even after I told him how scared I was of the ocean and its deceptive aquamarine waves lit by shimmering diamonds of tropical sun.

The horror of endless depths under the beauty terrified me. I'd seen *Jaws* and *Orca* and all the other sea horror movies as a kid. I'd watched enough to give myself a true phobia of the sea. Beaches were a path that led you to a monster's throat. No, thank you.

My Lia was fearless, though. Even at ten, she knew she wanted to be a marine biologist. She pored over every single book about the ocean and its toothsome dwellers, particularly loving the sharks and the stinging jellies.

"Look, Mama, the barracuda can take a hunk out of your muscle when a shark usually just tastes you and lets you go if they bite."

Every fact she read to me made me shiver, but I hid my fear. My fear wasn't hers, and I didn't want to infect her with my irrational phobia.

During *Shark Week*, Lia would make the family sit and watch show after show after show that vacillated between showing sharks as shy, misunderstood creatures and the perfect apex predator of the sea. She leaned into the images, oohing and ahhing with her daddy, while I tucked my feet up under me so my legs didn't crawl with goosebumps where Lia and Tommy could see them.

I'd always been especially scared of sharks.

Something about the dead button eyes.

The rippling slit gills tasting the water.

And the rows of triangular teeth.

They were the monster I couldn't laugh away.

Then Tommy suggested a vacation to the gulf. His buddies wanted to fish, and Lia wanted to see the actual ocean. We live in a landlocked state, so our fish live in rivers and lakes, brown as mud. But in Florida, we could go see dolphins and maybe even touch them. Lia lit up like a lamp when he suggested it.

I said, "Why don't you go fishing, and Lia and I will go to Disney instead?"

Lia immediately started to cry those slow, quiet tears that a child has when they don't want to look like babies but you've hurt them somewhere deep. Too far down inside for a tantrum and way deeper than a snit.

Disney wouldn't do.

"Please, Mama?"

Afterward, that's what I heard when I woke up every morning covered in sweat.

I stirred my coffee and sighed.

Her tiny coffin was empty. Her bedroom was locked. Her pictures and toys were in boxes in the basement. She'd disappeared into the depths in every way.

The coffee swirled in my cup and soon rippled, just like the waves from that day. My stomach lurched when I thought about it. I dumped it into the sink, then threw up all the brown sips and washed them down the drain.

"Sick again?" Tommy moved to the fridge, avoiding my gaze. The first time he'd seen me get sick, he'd gotten so excited. He'd thought I'd let myself get pregnant. He'd asked about it, smiling and encircling me around my middle, the hope radiating off him in waves.

I'll never have another child.

I told him so, though I could have been kinder about that.

"How dare you." I'd slapped his cheek. It wasn't hard and, honestly, it was so dramatic it felt as corny as an old fast-talking, black-and-white movie. Only, he didn't pull me into his arms and kiss me against my protests like Rhett Butler. He didn't sweep me up in his arms and carry me to the bedroom as the camera's eye wandered away. He stood there, gasping, as a single tear tracked down his cheek.

He hadn't touched me sexually since.

And he'd only comforted me with any touches after my nightmares.

"I think I need to go back, Tommy." I leaned against the edge of the sink, the cold porcelain chilling me into gooseflesh.

"No."

I shook my head because we had this conversation every morning.

It never changed.

When Tommy left for work, I went up and made our bed. I scrubbed the bathroom and vacuumed. The pattern of it all helped distract me, but at some point in my hurried work, I found myself outside of her bedroom. I stopped and touched Lia's door, feeling the chill of it through the pads of my fingers.

As I pulled my hand down the veneer, I left trails in the condensation drops that seeped through the door. I put my ear against it like I did every day, and I heard her splashing. I felt the pressure of the water and the humidity of the Florida afternoon right through the wood. It was in there with her. Circling. Following the trail of chum the captain had dumped for Tommy's buddies. Lia had hung too far over the side, looking for sharks, and I had been so far away from the edge because my heart beat like rapid-fire gunshots in my chest, and I'd taken a valium to even get on the boat, so when she fell it was like watching her fly . . .

I roll my forehead against the grain of the door.

I knew where the key was.

If I went in, could I finally reach her?

The bottom of the door pulsed with seawater lapping out onto our carpet. How deep was it in there?

Something meaty thumped against the door, and I fell back. I scrabbled against the wall and crawled toward my own dry, landlocked bedroom to weep on the bed.

When Tommy got home that night, I asked him if Lia might come back to us. Like maybe, if we go find her, we could save her from the bull shark that tore her little body to pieces. I asked him every night. He just shook his head and headed into the living room to watch sports or mind-numbing sitcoms but never any nature shows.

I went back upstairs. I thought if I took a valium, maybe I could lie on the couch and put my head on his lap. I'd try not to cry. Maybe I would let him tell me it'd all be okay and pretend I believed him.

As I walked past Lia's door, I heard the lapping waves.

"Mama," she gurgled around the salty sea in her throat. "It's beautiful down here, Mama, but scary too. Why'd you let me fall?"

I sobbed and pressed against the door. I jiggled the handle, even though I knew it was locked. Part of me wanted to run screaming. Damn the water and the sharks. Damn my sweet little Lia. But the other part wanted to drink the salty water down until the sea was in my blood. Until I was like Lia—blue-faced fish bait.

Like my poor girl.

The handle rattled in my grasp. It was Lia unlocking it.

"Hurry, Mama. Before Daddy stops you."

Like he did every night.

She wanted me to come. She asked me in a million ways. She didn't say it exactly, but that's what the nightmares really were.

Invitations.

I'd let her down before. My fear of the ocean still iced my muscles and slowed my blood, but I turned the knob anyway. All I had to do was push.

"Marla? Come on down, honey. I'll get dinner started."

He wouldn't wait long.

It had to be now.

But my feet were cement, and my heart squeezed harder with each beat like it wouldn't ever beat again.

I sipped the air a final time.

I wouldn't let her slip away.

Not again.

I pushed as hard as I could and . . .

The sea closes in. I sink into the sapphire depths. As I sink, my clothes flutter around my body like I'm flying. I look up at Tommy's screaming face above the rippling surface of the sea and say, "I love you, Tommy," with the last of my breath. The bubbles from my words float up and pop silently against the hull.

"Mama," Lia says, slick little hands caressing me as she slides by, cutting through the water. My baby's flat black eyes shine in the dark velvety blue, and her white teeth flash.

I stretch out my arms for her, even as I scream and suck in water.

"No, Marla!" Tommy screamed as he jerked me back from Lia's doorway. I tumbled away from the door. He pulled it shut and locked it. He knelt in the salty puddle and pulled me up to face him, wiping wet hair out of my eyes. "You know she's gone. You know she is!"

He leaned against me, clutching my body and sobbing. Shaking his head into my wet neck, he whispered that he was so sorry. That he'd take it back if he could. That he loved me, no matter what.

He was finally ready.

I hugged him close with one arm and reached for the doorknob with the other.

It rattled, and then it turned.

"Don't worry, Tommy. She says it's beautiful there. It only hurts for a little while."

And the turquoise wave washes over us as we begin to sink.

TOMMY'S BAG OF BONES

WHEN CANCER TOOK Louie at ten, I wouldn't put him in the ground. There's no law can stand between me and my poor boy. None. I went to court. I fought a good fight. Didn't matter that my man wouldn't stand by my side.

My little Tommy did.

"He's my brother. He's going to stay with us."

"He's ours," I agreed.

A taxidermist stripped his bones using dermestid beetles. Tommy and I watched them eat the pasty skin from his muscles and then the muscles from his small pink bones. The taxidermist let us help brush Lou's bones clean, bake them with white glaze, and then form a durable structure to house his bones.

"Normally, we'd make this from polyresin, but for your purposes, why don't we add some woodwork and rubber?"

By the time we were done, we had a fully articulated skeletal Louie with swirled pink and clear skin so you could see through to his grin. He was with us again. My sweet Louie.

Tommy carried him out to play because his friends liked to pose him on swings. They propped him up in soccer goals. They strapped him to bikes and sent him down hills. Kids took selfies with Louie and Tommy. Hell, the kids were more popular than they'd been when Louie was alive.

I bought rubber fill to fix scrapes and gouges.

It was all so beautiful.

Until parents started complaining. They carried petitions against us and formed marches that wound right past our house. My ex and his mother walked with them, carrying signs that read *Let the dead rest* and *Rest for Louis*.

They never did spell his name right—bunch of snobs.

When I'd tuck the boys in at night, I'd kiss them and tell them about their other family—the one in the swamp. I'd tell them about gators and airboats and the fullest moons they'd ever see.

When the cops came banging on the door with a warrant, I let them in. Tommy was sitting at the dining table doing his math, grinning with a gap-toothed innocence only an eight-year-old can achieve.

"Where's your bag of bones?" the officer asked Tommy.

"We buried them, sir. By my daddy's daddy under a pretty little angel."

"Just yesterday, sir. You can see for yourself." I held out a sales receipt backdated to Louie's death for the tombstone and another for the interment.

"Well, I guess that'll do. I'll let your ol' mister know where he can visit his boy."

We smiled and smiled until he was gone, then Tommy pushed the table out of the way. We twitched the rug out of the way and pulled Louie out from under the floor, where we'd hid him.

"It's time we visited Granny in the swamp," I told them.

Tommy gently folded his brother into a Nike bag I'd gotten him. We slipped out the back so neighbors didn't see, jumped on the train, and met my cousin at the bridge on Pontchartrain. Safe in his boat, we got Louie out to taste the sweet morning lake air. Wouldn't be but an hour, and he'd be sitting next to the ancestors. They'd be so impressed with his rubberized skin.

They themselves only had their own papery skin and Granny's woven braces to keep them upright in forever chairs.

"Think they'll like us, Mommy?" Tommy asked, as the airboat banked into the channel of swamp.

"They'll like you so much, they'll want to keep you forever, cher."

Louie's head bobbed.

Forever family.

FLOODS AND MELANCHOLY

MY TEARS BRING RAIN.

Used to be folks didn't know about the strange powers wrapped up in my moods. The dusty wind and bright summer sun, even if it peeked through the sullen gray clouds of January, confounded my neighbors. Made them blame the ill-tempered gods or the fickle fairy courts and their magics weaved from the breath of past seasons, stoppered up and saved in their cellars next to their bewitched dandelion wine.

Wasn't until the false spring Manny made with me that they put the waddle with the duck.

He'd been courting half the girls of the village. Promises and sweet secrets for every comely lass in the limits of the town. Only when I walked through town, he'd stop what he'd been pursuing and chase after me. I never knew why. I'm not as pretty as some of the gals, with their soft brown curls flirting with the planes of their faces. Or the gals whose bodies swung and hips shifted with the beat of their hearts and the rhythm of their steps. I'm not bad, just not gifted with any special flashing eyes or bright smile. My brown skin is dull in the sun, muddy. Many others have bright skin, shining darker or redder.

Still when his opal eyes set deep in the strong arches of bone and the dark frame of his perfect skin turned to me—me!—I nearly fell apart. I walked steps ahead of my baby brothers, dirty feet sifting the pressed dust of the trading road, and he smiled, slow and knowing, eyes on mine, hungry like he'd not eaten in years. Eyes full of my face. I felt his gaze roll through me, striking me within, warming me in ways that made me blush. I thanked the gods for my dark cheeks.

"Hullo, Miss," Manny's voice was like a drum thrumming low against the soles of my feet and the tips of my fingers, vibrating through me like a song I wanted to dance to.

Wasn't but a week until I had him in my bed, him rolling waves against my shore. New to love, we both spent so many hours sneaking away to places, stealing sweet wet kisses, making promises we couldn't keep. Even though it was midwinter, mud-flecked snow and trees drooping under ice diamonds couldn't stay cold with our warm embraces heating the village. The days grew hot, dry, and sweet as we carried on. Flowers burst through the crust of the December soil. Birds sang their mating songs.

At first, folk thought the weather a gift from the gods. But when the insects doubled in days, coming in swarms, we knew we'd have trouble. The cold kills them, makes them die back to reasonable. But this warm I made loving him brought them out of their hidden holes, to bite and plague and breed until black buzzing clouds thickened the air.

I knew it was me.

Manny came to me, smiling through his eyes, lighting that flame in my body. The heat of the air rose uncomfortably high that day, and as we pulled away, panting, he eyed me.

"Honey, the others say it's us makin' the heat. They say they feel it roll off of you in waves when you walk. That it gets hotter when we, you know, mess around the way we do."

I loved him. Couldn't lie to him, could I?

"Always been that way. When Momma died, I near flooded the town. When the boys fight me on chores, claps of lightning burn the field so close our hairs all stand up."

"You a weather witch or somethin'?" He leaned into me and took my hand.

I sure expected him to run from me like I poisoned the well, but he didn't. He loved me just the same. We laughed together some, but when I reached for him again, he shook his head.

"I love you, gal. I'll marry you if you'll have me, but the elders won't let us be together now they know what you are."

Folding my arms across me, I let all the arguments run around free inside my head. None of their business what we do. We love each other. They got no right to decide for us who we can and who we can't have. I paced the floor of my bedroom, peeking out the window only to see my papa leaned up against the stone fence, surrounded by the old know-it-alls glancing up at my window, waving summer hats in their hands. Wasn't any bitterness on their faces. Only worry. Worry I'd caused. The sound of the flies and skeeters filled the air by the stream. The poor cows groaned under their bites and the whirring torments. My fault.

"What we gonna do, Manny?" I turned back to him, my eyes full of the fear blooming in my belly.

He took my hand and led me down the steps to the elders to try and make a deal.

We married that winter under a blooming Jadal tree—tree of the Mother in honor of mine who been dead these ten years.

He kissed me and said the words in front of the elders, my papa and brothers, and all those gals he'd wooed—they gnashing their teeth against the bitterness of plain old Sadie winning handsome Manny for her own. Even the mayor's daughter Wenna been spurned and huffed every time Manny kissed me at the wedding party that night. I didn't mind her jealousy. Understood it even. Manny was the most beautiful man in our village, and he was all mine. We moved into a couple house near the stream, but we couldn't touch each other. Couldn't do more than press together our lips like cousins at church. We'd sworn it.

My body still longed for him. When he came near, I heated up like a smoldering campfire sparking up on a wind, but we didn't touch none.

The winter roared back harder than usual—full of raining ice and drifts of heavy snow. Killed those damned insects. Then, it started killing game. Cows froze in the night. Spots of chill passed over the skins of folk, leaving black dead spots needing to be cut away. Those spots were us, Manny and ma, fighting about not touching.

Wasn't long till the winter froze so deep and bitter that Manny decided to break the fast, to warm us up. That day, we made our first babe together.

"A balance," Manny said. "We just need to be careful's all."

So, we were.

$$)O($$

We went on that way, and three children later, he still made me hot like sun's blisters when he looked at me under his dark brow. But I don't think he saw me the same. My body thickened from carrying our babies. My voice not so low and lovely when it called to his kids. My soft hands got hard in the wash water.

He kissed me. Closed-mouthed, as was our custom. Still, he whispered words of love, not the hot ones we saved for winter's icy grip. We managed. Our house got bigger. Our kids got stronger. People came to him asking for weather boons, and he'd smile, say he'd see what he could do. It was a good life we made.

Still, I saw him watching the swishing skirts of the gals he'd courted before. Most of 'em married now, but you know how that is. Some folks don't take vows and mean them. Some mean them but still break them. My Manny fell for the worst one. The bitterest girl. Wenna. That loss never left the sharp tongue she used to lash me or the foul words she flung at my feet when no one but the women could hear.

The town told me when it got worse.

First, they whispered just out of my hearing. "SSS-SSS-SSS" like snakes with glances so piteous I looked to see if all my clothes were right and proper.

Then, they did nice things for me. Brought apples and jams and hunks of meat for stew. Offered to get me whatever I needed. Sweet of 'em. Too sweet.

"Someone die?" I'd ask.

They'd bristle, but then fret until something came out like, "You poor, poor dear."

I'm nobody's poor dear.

I stormed home, my babies in tow, threw open the door, and caught my brothers smoking herbs in the sitting room. Both snuffed out their smoldering pipes and leaned back, all innocent like. Playing fools for sister. Never did work on me. Not when they was little, not when they got big.

"Here now, what's all this? Tell me what folks won't say." I grabbed my younger brother by the shoulder, gentle, but enough to feel the tensions he held inside.

My brothers gazes filled with knowing, and a silent conversation passed between their eyes. The two of them knew me better than I knew myself, and their worries made my stomach clench and buck. What was a-comin' would hurt. I set my kids to playing in my old room behind the hearth. Then I pulled out a chair and sat with them at the table. I took the pipe snuffed on the tray in the centerpiece bowl and lit it against the candle burning there. I took a puff and watched the boys' faces. I think it was then I knew.

Outside a soft rain began to fall.

"Tell me."

They spoke together, took turns, paused, and breathed as the other rattled out all they knew, a serpentine explanation with stops and starts and sighs all woven through.

A damned terrible tapestry they made to hang off my heart.

"Manny took up with that Wenna. Sees her couple a times a week. Don't think he loves her, just—"

I waved my hand in the boys' faces, halting them. I tapped out the pipe in the hearth, kissed each of them on the head. "You keep my babies, hear? I'll be back for 'em after."

The boys knew not to argue. They'd seen the lightning strikes a time or two. I wasn't some knock-kneed gal to be trifled with.

The rain met me like a wall as I walked out on the trade road. The sifted dirt ran in rivers of mud, but that was none of my concern. I marched myself right past the houses, but the folk inside couldn't see me through the thick veil of the downpour, the monsoon my sadness made. Rain that fast got nowhere to go. It washes away crops and livestock in its hurry. Batters barns full of hay and wets the bottom so it molds. Seeps under door frames flooding houses. I didn't mean to hurt them but damn if my feelings weren't hurt.

I strode up to her door, rapping with an efficient, restrained tap. Didn't need to appear anything less than cool in front of my rival.

She opened the door, half naked and grinning, house warmed by the light of candles and a bright fire. The smell of sex hung in the air, meaty and cloying.

"What you want, gal? Nothin' here for you," Sadie said. Her ruby-tinged brown skin lit with the sheen of exertion. Thin and lithe still. Eyes with a frame of long lashes.

How I hated her then. Could've called lightning, but I didn't. Mommas didn't do such things.

I pushed past her, making her cuss me as I stepped in. "Manny, come on out now," I said. "Nothin' to this hiding. Everyone knows."

Tapping my foot, I waited for him to decide what was right. Sadie didn't try to lie. Didn't want to, I guess. Her eyes filled with triumph, and she tilted up her chin like she'd won some prize. My pain? Manny? She couldn't have either one.

"Manny, you don't come on out now, you can just stay right where you are. I won't have you a liar."

That did it. He pulled himself out from under her bed's edge, slithering like a belly crawler all the time. No shirt, and his bare chest looked just as handsome as the day we'd wed. Triangular and cut with muscle, squared up shoulders, and smooth dark skin so beautiful against the dancing light of her fire. A body built for love. I walked over to him and stood, eye to eye, staring into the face I loved more than any other. Then I slapped him.

Outside, lightning lit the church like a bomb, burning it down even in the curtained deluge of hot rain. Was gone in minutes like it'd never been—a river of ash running through the streets.

He took my hand gentle, sad as all the world. "You a goddess. You full of power. But I can't touch you like I want. They tell me . . . they say I got to put myself into other hands."

They. The elders. Damn fool old men making him take on a lover so he'd not warm my bed so much.

"You didn't have to do it, Manny. You could say no. Do something else. Manage your own needs. That's what I got to do between when they say we can be together. I don't go running after no man to fix what you can't do for me." Bitter anger laced in my words. I had needin' feelings too, damn them. Why's a woman's needs less important than a man's?

He moved closer, and I could see the pain there, in his eyes, in the way he held back from touching me more—always hesitating around me. "They said they'd hurt you, honey. Said your moods would kill us all if they didn't control you."

He'd been in someone else's bed, touched another woman, and it was because of their damned fear of me.

"We could leave." I said it in a small voice, mostly because I knew what he'd say. I rushed into the gap in our words before he could tell me no. "We could go where my moods wouldn't matter. We could travel and sell our heat. Bet others would want rain and warm and all the other."

I reached out and smoothed my hand across his cheek. For a second, I saw it, I swear. The fantasy of our leaving struck his heart. His eyes hooded with happy hope, and he wrapped his hands 'round me like he always did when we could.

"Don't you touch her, Manny. Not after what we just did." Wenna came at him, hands curled into claws, drawing blood arcs on his soft skin. He shoved her back then, one arm still wrapped around me. Sure enough, I was still mad to beat the band, but that made me lift my chin and glare at her triumphantly.

"Stay away from my man, Wenna. Stay away or—"

"Or what?" She drew herself up, all haughty on his other side, hands clutched behind her. "They won't let you go. Their monster. Their weather witch. They have you, and they ain't going to let you just leave. They have your babies, and they have your brothers, and now I got your man."

The lightning struck the roof of her house but didn't hurt it. She had a rod to take the hit. The crackling boom made her jump, but she came back at me, bitter smile and twisted lips.

"He calls you goddess. Calls out for you even when he got me on him. Me! This body ain't made babies. I still have my girl shape, and he calls for you." She spat. "Damn you."

She came at me, thick knife in her fist arcing down, glancing across my shoulder bone and cutting my skin in a long slit, and another bolt of lightning shook the house. Manny danced between us, trying to block her with his body. Trying to keep her at bay. But Wenna kept coming, slashing to get to me. His hands, beautiful hands before. Hands that held me, ribbons under her attack. She screamed and chopped and slashed. He fell against me, pinning me to the wall with his bulk, jerking and grunting under her blows.

That's when the elders burst in.

"Manny, you got to find your gal," the first elder screamed

before he saw the tangle of us on the floor. Blood and skin, and Wenna still swinging her knife, warbling some song no one understood. They pulled her away, dragged her out, and as they did, the bolt struck her—white hot and between the eyes. Ozone and heat sizzled through the air, and in seconds, wasn't much left of Wenna. But my poor Manny. . .

"Honey," he said to me through wet breaths and bubbles that came out through the cuts in his chest. "I only ever loved you. I'm . . . sorry."

Then he left me.

His beautiful, broken body. His ruined face tattered like granny curtains.

The rain stopped only because part of me died. We gathered up my babies and brothers and buried my Manny in our garden. Folks went quiet around me. No whispers, nothing.

The elders came one day as I sat on Manny's grave.

"Your brothers say you don't care for your babies anymore. They say you don't talk any or eat."

I turned to look at them, eyes unblinking. My body thin and dried out like a husk. Goddesses don't need to eat.

Another elder sat on the yellowed, dead grass next to me, stroking the violets I kept growing on Manny's grave. The lush purple with a watchful yellow eye on nodding heads lived well. They were the only thing that did. They didn't nod for the weather since I'd made all the weather cease but for their watering. No wind or rain or warm or cold. Just nothing. Dead air. That's all folks deserved from me.

"If you let us die, your babies will die too. Manny's babies." He waved his old veiny hand, ashy brown and sad. Not like Manny's hand. Not beautiful and strong. The others parted, and my brothers walked up to me, each of my three babies in tow.

They cried out, fat little hands clutching at me, fingers grabbing.

"Mama," they said. "Mama."

I ain't fit to be their mama. Not even a human. Goddesses don't love.

I put my hands out, and they ran to me, laced their arms around me, and cried against my breasts.

Goddesses do love. I felt it when I clutched them to me. They smelled like Manny. Their eyes shone like his. I let one tear fall, and with it, a gentle rain wet us and the violets with clean water from the skies. The elder cried out in happiness. It had been months since the rain.

"We'd let you keep 'em with you if only you'd let the weather come again. If only you'd help us" The elder smiled.

Fool thought he'd done me a favor and won me.

"Let?"

He nodded and stood, brushing off the dust that clung to everything.

"You don't let a goddess."

That's when the stones fell from the sky. Stones like fists, smashing them. Giving them the pain they'd made for me with their meddling. Wasn't long until they all lay, broken dolls. My poor brothers bled with them, mixing their blood in the sand. But my heart was like a stone.

The babies each wailed.

"Mama, don't let the stones get us," my boy —Manny's pride—said.

I shook my head. No, not stones. Not for my babes and the rest of the village. I reached into my heart and broke it open, letting my tears come. I let all my grief out. The rain started, and I clutched them to me hard. By my hand or by my rain flooding the valley and covering the houses, they'd be with their da soon.

But can a goddess die? As the water crept up the hill and covered my toes, I knew I'd soon find out. The water was warm, like tears.

IT'S A WEIRD TALE

MARGARET BROUGHT the soup to her bedbound mother. It was warm enough to soothe her aching bones but not hot. That way, Margaret didn't have to stay in the room, blowing on steaming spoonfuls before tipping the liquid into Mother's puckered, toothless maw. She pulled the door shut behind her, leaving Mother to read religious tracts and slurp.

Byrd drew at the table. Only seven years old, but already so like her.

How could he be like his father? He barely knew him.

With a huff to blow away the anger, Margaret sat next to Byrd and spread the newspaper out on the table, looking for want ads for illustrators.

None.

No fashion editorial artists need apply.

No part-time sketch artists.

Nothing for someone like her.

And her husband, Slim, was off with some other woman, useless wretch that he was.

The cupboard held enough flour and tuna and squirreled odds and ends to feed them for another week. Not two.

"Mama, what's a depression?" Byrd's gaze followed her movements, eyes as brown and deep as a dream.

Margaret allowed a smile, though the edges hardened around the bitterness of it.

"A depression is this, baby Byrd." She pointed to the empty cupboards. "A depression is people being hungry. People not getting work. Or like those little girls who lived under us that were put out when their pa left them."

"Like Daddy left us?"

"No, honey. Their daddy had the decency to die, but he left them destitute."

"They don't come to school no more."

"Anymore, Byrd. They don't come to school *anymore*. Because they have to work to support their family."

He put down his stubby pencil and stared up with bare admiration at his mother. That look was food enough, heat enough, air enough to breathe, and she reached out and clasped his little hand in hers.

"I don't have to work, because. . ." He drew in a deep breath and looked upward, seeking the words she'd told him so many times. "My mama won't have any baby of hers work while there's a breath in her lungs."

It came out of him so singsong sweet, Margaret giggled.

But past him, past the thin bubble of love between them, the thick stack of bills waited neatly on the sideboard. Margaret couldn't ignore them much longer. The rent. The grocer. The weight of living pressed down so hard, Atlas's burden couldn't have been heavier.

Her invalid mother. Her poor baby Byrd.

She looked down at her hands, knobby and red from washing glasses at the Dill Pickle Club. She used to waitress before Byrd came along. But absent Slim didn't think the mother of his son ought to be waiting on people, getting her tush pinched and boobs brushed by drunken schmoes, so she switched back to the kitchen for less money. And Slim had shacked up with the cute red-headed waitress for the last four weeks. Good riddance. If divorce didn't cost money she didn't have. . .

Byrd went back to his drawing. A childish little doodle, but for a seven-year-old, it was quite clever. A woman—by her shape and the exaggerated lips—stared out of his sketch like it had a will to see through her. Margaret, an artist by training, traced the sure lines his little fingers had drawn. The woman's body promised strength, curving on muscles and taking up space. But perched on her head, the strangest black blob stretched up and out.

"What's that?"

The boy kept scratching away, darkening the blob. "A bat. She's got a bat on her head, and it tells her things."

And just like that, the image flared to full-color life in her mind.

Only three hours, and she'd need to be off to the Dill Pickle Club to scrub pots and cups and bleach the toilets white and sparkling, but for now. . .

She grabbed her pastels and some art paper. Things she hadn't been able to use since the market had crashed and jobs for artists dried up in the economic desert they called the Great Depression. Now in her hands, the stubby pastels felt like magic humming.

The colors blended as she layered them onto the thick paper's weave. Green background as rich as a lake in the eye of memory. Black leather top that showed the shapely arms, round with strength and supple sensuality. Pouty red lips not parted for a kiss, but curled open on the last syllable of a word of power. And on her head? The skin of a bat perched with wings spread. Her eyes peeked from the mask-like holes in its body. And those eyes. They devoured Margaret. Sank in and held her like she'd cast a spell.

"Mama. . ."

And in the swirl of the colors before Margaret's eyes, the

woman pulled her hands up the front of her body, red-tipped fingers scraping upward until her hands framed that fierce face. Her lips muttered and moved across words beyond Margaret's hearing.

"Mama. . ."

Then she showed her. . .

"Margaret," the pastel woman growled at her, and the world exploded.

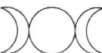

When she came to, Byrd had her head cradled in his thin nest of knees.

"Mama." He petted her with sticky, plump fingers. "Mama?"

"S'okay, Byrd. S'okay," The dream numbed Margaret's voice. By sweet promises, she didn't have the words to explain.

"You met her, didn't you?" Byrd asked. "Did she show you everything?"

Margaret glanced up at the clock. If she left immediately, she'd make her shift at the Dill Pickle Club, and all would be well. Or unwell and normal, at least. But the things she'd seen, the promises the bat witch woman made, those she couldn't forget. The sketch of her promised so much more.

"I'm going to start painting, Byrd. Will you keep Grandma company?"

He nodded and took his stubby pencil and paper with him.

Margaret started on the things she'd seen and the images bled from her thoughts through her fingers and onto the paper. Sprawled women with their souls in peril scraping at the sky with clawed fingers, bodies exposed. Bare-breasted goddesses sacrificing stretched, screaming women. Snakes and monsters all clutching and cutting and touching women. Women in the middle of their stories. Women on the cusp of their third act.

Naked women because the threat they faced wasn't something to hide from.

Frightened women because the monster before them wasn't some menacing shadow villain but their own anger—their own hate—made real. Hurt that they could hunt, kill, and triumph over. The bat witch woman showed Margaret. Told her. Filled her with all the old stories that all women know only in their dreams.

And then Margaret made a deal with the bat witch woman filled with knowledge and gain for both.

Womanly things that men don't understand but they hunger for.

And soon Margaret knew how to take care of her family.

"Where do you get these ideas, Margaret?" The editor of *Weird Tales* held the completed cover art in his hands. He flipped through the salacious images of women, naked and in danger, big-eyed with screaming red mouths. He brushed the edges of the painted breasts, face twisted in a primal shape so like a snarl pretending to grin. The power of it pulsed through the room. "These'll sell like crazy."

Margaret smirked as he handed her the check, and the bat witch woman, perched inside her, smiled with her own pointed teeth as the prospect of thousands of magazines with her on the cover tantalized her. The editor's gaze fed power to the bat witch woman with every glance at the paintings, and every cover would fulfill the promise. Margaret knew they'd both eat well soon enough.

PLAGUE BABIES

THEY SAY the children aren't affected by the virus, so the rest of us wear masks and hunker down. We send our kids out to do the essential work that needs doing.

We lower the driving age and the age they can have a job.

We work at home and hold our breaths.

My boy Moe works fifty, sometimes sixty, hours a week at the grocery, cutting meat and delivering it to doors that stay closed when he approaches.

He comes home every night deflated, with his sweat-stained smock dangling from bandaged fingers.

"They're letting ten-year-olds drive and work with customers but not the slicers. Have to be fifteen to work with those."

Butterfly stitches become a mark of service.

We put up signs in our yard.

A hero sleeps here.

Thank you for your service.

People peek through their blinds or speak through masks from a distance when they catch sight of us.

"Tell Moe we're proud of him."

"What would we do without the kids?"

And all along people die. First, the oldest of us. Then, age doesn't matter. Anyone over eighteen is at risk. We watch percentages grow. Death tolls climb.

How can it still be spreading? We've been so good. Closed all the shops. Order takeout and have our needs delivered by the kids.

"Did you notice how the Rogers girl—Vicky, is it? How she looked yesterday? Angry little thing. I know she's only six, and it's tough carrying boxes to doors eight hours a day. We have to do our part. But she looked like she wanted to kill me when I waved as she passed. Not just tired. . ." My husband John's words trail off as he points.

There she is in the backyard in her little brown uniform. If I hadn't seen it myself, I guess I wouldn't have believed it. Her little chubby face is twisted up in a bitterness I've never seen on her. She's always been such a sweet baby, really.

Nora Rogers, Vicky's mama, opens the kitchen window a slit. "Come on in, Vicky. Mama's got your breakfast ready. Can't be late for work."

The child's chubby little fists unclench, and her body seems to sag into the idea, and she goes inside.

Before all this—just a year ago, but it has been one long damned year—children were ours to keep and care for. They'd been treasures we brought up to be just like us. Little lumps of clay. But now they keep us.

The virus's grip has changed us all.

Even my Moe.

He is seventeen when he starts coughing. They take him away to the hospital.

Seventeen.

They told us kids weren't affected. They lied.

I remember holding him in my arms and promising I'd always take care of him. That I'd be his rock. And now he's in a hospital hooked to a machine that makes him breathe. Or maybe he's dead. I can't think that. We need him to come back.

I dream about how his breath must sound to him inside his head. A rattling wind that forces the caverns of his chest open.

My poor boy.

And my youngest, Shelly, is just old enough to start working in his place.

I bundle her up in his too-big smock and send her into work.

The worker tram drops her off in front of our house on the first night. I mask up and meet her in the garage to spray her down and give her sanitized home clothes. Her smile comforts me immediately.

"Mama, they put me at the hospital. I get to run the mop machine and bring bags of fluid to the rooms."

I hug her and settle onto my knees, eye to eye. "Did you see Moe?"

Her smile fades a bit. "They told me not to ask and that I couldn't tell you anything anyways. They said it was part of my job to keep secrets."

I know my little one. She can't keep a secret. If she's seen him, she'll tell. "Okay, sweetie. Let's go eat."

John makes her favorite—spaghetti and hotdogs—and as she shovels it in, I silently run through our blessings. Our house, each other, food, and—

A scream splits the quiet of our neighborhood.

"Stay here, baby," I tell Shelly.

John and I run out onto the back patio in time to see Nora Rogers tumble out her back door, clutching her throat.

"Is that blood?" John asks. "Nora!"

But he doesn't run to her. She could have the virus.

I call 911.

"I'll send the police." The operator sounds like a boy whose voice hasn't changed yet.

Two teenagers pull up wearing blue uniforms and badges, guns drawn. They rush into the backyard and glance back at the house. They nod and drag Nora back inside, though there isn't much life left in her. Other than the streams of red staining it, her skin is white as Wonder bread.

"What are they doing?" John asks me.

Little Vicky stands by the back door. She is covered with blood, presumably her mother's. The fire in her gaze and the tiny gritted teeth project hatred.

"Oh, John. She killed Nora. I'm sure of it." Just then, I glance back.

My baby watches from the kitchen's sliding doors.

I rush inside and grab her away.

"What, Mama? What's wrong? I saw that much blood a bunch of times today at the hospital." She hugs me. "Don't worry. I'm not mad at you guys. Not yet."

She skips back over to her spaghetti and hotdogs.

Weeks go by. My little girl changes.

One night, she asks for seconds and then thirds. "Moe is dead. For sure." The words are flat and come out between bites of mac and cheese. "I found his room last week, but I couldn't get in to see. I didn't want to tell you 'til I was sure. I saw him when they wheeled him out. Can you pass me some ketchup?"

John stares at her wide-eyed and sucks in a great gasp. "They said, they told us. . . It can't be!" Then the tears.

"They lied, Daddy. We just get it different. I hear them talk about it when I'm bringing in the bags of medicine. We all have it. It's just not killing us littles. They just figured it out, you know. But we kinda knew."

Her little sweet mouth stretched oddly as she fills it with more cheesy mac than should fit, and the pit of fear in my stomach freezes.

We're doomed. It was all for nothing.

I take to my bed, leaving John to weep and Shelly to pack her rubbery cheeks with noodles.

)O(

Something wakes me suddenly, and my heart lurches.

John lies next to me so still I can hear the house creak.

On the other side of me, a warm breath. "Daddy's dead, Mama."

I jerk up and gasp.

Shelley stands next to me, mouth wide in an alien grin. "He kept eating pills and telling me it was better. You won't do that, will you, Mama? Not now that you know it's just me and you?" Her face twists in a sad bow, and she stretches her arms toward me like a baby wanting Mama's lap.

I pull her into bed with me. No need to call the cops.

John's body cools in the bed next to us as we sleep, and my baby's body changes next to mine.

)O(

When I wake in the morning, John's body looks like a carved grave marker. His cheek feels like ice against my fingertips. That doesn't surprise me because I have a plague fever.

The inner fire that the virus stokes burns away my need to cry, but on the inside, I mourn everything. My life, my babies, John. I especially mourn that I'd let it all happen. Could I have done something differently? Refused to send out my kids? Questioned the disappearance of the scientists and doctors? Asked about the teachers and the nurses? But then they'd have made me disappear too.

I stumble through the house looking for my Shelly. She's gone to work. I have to see her.

I make my way down the empty streets to the depot and climb on the train that passes by the hospital where little Shelly works. My skin crawls with fear as the other occupants stare at me. None of them are . . . normal. Like my baby, their skin stretches, flaking large, discolored chunks. Like my baby, their eyes are all sunken but shine with the brightness of internal spotlights.

A few are all of the things that mark the plague. Skinless, bright glowing bodies that move like liquid cells under a wet slide cover. Plague babies, all. Becoming something that only they could be.

I get out at the hospital's station and collapse, my fever crushing me to the cold concrete. When I awake, I am in the hospital and creatures of light surround me, all touching my face with their flagella. One of them feels like my baby. Something about the way she leans or croons or bubbles.

She presses against my ear. "Can't save you, Mama," she says in her sweet voice. "Only the little ones can take the change. But I love you."

Then, they all withdraw and leave me to lie on the bed with my plague. Death is coming now. My body fights like hell, but the virus inside me will win.

Minutes—or days—later, I see her.

She's so bright.

I raise my arms to her like a baby wanting to be held by Mama.

She slides onto the bed next to me and wraps around me with her many bright arms.

"You're so beautiful, baby," I whisper. "So . . . beau . . ."

I'm slipping away. As I do, I wonder if this world will be called conquered or if it will be called cleansed. Shelly's in it, and that's all that matters to me.

Shelly's the whole world.

EVERY ROSE

COLINDE'S FATHER, King of the Summer, demanded she come before him at court with haste. After she was formally introduced and genuflected to the floor, her father called her to sit at his feet with a flick of his thin fingers.

"King Rodget's wife is dead, and he is in mourning. His child is a babe. Win him over, ensnare him with your beauty, get rid of the heir, and you will rule there in my stead forever." As ever, his instructions were cold and unfeeling. "Fail me, and I'll take your immortality."

Princes and princesses of immortal witch kings didn't ever inherit. They fought their way into ruling, or they assassinated mortals fool enough to stand in their way. The tradition was a tried and honored one, but Colinde hated it just the same.

She'd grown up with her dawn-fairy mother in the meadows of summer. She'd played in purple coneflower fields and worn a crown of ivy upon her head. She was the beauty of a budding summer, burning bright with purple hair and ruddy bright skin. Without an order from her father, she might have lived forever as a sprite dancing in spots of dew-soaked sun or whirling the dusk into a night of fireflies and whispers among the folk.

But her father held a geas on all his children. Any he called must fulfill the ancient role of conqueror, and Colinde among all his children was the smartest, bravest and most beautiful.

She arrived in a golden carriage pulled by butterflies. Swarms of honeybees carried her trousseau and dowry treasures, following her loyally as the servants saw her to her quarters. They'd come to the cold, though she'd asked them not to. She dismissed them with a smile as warm as home once the dresses hung neatly in the tall chests.

When they flew off, she watched them fall to their deaths, starved and cold in the northland's winter. "Goodbye, my brave summer friends," she called after them as they fell. Their deaths marked the last of her home.

She went that night to the table of the king, a ridiculously long, formal table. He and his advisers at one end. At the far other, his lovely little girl, as white as Colinde was red, hair black as night, and eyes that saw everything for what it was. Colinde sat with the child.

"I'm to be your new mama." She studied the child.

The little one looked up and smiled, lips bowed and red as a rose. Red as blood.

"I miss my own mama," the girl said. "She died in the snow running away from Father. She didn't like it here. I was born in the snow right before she died."

Colinde knew the story from the whispers of the mice in the walls.

The girl stuck out her hand to be kissed, as was the custom. "I'm Loline, but most people call me Snow. My father likes that."

The girl's mother had been an ice maiden. The heat of the king's love made her sickly, and she'd gone into the ice to escape with her soon-to-be-born babe.

"What do you like?" Colinde held the girl's hand softly in hers.

"Loline, if you please. It was my mother's name."

The mice thought the king had her killed. She'd have to be

very careful with him. But the child might be a boon, sweet as she was.

Colinde pressed her lips to the girl's palm and said, "Thank you, Loline. You may call me Colinde, if you please. Perhaps later, you might call me Mother."

The girl smiled prettily, giving Colinde's palm her own little kiss with lips as cold as ice.

"Ah, you've met."

The king stood suddenly in the space between them. He bowed, only slightly, and took Colinde's hand. He jerked it up to his lips and planted a kiss of greeting there.

"Colinde? I'm Rodget. We will wed tomorrow, if it pleases you."

None of this pleased her, but it was her geas. Her destiny. She nodded her assent with a shy affect pleasing to most men of power.

)O(

The wedding was short and beautiful. No time for her mother or sisters to come, though a herald was sent to the summer lands with announcements and gifts. Rodget often pulled her into pantries or excused the court so he might taste the summer in her kisses. So that she might enchant him with her eyes.

It wasn't difficult. He was a strong man, but he wasn't deep.

Soon, she had him enraptured. A puppet that she directed with a smile, a whisper. Soon, she wore a golden crown and sat by his side, issuing orders.

But Loline was her joy.

The child grew bright and lovely, but even more interesting to Colinde was her natural wisdom. Colinde's father had charged her with killing Rodget's heir, but she wouldn't do it. She'd come to love the girl so much that if her father came to take her immortality, she'd give it willingly to keep Loline safe.

The girl charmed birds from trees to sing with her. Forest

animals danced and played at her feet when Colinde took her for their daily lunch in the queen's rose garden. It was there that Colinde learned of Loline's geas.

"I'm to kill you one day, Mama."

The girl had been plucking wilted roses from the bushes, pricking her fingers on the thorns and licking away the drops of blood. Nothing Colinde said could stop her from the ritual, and she understood the power of blood better than the foolish human nannies. Besides, the girl's perfect creamy skin healed nearly instantly.

"What do you mean, sweet Loline?"

"When my mama—my other mama, you know—when she lay dying, she promised that I would kill any queen who came after her. That I would never give my father peace. Sometimes, at night, shadows come and tell me the story. They touch my face, and I see what happened to me and Mama when he killed her in the snow. He stabbed her and I came out, then she cursed him. I'm sorry that she was so mean, but my father hurt her, so she hurt him back."

Colinde sat in the green grass next to Loline and pulled the girl into her lap. The story was an old one. Stepmother becomes villain, then the victim. New girl replaces old. The circle renewing with the blood of wronged women.

"You don't have to kill me right now, do you?"

Loline, whose face had been sad as a marble grave guardian, lit from within. "No, I don't have to. Not now."

"Did she say when you had to kill me?"

The girl's head tilted, and she grew thoughtful. "No. But I am to punish Father. He's old now, you know. I should do it soon." The girl's features stirred and collapsed into a sad mess of confusion.

"A geas is a powerful thing. But maybe together we can stop it. There might be another way we can please your mother's ghost."

Loline leaped up and threw her arms around Colinde's neck. "Yes, Mama. Please?"

The next week, Rodget choked to death in his bed, wife standing on one side, daughter on the other. When he stopped thrashing and blood ran from his eyes, ears, nose, and mouth, they knew Loline's promise had been fulfilled. They poured the remains of their poison into the fire and called for servants. Both were crowned co-queen, and together they ruled though the shadows and cold of the ice kingdom, still whispering together about deaths they owed and the geases that hung like rotted garland in the rafters above their crowned heads.

From then on, Colinde spent her spare hours searching through books, talking to birds and old women of the woods, and sending messengers to the witch guardians about how to break their geases. The answers that came back were bleak. By the time they had exhausted the search for all the knowledge about overcoming geases, Loline was nearly grown. They pored over their final plan side by side.

"To break both our geases, we must give up our lives. A false death, you understand. We will drink a concoction to sleep the sleep of death, but the magic will expire, and we will both rise. It's the only way for us to be free."

After Loline studied the plans, she realized Colinde had lied. Colinde intended to foil both their curses by poisoning herself in such a way that her immortality was stripped and she'd die at her own hand. Loline would be left queen, her geas fulfilled, and Colinde's witch father would have no sway over the kingdom.

It was all woven into the magic words, deftly, of course. Hidden, but she found it and understood why. Colinde believed she had to die to stop her witch king father and didn't want Loline to suffer with the knowledge. Colinde was her real mama, through and through, and would do anything to keep her safe and free of the grief that would come from murdering her.

Loline ran away to save her mama from the geas. She found a forest dwelling with hard-working dwarves who protected her and sang her into a deep sleep like death. They had to. She was Snow, and they were summer. They encased her in an icy diamond so she wouldn't melt away in the heat. Then, they mourned her, praying by her casket every day.

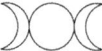

Colinde searched the castle and the towns, knowing that clever Loline had found Colinde's death in the plan and ran from it to save her. Months passed. The kingdom mourned, but Colinde wouldn't give up the search. She used her magic to make a scrying mirror that traced her daughter's fading steps. She saw her girl encased in diamond in the summer wood.

It was as if she were dead, but not truly.

When Colinde glanced up at the rafters and saw the shimmer of Loline's geas, she saw no trace of her own. Colinde's was gone with the stopping of Loline's breath, just like the old witch she'd paid with coneflower seeds and butterfly cocoons had promised.

There was but one thing to do.

She filled red apples with her eternal life, the gift of her father, the inheritance for a conquering queendom. She donned a hooded cape and set out for the dwarves' house, knowing that with each step, her beauty would fade.

She didn't care.

With each step, she aged, for she'd lived a long life in summer before she'd come.

She didn't care.

The dwarves opened the diamond casket at her command. They were summer creatures, so they had to obey.

She knew her face was lined and cracked and twisted with the ravages of her sacrifice, but she'd have it no other way.

Loline lay in a bed of ice, frozen and white as the snow she'd been born to, but her lovely hands and slim arms sprouted thick thorns from all the spots she'd pricked as a child in the queen's garden. Perhaps it was a curse for her disobedience. Or maybe her first mama was turning her into a rose the way gods did to their lovers and children when some piece of their destiny went awry.

It wasn't good enough for Colinde's sweet girl.

She bit into the apple filled with her life and chewed it, then pressed the mash into Loline's mouth with a sweet kiss.

She fed her life the way a mama bird feeds a chick.

Eternity infused Loline's skin with vitality, warming her cheeks and lighting breath in the furnace of her lungs and heart.

"Alive?" Loline breathed. "No!"

She sat up and grabbed Colinde in her arms, drawing blood with her thorny arms and hands. "Mama?"

Colinde wasn't dead, but she would be. Tomorrow or next year. Who could know when her mortal life's thread would be cut? Immortality imbued Loline's body as Colinde had hoped. She would die for Loline, as the first queen's geas demanded, in the fullness of time. And Loline had died for her, as the Summer King had demanded. The swirling showdown of the dead queen's geas dissipated in the bright summer sun.

"I'm still your mama, if you'll have me."

The beautiful young queen dropped to the ground next to her stooped old mother and offered her a thorny arm. Thorns were a small price to pay to be together.

"I'm still your daughter, forever."

And they ruled together until they didn't, but together was all that mattered to them.

ORIGAMI: THREE FOLDS

She folded up her features
Pressing lines in her cheekbones
Puckering her lips
Deepening the folds in her eyelids

Blood doesn't stain skin

MONA SAT in front of her vanity, tugging at the loose skin that hung from her jawline.

"Come on, Mona." Jerod leaned against the doorframe. He still looked so young. Just a little gray at the temples, a few smile lines around his eyes. He knew he was still hot. He was quiet about it, but he worked out every day and wore his clothes a little tight so his muscles pressed against the sleeves of his dress shirt.

She sighed and grabbed the thick foundation she'd been using to cover the cracks and fill the holes age had put in her face.

"Seriously?" He glanced up at her as she brushed on the thick brown paste. "Just put on some mascara, and let's go. The lines are only getting longer."

She sighed and soldiered on, smearing the paste into place.

"They won't start without me, Jerod. Just let me work my magic."

He grunted and headed into the living room to wait.

As soon as he was gone, she slid open the drawer and pulled out her evening face. It shimmered with the promise of youth. Rosy cheeks and plump skin. An aquiline nose framed by bright eyes. It fit like a glove after the edges dug into the white facets of her bones. In minutes, the features would settle on her bones and remake her beauty, as they always did. Finally, she felt herself again. A new face always did that for her. The press would take picture after picture and wonder why the camera loved the two of them so.

She pulled on the red sequined gown and took a moment to thank her god for all her gifts.

"Done?" The approval in Jarod's gaze as it skimmed the planes of her new face and down the lines of her tightening body was her reward.

She sent an extra thanks for sending the cute little delivery girl for her to peel.

"I'm ready," Mona said. "Let's put our game faces on, sweetie."

He chuckled. "If only they knew."

> The skin folds under her breast
> Under her ass and across her stomach
> The skin folds when she bends her neck
> When she smiles or frowns
> Why doesn't it fold into something beautiful?
> A butterfly
> A crane
> The skin folds
>
> Blood doesn't stain skin

Arlene spent every penny of her inheritance on liposuction, tummy tucks, a stomach sleeve, a wired jaw, and she lost over two hundred pounds. But then she put it right back on. The numbers on the scale crept up from goal weight to "okay, that's livable" to "I'm a complete failure" and sat on her heart like a weight.

She had a closet full of clothes she'd bought when she'd been her lowest. Clothes that she couldn't wear but couldn't bring herself to get rid of. Clothes that were like an accusation every time she looked at them.

Failure. It was written in every dimple, ripple, and sag on her body.

Every time she went past a mirror, the guilt squeezed her heart. Why couldn't she control this one thing?

Control.

God, what she wouldn't give to look in the mirror and be pleased. To get into the clothes she bought without worrying about the buttons and gaps and rips. To just feel beautiful and not worry about the scale.

Control.

It occurred to her that throwing all that money away and then regaining all the weight gave her a unique opportunity. Instead of giving control to doctors again, only to have her body fight back like a rebellious teen on a rampage, she could handle this. She'd take care of the whole damn problem.

Control.

Arlene grabbed a butcher knife from the kitchen and headed into her bathroom.

She'd take control over this body. She'd shape it and cut away all the rebellion.

She'd fit into those clothes again, even if it killed her.

A daughter is a fresh page
A sheet of virgin paper
Never folded.
Nothing written on her face.
The crisp edges and uncurled surface
Next to her, a mother is a novel
A thick file full of scribbles
A piece of origami
Folded again
And again
Until all she is
Is folds
Folds that cut
Folds that bleed

Blood doesn't stain skin

The room smelled like a whorehouse. Salty and that odd mixture of hot fabric and alcoholic man sweat I knew from my own experiences with Joe.

Damn him. He'd been at her—that fucker! The rage in me roasted away the weepy bullshit until everything was sharp and clear. My baby needed me.

"You okay, honey?"

She was curled up on her bed, her body a comma in the middle of a thought. She had the covers pulled up tight around her throat, and she shivered even though the night was as hot as a July night ought to be.

She stared off at the wall, back to me. "Mmm, fine."

I went around to sit next to her curled-up knees and touched her forehead. She jerked under the pads of my fingers like I'd burned her. The thick layer of foundation couldn't hide the bluish bruise.

"What happened?"

"Nothing, Mama. Just . . . I fell and . . . I . . . and . . ."

"Are you sure?"

She nodded. "I love you, Mama."

She sounded just like she had when she was four. We'd been alone then, living paycheck to paycheck. Shitty apartments and couches of friends, but we'd lived happily. My little girl.

Then I met Joe.

He put her up on his shoulders and made her giggle. He paid our bills. Bought the house. We had a nice white wedding with my baby girl as the flower girl, and we set up house.

The years went on.

Joe got a little more demanding by year two. Started shoving me, drinking every night. But my girl had a roof over her head and clothes and good food. I turned up the radio so that she didn't hear our . . . disputes. Covered up the bruises, tried to keep him happy.

It was all for her.

But he'd been different lately. Nicer. Bringing home dinner and presents.

I just thought . . . I don't know. I thought he'd changed. Settled down.

"Did he touch you, sweetie?"

She squeezed her eyes shut and gasped in a deep breath. She sobbed. I heard everything I needed to hear in that one sound. It folded me in half. Twisted me into something I hadn't been before.

Ripped and tore and wrinkled me.

"I'm sorry, Mama." She said that to comfort me.

Me!

That fucker had to die.

"Stay here, baby. Don't you come out, no matter what you hear, okay?"

She nodded and curled up tighter under her sheets.

I pulled the door shut behind me and headed down into the basement, where he liked to sleep it off when he drank. He was stretched out in the middle of the room on the La-Z-Boy, snoring as the game played on the flatscreen.

Those hands had touched my daughter's skin. That body had pressed her flat, then folded her against him.

I looked around for something—anything that matched what he deserved. It only took me a few minutes to put together a plan.

He'd cut me. Bent me to what he wanted. Pressed me into a shape, and I'd let him. Now he was doing it to my baby.

I found fishing line. Heavy-duty stuff from the trips he made to Florida chasing sailfish and barracuda. I walked in circles around the chair, wrapping the thick, clear line around his middle like a tight belt. I kept going, walking and looping, and remembering everything I'd done for him to keep him happy, every time I took a hit or said yes to his sexual demands, ducked my head and took heat. All to keep my baby safe.

And I'd failed.

He snorted and tried to turn, but the fishing line held him in place. Pressed him down.

Like he'd pressed us.

Behind him, I set up a surprise. I pulled a rickety old shelf behind the chair and piled it with all his detritus I could find. Bowling ball, tool chest, boxes of *Hustlers*—everything that I could think of that he'd brought in into our lives. Everything heavy I could find.

"Joe, wake up, you fucker." I kicked the swing arm of the La-Z-Boy so the leg rest collapsed.

"Wha. . . Whasz goin'—"

"Shut your mouth, monster."

He woke up real quick when I said that. "What's wrong with you? What. . ." He struggled against the fishing wire biting into his flabby white gut. Bloody red streaks wet the front of his shorts. "Let me up, you bitch. This ain't funny."

"You know what's funny?" I got right in his face and leered, but he couldn't touch me with his hands lashed to his side. "It's funny that I let you treat me like trash for so long." I pulled a trash bag from behind my back. "But it turns out you're the trash."

I slid the trash bag over his head and twisted it until it he thrashed, and the bag sucked up against his mouth and nose as he gasped.

"I know what you did to my baby. I saw your fingerprints on her skin."

He shuddered and bucked against me as I held the bag closed and grinned at his pain. I didn't see his fist until it was too late. He'd freed one hand and caught me in the temple, knocking me back. He pulled the bag from his head, red-faced and wide-eyed. Rage split his features as he wheezed in breaths.

He tugged at the fishing line, plucking at the strands as he spat curses at me. "I'll fucking kill you, bitch. Watch me. And I'll hurt her again."

The fishing line split and tore under his bloody fingers, and I pulled my knees under me to crawl away. My head swam, but my surprise still waited.

"Don't. . . touch. . ." My words were slow. Thick and slurred. He'd knocked me right to the edge of consciousness, but I wouldn't go down.

I got to the backside of the shelf. I put my shoulder against it and pushed with all my might, but I guess I'd made it too heavy.

His other hand got free.

"I'm coming," he said, his rage near gleeful. "Oh, damn I'm going to hurt you."

I shoved again, and the shelf wobbled, but the strength had gone out of my body. I pulled myself up to standing and tried to rock it, but I was so damned weak.

Always so weak.

"No," I wailed.

I closed my eyes and put all my weight against it. At first, nothing. I knew there were only seconds. But then I felt it rock.

"Here I come—" The sneer in his voice sounded near joyful, the fucker!

"Come on, Mama."

I opened my eyes, and my girl was next to me, pushing the shelf.

We pushed together.

The shelf fell. It crushed his chest and the chair to the floor with a crunch. I couldn't see his head. I couldn't imagine there was much of it left under the pile of shit we'd dumped on it.

I heard him take one last soupy breath.

My baby turned to me and sighed like the weight of the whole world had lifted.

I took her into my arms and folded her against me. "It'll be okay now, baby."

Women fold their hearts
Press secrets into their lines
But lines aren't weakness
Folds are places to hide our fears
And the other side is an edge
To cut with.

And blood doesn't stain our skin.

CRONE

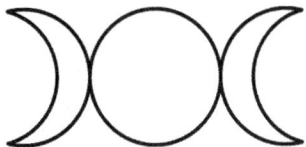

Women are wise. They are the soil that we rest in so we can rise again.

AFTER SAVING HANSEL, GRETEL FOUND HERSELF

CHILD ABANDONMENT ISN'T NEW. Since the first people walked, babes have been tossed from cliffs, left on temple steps, smothered—shut the mouth you didn't want to feed. Like so many before him, my father dragged me through the woods, laughing at my tears. He left a crust of bread and not a backward glance.

I rocked in the dark, trees tight woven over my head, holding my cries inside the wood, sipping my tears. I was only ten years old.

Hunger drummed a mellow throb in my gut like it always had. Three brothers and five sisters—did I eat so much? But being the ninth wasn't the only reason he'd turned me out. He damned me because winds followed my feet and crops sweetened where I walked. You'd think a farmer might value my gifts, but no. He'd taken his vows in a church and read from the book of the risen God every night after our porridge. Suffer not a witch to live.

The forest took pity on me as I wandered. Ripe fruits landed in my lap. Butterflies flitted by, drawing me to clean water. My gifts pulled sweetness from green plants I grew in a clearing.

Their sugar turned into walls, doors, and windows in a house of my making. My home. What softened in the rain, the forest regrew, and the bees and the hummingbirds took nibbles to fuel their flights each day. But the little ones always came to my doorstep, and I'm no mother.

Every time parents abandoned their child to the forest, I wished another child would be brave enough. Would withstand the winding paths and the starvation. I'd been in the woods for so long.

But the children didn't survive my tests. My house and my oven tested them, and they failed again and again. It's easy to judge from outside the wood, but inside, mettle is tested. Nothing is given unless a price is paid. Nature isn't kind, and neither am I. So many little bones buried in my garden, I hear them clacking together at night.

Many almost made it. If they had, what would they do with my candy house? Would they leave it to rot and go home to parents who'd abandoned them? Revenge themselves on the careless village that allowed them to be treated like trash, pitched away and forgotten? They'd have the power to do it.

Or would they step into my shoes and test others, as I'd learned to do. They called me a witch, but I had a job to do like every other creature of the wood. Couldn't have little children wandering free, destroying the balance with their thumbs and their needing. Besides, I was kind. I released them from pain. Their reed spirits, baptized by fire, found the next place. A place where maybe they'd be loved. Valued.

But I was tired.

Steely-eyed Gretel offered my deliverance. She passed my tests and saved Hansel, setting him free before I shoved him into the oven. She stood so tall for a girl, clutching the broom she'd swept with as a cudgel, pushing me to the oven. Oh, how she shone, and I knew I'd finally been bested. I whispered secrets, so my gifts passed to her between the breaths she took for strength.

Then she revenged the souls I'd freed with one great shove as
Hansel, the little fool, danced around the oven with glee.

The world turns. Wintery death gives room for spring.

So I let myself burn.

DESCENT

MADELINE CROSSED over with little fanfare. Closed her eyes and ceased to breathe. Her heart slowed until the beats were punctuation, ending the sentence of her life. Each rest between changed her. Her eyesight, blurred with the haze of age, cleared. Beat.

Her skin, frozen from the bitter bite of January frost, drew away, releasing her from its tyrannical embrace. Beat.

Feet that had failed to carry her to safety in the storm found purchase, though Madeline was sure she actually floated above it all. Beat.

Before her, the crusted snow and icy paths of Midtown Park divided to reveal a place she'd only dreamed of. And there were no more beats.

She stepped into the fold where the light was bright, blue, and welcoming. Two paths. Choices had never been her forte.

Her mama, dead these forty-five years, used to tell her, "Maddie, you got no more sense than a peapod. Find a man to decide things for you before you find your own ruin."

Madeline snorted. Mama had been so right. Never had she had a man decide for her, and never had she made a good decision.

"So here it is," she said.

Two paths.

One seemed beautiful and welcoming. A bright light. Singing. Madeline imagined all she'd lost waiting on the other side. All she'd been promised as a reward.

The other path was dark. Her stomach squeezed around her midsection as she moved toward that fearful path. Where the bad ones go. That's what the men at the mission had told the drunks when they stumbled in for broth and blankets.

Madeline knew this choice was the most important one of her life. These past few weeks, with the cough and the blood, she'd really thought about her end. Who would be waiting? Mama? What'd she know about Mama anymore? Hadn't seen her in forty-five years. Her sisters? They'd died without a word to her. Ignored her when they lived.

She remembered what her sister Lissie had said last time she saw her. Lissie and her churchwomen had volunteered at the soup kitchen. "Didn't expect you to be here, " she'd said as Maddie reached to hug her. "Crazy Maddie," she'd said to her tittering church friends loud enough for the sleeping drunks to hear. "Maddie is so slow, she'd chose the devil for fear of choosing wrong," she'd said.

Here she was, going to make Lissie's words truth.

Madeline's spirit feet found their way into that dark tunnel, and her stomach, at least in spirit, turned and twisted, but came along for the ride.

"Yep, choosing the devil," Madeline said to herself as the passage narrowed to her shoulder's width. The walls were spongy to the touch. Wet. Like insides.

The passage opened up into a yawning cave so filled with dark it ran over into her soul. She wanted to turn and run, but the decision had her now. So, she moved in further, hoping something would make sense. Hoping for . . .

"Hey, stop that!" A voice from behind.

"What?" Madeline was afraid to face whatever she'd offended.

"Stop that hoping. We don't want that here."

A beautiful young man, maybe fifteen, shook his finger in her face. "There something wrong with you, Lady? Didn't you read the sign?"

Madeline's eyes adjusted to the dim, and a winding path loomed in front of her with cavernous valleys, and a glow cast twisting shadows of pain and suffering on the rough cave walls. Sign?

"There's no sign," Madeline said.

The young man made her nervous. The young always did. So little life lived and so sure of their ideas. Life hadn't knocked them down enough to know how stupid and dangerous they were. This young man seemed the same as any who'd mocked her in the park, told her that she was lazy and should get a job.

"No sign? Huh. It's right in front of you."

She blinked, twice. She dragged her hands along the walls hoping to find the sign. If she could feel it, then maybe she could trace the letters and make the boy happy. Happy boys don't kick you or hide your cart. No matter. She couldn't find the sign.

"Never mind," the boy said. "I'll read it to you. It's our one rule. It says, 'Abandon hope, ye who enter here.' A simple rule, and you have broken it."

"I didn't mean to. I'll try to watch myself. Say, didn't you steal that line from somewhere? Supreme Court building, maybe? Can't quite remember."

"What of it? Just do as it says. This place is anti-hope. It's eternal and it's fruitless and that's how we like it."

"That's nice," was the only thing Madeline could think to say.

The youth smacked his forehead. "No nice here either."

She didn't want to say the wrong thing again, so she kept her mouth shut. One of her great talents, the minister used to say when she'd see him palming contributions or paying night visits to the other street ladies . . . the ones who didn't push a cart. She nodded.

"There's really something wrong with you," the young man said. He tilted his head, smirking at her. Madeline shifted her gaze away. It was always better not to look boys straight in the eye when they appraised you. Gave them ideas about your vulnerability. On the street, it was better to look crazy than vulnerable, so Madeline muttered to herself. Best to keep them guessing.

"What's your name, lady?"

"Madeline." Always answer; never hesitate.

"You smell, Madeline. In fact, you reek."

"Sorry, I haven't really showered since . . ."

"No, I mean you have a sanctimonious scent. You don't belong here." The young man tapped his long finger against his chiseled chin.

Madeline hoped he'd just dismiss her.

"I think you should come with me."

Madeline nodded. Maybe this was the man her mama always promised would choose things for her. He moved forward into the darkness, and Madeline scrambled to keep up with his sure-footed steps.

"I can't see," she complained. Mostly to herself.

Often in life, Madeline had found herself in tough situations. A day without food. A downpour. An overturned cart that left her possessions exposed for all to see. Talking to herself about the problems helped her to focus on the solution, and it never seemed to bother any people who were around her at the time. In fact, it hurried them along their way. The youth here was different.

"Oh, well, we can fix that."

He waved his hand, and a ball of flame hovered between them. It lit the entire cavern with its brilliance, though Madeline was sorry it did. Splintered bones marked the path they followed, hemming out the sliding rocks that looked suspiciously like skulls. Madeline's stomach clenched as a rat the size of a Rottweiler scrambled up the wall carrying a stringy bit of flesh in its mouth.

In life, pigeons, squirrels, mice, and the occasional stray cat had loved her. She had saved them crumbs from her meals and fed them by hand, all the time talking about what their eternal reward would be. A life full of nuts and trees and peace. She loved animals. But rats . . . they were thieves and biters and hissers. So much like the boys who tormented her on their way from playing ball, or whatever it was that boys did. She shivered, though the air was hot. Shivered deep until her hairs raised.

The boy walked silently in front of her. She hoped . . . scratch that. Maybe he would help her understand why the dark path had called her more than the light one.

"What's your name, Boy?"

"Gebrek Aan Hoop."

"Gebrek? That's a strange name."

"I have many. Would you prefer another?"

Madeline shook her head. "What does it mean?"

"Nothing." The boy's voice aged in that word's delivery. Deepened into a timbre of utter despair. "They call me Lack. If you'd like, you can call me that too."

She felt the weight of a thousand stares. What she said mattered deeply—to her, to the boy, to others she couldn't see.

"Can I give you a name?"

The boy's eyes filled with the eager watchfulness of youth. He nodded.

"My brother was named Edward. He was just a whip of a thing when he died. Polio or some such. So long ago, I can't rightly remember. But I loved to call him Eddie. Made him mad, so I did it all the time. I'll call you Eddie."

"Fine. For you, I will be Eddie. Now, follow."

The young man turned from her and beckoned as he cleared the first rise. She followed, though she hesitated just at the crest.

The light that shone like a halo around the hilltop was hectic and angry. Diluted waves of heat and fear, things her skin could feel in this place, seeped over the rise.

Why had she chosen this path? A warm, sweet reward had been the promise of the other path, and yet she'd come here. No sense, like Lissie had said. She found her feet and willed them forward, over the rise.

The path descended into a pit lined with cubicles of rough-hewn wall stretched into the horizon, so deep that the lines joined into a solid. Inside each cubical were souls participating in the business of the place. She expected screams, moans, something. Maybe even elevator music. The silence was devastating.

"Eddie?"

He shrugged his shoulders. "Hell is personal. Pits of fire and brimstone were just . . . well . . . metaphors. No offense, but humans don't get much right."

They wound down the path to the nearest row of cubicles. The stench of bodies, sweat, and pain blended into a vile mist that wound around her ankles.

"Purgatory. Sinning is a purchase on credit. You can buy big or small, but someday you have to pay. Most people come here on their way to the next place. Gotta pay your bill before you leave . . ." He led her into the nearest cubicle.

An older woman sat with her back facing them, legs folded neatly to the side. She was naked, skin sagging and pooling around her old bones. Madeline's heart cracked a little as the old woman turned toward her, face distorted with the ravages of her age. Beneath the wrinkles and the sag, the woman had been a beauty. Now, her deep brown eyes were shot through with broken blood vessels. A petite nose, slightly turned up, crusted with dry skin. Cheekbones so high, now just hangers for loose flesh.

"Her bill is for vanity," Edward said.

Madeline walked into the cubical, and the silence changed—as if she'd walked through a membrane.

Suddenly, she was surrounded by screeching voices. "Ugly." "Homely." "Disgusting." "Plain Jane."

Madeline stepped back, escaping the bubble of voices that surrounded the woman. "Her own voice, right?"

Edward nodded and turned to leave.

Madeline fought the urge to walk away. So easy to ignore her. So easy knowing that this woman was just like the many who'd dismissed, insulted, and ignored her all her life. A bill to pay, Edward had said. Madeline wasn't a wizard of finance. She'd never been good with debts, and this was no exception.

She kneeled next to the woman. She put her arms around her and hugged her tight, hoping she didn't smell in spirit as she had in life. The thundering voice was a stinging slap this close.

"Can you hear me?"

The woman's eyes cleared and focused on Madeline's face.

"Come away from her," Edward said.

"Can you hear me? What's your name?"

"Helen."

"Okay, Helen. I see you. I know you are beautiful. Can you see me?"

Helen nodded.

"I forgive you, Helen."

The voice, Helen's own, repeating over and over the insults she'd offered in life, crescendoed and crashed against them, battered Madeline as she clung to Helen.

"I forgive you for the things you said, Helen. Forgive yourself now."

The woman wailed, drowning out the sound of her insulting voice.

"I . . . I don't deserve it. I only loved myself."

Madeline nodded. "I still forgive you."

The silence returned, though now it was a relief. Madeline

touched Helen's cheek and pushed herself up, dusting off her knees on the way.

She turned to Edward and crooked her thumb back over her shoulder. "Her debt paid yet?"

Edward stared open mouthed as a flash of light blossomed from behind Madeline. Helen was gone. "Yep, I guess it's paid. You coming?"

Edward turned so quick, Madeline couldn't be sure what he thought of what she'd done. Could she do it again?

"Now, look, you can't go changing how this works. People who did wrong have to be punished. It's the way of things."

Madeline nodded but smiled.

Edward hurried her through the rest of the row, not stopping to show her anymore. Madeline could feel change in the air. Hope. It was like a gentle breeze following their steps. She didn't have to reach them all. The hope would bloom and flow and—

"I thought we had an understanding." Edward hurried up a steep rise and into a tunnel.

"We do."

"You will not do it again. I can feel your satisfaction at throwing purgatory into a panic. That's what I get for showing you redeemables. Your smidgeon of hope helped them, but it will have no effect in the next realm."

They stepped into a narrow gray hallway lined with white doors. It reminded Maddie of the welfare office that Rev. Jack took her to. He'd said that it was the path to normalcy and plopped her down in the hard, orange plastic chairs that hooked together. She'd sat in that room for hours, filling out forms in triplicate. Nasty place.

"Crimes against love," Edward said. "Nothing more deadly than someone who will destroy love. It's soul murder."

Maddie nodded because he wanted her to. What crimes were so bad? Maybe spurning someone's love or hurting a friend. How could those things deserve hell?

They skirted the winding ropes that marked the queuing area. Wispy, insubstantial folk shuffled forward in inches but never seemed to really move. The queue shifted and doubled back upon itself until Maddie was sure it was a trick, like those Escher prints she'd seen in shop windows.

"I just can't see where they're going."

"Right. Too sanctimonious. I told you."

Maddie squared her shoulders. "I'll try not to be."

Eddie laughed. Maddie wondered what got such a nice boy damned to eternity as a tour guide in hell. She hoped it wasn't . . .

"I told you, Maddie."

"Sorry. That one just slipped."

Eddie grasped a shining brass doorknob, the first in the endless gray hall of chairs, doors, and queues.

"This is the hell of broken promises."

She stepped into a vast conference room lined with hooked orange chairs in tight little rows. Vaporous figures sat in the seats, writhing in the glaring florescent lights. The geometric carpet, done in pink, green, and orange, seemed to lift and recede in a shag wave. A fifty-foot projection screen sat atop a wood plank stage and showed bright scenes of pain, loss, and heartbreak. A man neglecting his children. Pain on the tear-streaked little face. A woman in bed with a man not her own, her wicked smile a beacon flashing. A fiancé walking away from his bride at the altar. A friend stealing. A partner betraying. Love crushed. Shattered like a lightbulb.

The weight of it made Maddie stumble. Eddie steadied her. He led her to the front, though Maddie wasn't sure how they reached it. It stretched in every direction to accommodate all the thousands of souls. Maddie's eyes skimmed across them and couldn't count. So many! Eddie led her to the stage where the forms congealed. Faces in anguish. Hands hooked into claws. Hair tangled. None closed their eyes . . . even blinking seemed beyond their abilities. No interruptions to the continuous flow of heartache. No respite from the pain they'd inflicted.

"Did they never learn to love?"

Eddie nodded. "These are the selfish. They took love and shook it 'til it was dead. No way out for these fools."

She watched the images flickering and felt her breath catch in her teeth. She saw herself over and over, mixed in with the random nudes and tears and shrieks. Maddie, as a child, getting her dolly yanked away. Maddie, as a girl, dress torn. Teenaged Maddie watching her best beau walk away. Maddie as a bridesmaid when that beau married Lissie. Maddie in the soup line, shame burning on her cheeks.

Maddie searched the figures seated and moaning before her. "Lissie?"

"You'll only make it worse," Eddie said.

"Not Lissie. She was God-fearin' and straight as an arrow. Married and three kids. The rock upon which Main Street Baptist was built. Can't be here!"

At least Maddie hoped she wasn't.

Eddie shook his head but didn't chide her. Probably figured hopeless hope was the same as a lack of. Maddie searched the crowd for Lissie. Maddie's eyes lit on her finally, still the same pinch-faced prune she'd been near the end. The same judging eyes. The same bitter mouth. Now, those features wilted with regret.

Regret had to mean something! Regret was nearly repentance. And forever? Not if she had a say.

Maddie launched herself at the screen. She tore at it, though it felt like it was anchored in concrete. She lifted and cussed it and kicked it until it finally loosened in her grip.

"Maddie, it won't work."

"It's got to work. I just won't have it! My Lissie . . . all these folk. They messed up. Learned a lesson at another's expense but learned just the same."

"No, these folk never loved. Never. Not their babies, not

their mamas, not even themselves. Nothing freely given in love, no love returned without a price, no love lost or tears shed."

Maddie shook her head and shoved the screen, toppling it. The images shuddered as the screen fell, then flickered mid-air. A groan swept the crowd so pained that her eyes stung. The images, flat and lifeless before, found form. Where before they'd been shapes and memories, now stood people with blood and bodies.

"What have I done?"

"You know what they say about the road to hell. Good intentions and all," Eddie said.

Maddie stepped off the stage and moved close to the souls. Husbands wept as wives packed up bruised children. They wept tears that, in life, had never formed. Like ripples spreading on a pond, each soul saw the effects of their lovelessness carried forward and forever.

She knelt next to a youngish man to watch his vision of hell. His face was charming. Not handsome, but sort of weather beaten and manly. Crinkles around his eyes and deep laugh lines framing his mouth made Maddie wonder what kind of love-killing such a smiling face could commit. As she turned to watch, his hand shot out and took hers.

"Poor Dell," the man said in a voice like an autumn wind's sigh. "He's gonna die because of me."

Maddie turned to watch the man, as a youth with . . . a brother? No, a friend. Thick as thieves playing at baseball and peeping in windows. Then in high school, the boys turning to men, playing football, drinking, and smoking together. Raising hell but doing it together. In college, Dell becoming different. Dell going to meetings. Dell coming out.

The replay slowed as Dell approached the man at a frat party. His drunken eyes shifted from his lifelong friend to the frat brothers sitting stiff in silent judgment.

"We need to talk, Ronnie," Dell said.

"Nah. I know what you're gonna say. Don't give a shit," Ronnie said. His features twisted like a knotted rag.

"Look, I'm still the same guy. It doesn't say anything about you. I'm gay, not contagious."

"Get away, fag," the man said.

Dell backed away, tears in his eyes.

"Look at the little fairy crying. What's wrong, tink?" The frat brothers laughed and toasted with their mugs.

She could feel him then, with his brothers, not caring about Dell—hating him. The scene shimmered into a dark place, a meadow lit only by the soupy light of a new moon. Dell was tied face-first to a tree. The frat circled him tight, pulling his hair, punching him with thudding blows, and mocking him with razored epithets.

Maddie watched Ron's eyes, not yet crinkled from a long life. They reflected no love, no pity . . . nothing.

Ron's buddies jeered and taunted. In those words, Maddie heard an echo of the insults she'd faced from similar young men. She could hear the edge of their voices—the promise of violence.

"I know what he wants! He wants something up his ass," the biggest boy said. He lumbered off, weaving, and rustled through the bramble bushes.

"No!" Maddie shouted. Cruelty blackened the hearts of the young. She'd seen so much blood and pain, some her own, from unanchored youth. She knew what was coming.

"Huh?" Young memory Ron turned toward the sound of her voice with a jerk. "Hey, didn't you guys hear that? Someone's coming!"

Sudden clarity in his voice. Maddie wished it was from the guilt he should be feeling for his friend, but it wasn't. It was from fear. But he'd heard her.

Ron's head swiveled to see where the voice was coming from as his frat buddies jerked Dell's pants down to his ankles. The biggest boy returned from the bushes, clutching a thick knotty branch.

Maddie couldn't watch. She twisted away from the scene and from Ron, tumbling into a pile at Eddie's waiting feet.

"That was bad," Eddie said. "Wasn't the worst." His eyes distanced.

Maddie had seen that look on those with burdens—mommas with dead children, ladies at the soup kitchen missionizing to addicts. It was a hopeless look so deep that it stretched up to swallow her.

"Why, Eddie, you look so sad 'bout this. Was he your kin?"

Eddie shook his head. "He's no one to me. It's just a sad story I know. Dell didn't die from the attack. They sewed him up and sent him back to school, where everyone knew what happened. They knew because Ronnie told. Dell killed himself that year—another broken-promise sin. Then his mother stopped loving, withheld love from Dell's sister. She abused her baby. The sins keep on coming—an unbroken line to this day."

"That's not fair! All of them are here?"

"Yes," Eddie said. "The sins of broken promises create fallout.

"But Lissie is here. She only ever picked on me. I didn't wind up like Dell."

Eddie shook his head. "Sometimes it just rolls off. If you asked the people up top, they'd say you lived your hell on your park bench with your pigeons, but you and I both know that you were doing the best you could by staying out of Lissie's kind of life."

"I don't know any such thing. Just never got around to marrying and settling down. My loss, I always said."

"Maddie, be honest. If you'd been born Catholic instead of Baptist, they'd have recognized your saintliness and stuck you away in a convent where you couldn't have done any harm to their sensibilities. But perched on your bench, you were the scathing indictment of their lives and their sins that wouldn't just be stashed away."

"It wasn't that way at all!"

"Blindness to your own worth isn't a sin," Eddie said. He ran his hand through his tousled hair. "No amount of threatening or harassing or embarrassing from the regular God-fearing people kept you from ministering to birds and bums."

Maddie's cheeks reddened. None of it was true. He was trying to distract her . . . so easy to get off the track. She backed away from him and returned to Ronnie. He'd gotten up and shadowed his younger self, again and again. Bitter regret, tears, even cusses for his own stupidity burst from him in spurts.

"Ronnie." Maddie reached for his shoulder. It had no solidity, but she felt it all the same. She needed him to be flesh again, and he was becoming. "Make this right. Fix this once and for all."

Ron's red eyes turned to hers. Disbelief softened into a bright hope. A change in him swift and sweet, flesh and love tied up in the salvation of one but not himself. Dell. "Can I save him?"

"Can't hurt to try, right?" Maddie asked.

Ron smiled. "Right."

Ron stepped up to his young self, the one by the tree watching. He stepped up and in.

"Dell!" He launched himself at the boys surrounding his friend. They were too big to fall at first, but they were drunk too. Ron threw his weight into his fist, knocking one and the other to the ground. "I'll save you, Dell. Just don't leave me. Please?"

Dell's face pressed against the bark of the tree, but his eyes swiveled back, suddenly open and full of life.

"Ronnie, just get out of here! Get help!" Dell muttered around his broken teeth.

Ronnie pinned one of the boys and swung his clenched fist in an arc, smashing his upper teeth. Ronnie wheeled on the other boy, but the thick branch that the lead boy had intended for other things bashed his back.

Ronnie struggled to remain conscious. Lead Boy brought the branch down again with a crunch and broke Ron's skull. The branch pulled away, taking with it a hunk of Ron's scalp, clinging and waving like a flag.

"Missed you, Dell," Ronnie muttered with the last of his breath.

"Oh, Jesus, Ronnie."

Maddie tumbled out of the moment. Her legs sagged, but she stayed on her feet. She looked around for Ronnie. Eddie was next to her, shaking his head.

"You're like a virus, Maddie."

"Ronnie's gone?"

"Yep. Dell too."

She looked around at the crowded souls and watched them step into their own memories. Some quicker than others, but they flickered away one after another. She watched them go, happy that they'd found a way to love.

"When Ron and Dell went on in their lives, were they friends again?"

Eddie shook his head. "They died there."

She remembered, then. The lead boy clutching the gore-flecked stick.

"But what good was it, then? They died."

"No greater sacrifice than dying for love."

"But that other boy, the leader. Is he here now? Can't imagine how to save him."

"No need. He did the murder, but the murder freed so many. His own soul included. He couldn't stand the guilt. Changed him into a real, true man. He took the police back to the site. Did life in prison and taught others not to hate."

Maddie's chest knotted when she looked back at the crowd. Almost all of them were gone. Like Ronnie, they'd learned, fixed their lives, and went on to what was next. Almost all of them.

"Lissie."

Eddie nodded grimly. A few were left. A few that couldn't seem to fix things.

"Hope can't fix this one," Eddie said. "How can she go back?

If she changed herself, she'd change you; then you wouldn't be here. Paradoxes don't work in a mechanical universe."

"Don't know about any mechanics. I just know that she didn't do anything to me I wouldn't 'ave done to myself." Maddie started forward with Eddie trotting at her heels to keep up.

"She took all the affection, your beau, your self-respect. . ."

"Didn't take anything I didn't want her to have."

"That's not true," Eddie said.

Maddie wasn't one to be rude but, for Lissie, she'd trample poor Eddie if he tried to stop her. She weaved through the empty chairs and then realized that the chairs, like the people who'd filled them, weren't real. She cut a beeline to Lissie, who was wrapped up in her own memory replay. She seemed to be trying to change things, but the universe was getting in the way.

"Lissie." Maddie grabbed her sister's hand. "I'm here. Look to me, Sissy Lissie."

"She called me that, but I hated her. Blond curls. Why didn't I have blond curls? My daughter had blond curls, and I cut them off. Maddie never did nothing right and never suffered. Maddie always so good. Maddie wound up on the streets. Maddie, my Maddie. I pinched you to make you scream so Momma would hit you."

Streams of anger from Lissie's twisted mouth washed across Maddie like scummy water. Her soul recoiled. What was so bad that she couldn't fix it? Sister hate was just like sister love misdirected.

"Lissie, I'm here."

"Hate you, Maddie. Hate you, coming in here making things better but can't save me. Never saved me, not once. All those years, you were right. I married that fool to spite you, and he hit me every day. Had his ugly children, and they never treated me right. Only you, stupid little Maddie. Always loving me when you should've hit me. I wanted you to. I wanted you to be real, but you never were. If you were real . . ."

Maddie understood. Life had been for learning, not for living. Fitting in had been for others, for Lissie. She'd known from when she was just a whip of a thing that life was an illusion, a temporary state. Without much effort, she'd avoided all the excesses and temptations. Pastor said she was a balloon a way up high, just a thin, fraying twine keeping her connected to the world. Maybe that distance had been her sister's undoing.

"How's it her fault? Fault's mine. Never gave her a chance because I never let her in."

"It's not in my power to save her, Maddie."

He let it dangle there. Not in his power. It must be in hers. But what could she do? She'd go back for Lissie and change her life, but all those folks would be right back in the chairs, watching with horror and suffering. Even Lissie wouldn't be enough to balance that. She could take her place. Sit in the chair and suffer for her, but somehow that wasn't right, either. If she did that, how would Lissie learn love? She'd not solve anything that way. It came to her. Lissie wanted to love her, but she needed Maddie to do something first.

She drew her fists up into balls, scrunched her eyebrows like the angry shopkeepers who'd attacked her when she dug in their cans for food. She gritted her teeth like the cops she'd angered with her doorstep sitting. Would it be enough?

"Shit on you, Lissie!" Maddie screamed with all the anger she could muster. She hoped it would be enough, because anger wasn't her strong suit. "Shit on your whoring ass."

The cusses felt dirty but right. Lissie stopped, eyes wide and focused on Maddie. Just to be sure, Maddie flattened her palm and slapped her sister right through her spirit cheek.

"Well! You . . . you . . ." Lissie stammered with more life than Maddie'd seen since childhood. "You are a right willful bitch, Maddie."

Maddie nodded. She smiled brightly at her fleshy sister whose years were falling away.

Lissie's eyes hardened for a moment. She flattened her own

palm out and pulled her arm back to slap but halted. Froze in mid-swoosh.

"I guess I deserved it." She rubbed her cheek. Young Lissie's shoulders sagged, and she reached for a hug. "Sorry I've been such a hag to you. Sorry for it all."

Maddie nodded as her sister's form softened in her arms and swirled away as mist. Lissie's soul lifted, and so did the pall of dread. This felt right. Her soul sang a triumphal march. The oppression of the air thinned, sweetened into a fragrant warmth.

"You don't have to keep going. Look." Eddie pointed.

Maddie's gaze followed Eddie's finger. The gray walls softened, and the shimmering white light that promised so much reappeared. Why not follow that path to the reward that she'd promised the pigeons? Though her soul longed for it, it didn't seem right. She imagined facing her maker, knowing suffering and pain continued here. Maddie shook her head.

"The rest . . ." Eddie shuddered. "Even a saint shouldn't see what remains."

"Show me, Eddie."

He nodded and turned, but before he did, Maddie was sure she saw a glimmer in his eyes—hope. He led her through a door and into a cavern that the light didn't penetrate. The echoes of pain before were laughter compared to the sobs and sighs this cavern contained. Their sorrow seeped across her skin and into her gut, loosening it. If she weren't a spirit, she'd have sprinted to the bathroom. Everything good in her told her to run away from whatever was swimming in the darkness beyond the cavernous entry they passed through.

"I'm scared, Eddie."

Eddie touched her hand. There was no warmth, but the gesture made Maddie smile.

"I don't want you to get hurt. Some who get this far don't make it through." He squeezed her fingers with such tenderness, so much more care than had ever been offered on her behalf. "You can go. There's no shame in it."

"How many like me have come?"

"A good number since the beginning. Some make it all the way. Others don't. Don't go any farther. You aren't like the others. They were so sure of what they were doing."

Maddie withered a bit. She'd never been considered competent before, so why should this boy think differently? She dropped her eyes because it still hurt a little.

"Wait, I didn't mean that in a bad way. I meant that they were prideful. Arrogant. They sort of deserved what comes next, and I don't think you do."

"Oh." Maddie smiled. She patted his cheek. "It's sweet of you to worry, but I'm tough."

"You are. But tough doesn't describe these souls. They are horror." His hand swept the velvety darkness as if he parted a curtain. "You don't want to save these. Really."

His boyish earnestness was almost enough to turn her, but fear had no place here. She lived to help others find their way. She was a signpost on a one-way street. If she didn't collect them, why had she come?

"Go on, Eddie."

He led her further in, though his steps were tentative. She sensed movement, furtive and quick, beyond the globe light's reach.

"What's here?"

Eddie shrugged and slowed but didn't face her. "I called the others irredeemable, but this is the lost. I wish . . . no, that's too much like hope. I think that even you can't save this one. It ate souls to fuel its lives. Dictators, destroyers, and demons in life . . . now it's nothing but the anger left from each burned-out life."

Maddie stepped off the path, automatically seeking pain to salve. Her foot touched the soil and jerked out toward the deep dark. Eddie grabbed her just as the beast got hold. For such a little thing Eddie, had so much power. He pulled and pulled to steal her back from the beastie's claws. Her eyes teared up, but before the mist clouded her sight, she looked into the eyes of her attacker. Ruby fire and angry black points. Her soul recoiled. Its goodness was not enough. Eddie yanked, and the creature pulled back and Maddie's body stretched between them. Dirty claws lacerated her, leaving flaps of skin. Flashes of its memory smeared across her consciousness, images so sickening that Maddie's stomach lurched.

"Let go!" Eddie screamed at the monster as he kept pulling. "She's not yours."

The creature growled deep; the rumble crawled into her skin, making her bones shudder. Its grip tightened, shredding her ankles and feet. But the pain was nothing next to the images flooding her mind.

This thing told its story in rapes that left the woman, child, boy, grandma dead and bleeding. Decapitations by sword, by ax, by guillotine, by saw. Limbs rendered from shuddering bodies. Burning. Staking. Armies marching. And all the while, the beast with the claws showed itself, one soul with different faces. Faces that were so handsome, words like honey convincing folks that bad was good and evil was necessary. The victims of their works cobblestones underfoot.

Maddie shrieked as the creature jerked. It craved her soul. It needed to hurt her.

"Mine," the creature bellowed. The sound that crawled from its gut was more like metal scraping itself.

It would never let go, Maddie realized. She was its Sunday meal. The thing fed on the innocents it consumed.

"I don't know what to do! I can't stop it," Eddie said.

She thought for a moment and went limp. "Let me go, Eddie. I don't want it to get you."

One tear broke from Eddie's eyes, and as it did, he heaved backward until all but her ankles were free of the shadow zone. Eddie launched himself across her legs, anchoring her. "You can't have her. I won't let you."

The creature screamed. Maddie pulled herself up to sitting, though the spirit muscles in her trunk weren't happy about it.

Eddie hugged her calves and flinched as the creature loosened one claw to rake his face over and over. Deep gashes crisscrossed Eddy's forehead, and his handsome cheeks flapped loose from the skull. The creature hooked its claws into Eddie's nose until it shredded.

"Stop!" Maddie twisted in the creature's clawed grasp until she was able to throw an arm around Eddie. She remembered this creature now. The last time it was on the earth, it cost millions of lives. It would not be saved or satisfied.

Eddie gasped in pain but threw a fist out that glanced off the creature's face.

"Fight it," he muttered, though his lips had fallen away.

Maddie nodded. It only understood pain, so she threw her fist at it. Her knuckles connected with its eye ridges. She drew back her bloodied, aching fist and punched again, as Eddie did. Again and again, they hit the creature, their own blood flowing faster than the monster's.

Their streaks of blood mixed; their combined resistance fused onto the skin of the creature and began to burn. Bright white smoke rose from their blood. The creature's eyes rolled as pain climbed up its limbs. Maddie broke from the creature's grasp. The creature's interest in her was gone. Instead, it was interested in trying to hold the pieces of its burning flesh onto its rapidly decaying body. Smoke oozed across its skin like mist skimming a lake. Bone broke through the blistering surfaces, pulling the splits into widening chasms.

Maddie could watch no more. Eddie needed her. She held him. Rocked him.

Through his ruined features, one beautiful eye sought her gaze. "Maddie, go on alone now." His voice was steady, though the breath behind it was running out. "I'm just going to lie here a while."

"No. I'll carry you," Maddie said. The boy had saved her. For the first time, someone had risked his neck for hers. "It's the least I can do."

"We did it together. It's the only way to stop the lost."

"Never killed before," Maddie grumbled. She trailed her fingers across his hairline, soothing his pain.

"Sometimes you have to. Follow the path . . . nothing to be scared of. Just an old ghost."

Eddie's words fell like puzzle pieces. His eye closed.

"'kay, Eddie." Maddie lowered her head and kissed his good eyelid. "Love you."

The words fell in a vacuum. No movement or breath or shuffling. As she lay his head down on the path, his skin seemed to flow back together, regenerating and glowing.

She stood over his lifeless body for a while. Alone again but, in life, alone had seemed normal. Now she felt like she should tend to the one creature who'd ever risked a thing for her. A shiver passed over her as Eddie's skin tone faded to alabaster white. Death marked its own, even here. Her Eddie. Not like a son but a brother. Prodigal, and come home to heal all wounds.

"I'm hurting now, Eddie. You made me care for you in a new way. You for real, not you in general. Feels bad in a good way." Maddie ignored the tears that slid away down her cheeks and chin. Salty little traitors. "Guess I better keep going."

She limped down the path, thinking on why Eddie's body became so beautiful but hadn't faded away. What was he? A guide like in that Inferno story she'd read once? His name . . . she flipped through her memory. Cobwebby, her mind shuddered through all she'd seen and heard. Then it was there. Gebrek Aan Hoop or Lack, he'd said. Strange.

The path she limped along changed. Rough cobbles smoothed beneath her feet. The dark cavern gave way to something bigger. Wide green fields waving with stalks, lily leaves, and daffodils, but the tops nodded without flowers. Trees waved in the breeze, but it refused to touch her face. The lilting fragrance only flirted with her nose. Puffed white clouds littered the sky with no sign of breaking for a ribbon of light.

Maddie paused. What was missing? Such a lovely place but

nothing vital. It was like entering a room when the conversation hit a lull. Or the silence that follows the last note of a marching band. An upswept breath waiting to exhale. She noticed that the stones beneath her feet were metal—dull gold.

"Streets paved with gold," Maddie mumbled as the road climbed up a steep hill. Her ankles were aching, but not any more than in life when the cold was bad. "Sure miss my Eddie."

She crested the hill and paused to catch her breath. The hill folded into a marble avenue with silver risers and pearl fountains. Maddie's breath caught as she recognized the place somewhere deep. Home. That place she promised the birds and the bums, but here! But not.

She limped toward the center of the place, where she knew she'd find it. A throne, all encrusted with precious things, meant to cradle the most precious one. She found it beautiful and empty. Empty of all but the small sign set in green stones that read *Hell is an absence of God.*

She read the sign over again and felt the anger well. "NO!" Maddie shouted. "That's not fair!"

"Fair?" Eddie's voice echoed in the empty chamber.

Maddie spun, sending blazing pain through her leg. She shuddered through it. Eddie, her Eddie, wasn't some sweet guide. She understood now. This was his punishment, his prison.

"Come on out." She limped toward the throne.

"I don't want to. I don't want you to see me anymore."

She could hear the pain in his voice, the desperate ages, but at the same time, he sounded just like her little brother when he was full of hurt.

"Come out." Her voice was quiet but convincing. She settled at the foot of the throne.

Eddie stepped out from behind the throne and sat next to her. "You saved them all, but I don't mind being alone. Others will replace them soon enough. It's happened before."

"Others . . . This happened before?"

"Saints come. They come empty it out, but it fills back up. I'm never alone long."

Eddie shuffled his feet and glanced at the throne. "Do you think he misses me?"

Maddie wondered. She knew the story. Eddie had been the light bringer, highest of the high, and in a moment of pride and doubt, he'd been cast out forever. An example, kind of like the example she'd been for the volunteers at the soup kitchen. Better watch out, they'd said as they'd ladled out the watery broth into her bowl, mind your Ps and Qs, or you'll wind up like Eddie. They'd taught against him on Sundays. Said he was the enemy, the tempter. But Maddie saw more than that.

He'd had his eyes on God. He'd spoken and walked and worked with God. Then, he'd lost it in a moment of weakness. Like being born with sight, only to lose it once you'd seen a sunset. The loss of love once it sat warming your heart, but oh, so much worse.

"You must be the saddest creature in the universe," she said.

He squeezed her hand. She covered it with her other, trying to warm it.

"No matter what, you're my favorite, Maddie. All the others knew what they were and didn't care about me. To them, I was my name—Lack of Hope, Splitfoot, Satan. They saved everyone like you did, but they realized from the beginning who I was, and they were so sure I wanted to hurt them. Made me hate good for a while. They told me all the stories about what I had done on earth and spit in my face. They didn't see that I've been stuck here too. But you are different. I'll remember you for that."

As he spoke, the passage of blue light reopened, so much brighter and more welcoming than before. The pull was near irresistible.

"Time to go," he said and dropped her hand.

She felt it—a song that soothed her bones. A hero's welcome waited for her. What more could be done? If God wanted Eddie, wouldn't he fetch him? She thought back to her Bible learning, to the garden. She'd never much liked the story—poor old Adam and Eve. That tree was what her mind found in its wandering. The tree of knowledge of good and evil. It was there all along. And God put it there. All she'd saved had the knowledge, just like Eddie. Why not save him? Maddie turned from the light.

"Nope. Think I'll stay. They don't need me up there."

"Your work is done!" Eddie grabbed her hands, pulling her up. "Go on. Get out of here."

"Nope."

"Look, you did it. You walked among us and freed those you could. It's what you were made to do."

Maddie nodded. She didn't want to choose wrong this time. Something big hung on what she did here. Something so special that if she thought too long, she'd get it all mixed up.

"You go, Eddie. Get on up there."

Eddie's mouth fell open.

"You'd stay?"

"It's the only way to get you out, right? That's the problem. As long as you're here, others will come fill the rooms back up. Then what've we done? But me . . . They won't come here for me. I'll serve this out," Maddie said. She smiled and sat back down.

Eddie shook his head. "Aren't you afraid of forever? It's long, Maddie."

"Nah. I love you, boy. Can't be heaven if you're not in it. It'll be enough just to know that you're up there. I can imagine the rest."

"Don't even know if he'd take me back. I. . . I fell."

Maddie looked around at all the lacks surrounding them. She remembered how Pastor chided her for never "getting better" and for staying on the street. He had told her that she was punishing herself. Even now, his explanations seemed out of tune, but maybe for Eddie they worked.

"Did you ever try?"

Eddie shook his head. "Never been an opportunity."

She smiled and pushed him gently toward the lighted entry. "Go on now. I'll wait here."

Eddie took a deep breath and made his hands into fists. He walked toward the door, mumbling. Maddie couldn't hear what it was he was saying. Maybe he was apologizing. Maybe he was talking himself through it. She wasn't sure. But she was proud he was walking.

As he passed into the doorway, she smiled. No horns or pointy tail on that one. No hatred. Maybe it had been there once, but sure enough, now all those stories they told her were plain wrong. He wasn't any bogeyman . . . just another lost soul waiting to be found.

She watched until he was out of sight and the light winked out. She picked up the jade sign and held it in her lap to wait. It wouldn't be long. The daffodils were starting to bloom.

GRANDMA NEEDS A VISIT

ELLEN'S BONES BURNED. She waited for the nurse to visit with pills or even a pan of cooling sudsy water. Any visit was better than nothing, and at least she'd be less alone.

A blood moon lit the sky, but Ellen had no one to share with, what with George dead going on thirty-five years. Dumb luck she'd lived so long. The kids, too busy to take her shopping or help her count pills, sold her furniture and moved her to the old-folks home. They visited on her birthday, but they had little time for an old woman's loneliness.

So Ellen read. The nurses taught her to check out books online. She read romances when they were looking. Horror when they weren't. Summoning things from another world tickled her to no end. She was a God-fearing woman, a devout Baptist. She'd never harm anyone. But the thought of having a beastie do your bidding? Ellen couldn't resist.

She scratched symbols on the floor and said the words she'd found online. There was a book for everything, wasn't there?

Between nurses, Ellen lit candles and sacrificed—rubbery chicken nuggets.

With a belch of sulfur, the demon appeared.

"What deeds will you ask?" The demon rubbed its spindly hands together. "Revenge? Murder?"

"No, dear."

The demon looked at her and grinned. "Ellen! Wonderful to see you. Shall I whip up tea?"

Ellen nodded. Nothing like a demon to fill the lonely hours. They knew the best stories.

WOMEN OF A CERTAIN AGE

By the time they saw the smoke, it was too late. The walls never burned but, inside, the heat melted metal into puddles and rendered any biological matter into powdery ash. Three kids who'd been asleep in the basement now mixed with the filthy water that washed down from the smoking roof and into the cavern within. Their mother had been up on the second floor, where the fire started.

Joseph, fire chief of the borough, sprayed water on the roof and wondered at the still-intact shingles. They smoldered in the afternoon sun. Water turned to steam or sizzled as it ran down the walls.

It was always the same.

A woman, a house, a blackened maw on the inside. Nothing remained when the fire exhausted itself. Burned too hot and fast to leave any clues. No accelerant or bomb could be more thorough. They would pore over the site like they always did, looking for anything that would explain the spate of fires. Thirty in the last six months.

His phone never stopped ringing. The press wanted to know what he was doing about the fires. The mayor demanded action. Then there was Martha.

Since the fires, Martha called him constantly. Always wanting to know he was safe. Always asking about the women she knew—the ones who had burned. His wife hadn't been an easy woman to please before all of this started, but now, she never stopped fussing.

At least when he was putting out the fires, he got away from all of that bitching and questioning.

That night, at home, he switched his phone to silent so all he had to listen to was Martha. And she was on a real roll.

"Joseph, have you considered that all of the women lived north of the river?"

"We have a map with all sorts of pins in it at work."

She rattled dishes and shook something inside the kitchen and then returned to the living room. "What about kids? Do they all have kids? Macy did and so did Joan, but I don't know all of them."

"No, they don't all have kids or husbands. No pattern we can see." Joseph hoped that would be enough.

Of course, it wasn't.

"There has to be a pattern. Something no one has thought of, right?"

He wished she had a mute button. He flipped on the news and turned it up, hoping she'd take the hint.

But she didn't.

"I mean, I don't know the others, but Macy and Joan seemed so normal. Things like that shouldn't happen to people like them. They didn't have any enemies. They didn't do anything wrong."

He turned up the news volume.

"Joseph, are you listening?"

"Mmm-hmmm." He turned his attention back to the news.

"Macy used to say all she ever did was what they wanted. That they pushed and fussed and made her suffer, then they didn't thank her ever." She moved into the living room and sat on the couch next to his recliner. "Joan used to be so lonely. Just her in that house. The kids never visited. No one to talk to. She used to say women of a certain age needed to be heard. Appreciated. That at a certain point, we come into our own, but we don't know what to do with our power."

"Joan is fucking dead, Martha. Who cares what the looney bitch told you? She's dead."

Martha flinched liked she'd been struck. Maybe the silent treatment was kinder, but she'd never shut up about it if he didn't put his foot down.

"Why are you so cruel? I just want to talk. It's not like I have many people to talk to. You wanted me to stay home and be a housewife. You wanted—"

"I want quiet, okay? After such a fucked-up day, just a little quiet. Can you get dinner and let me have some peace?"

Martha stood, blocking the view of the screen.

"See me, Joseph. Just . . . listen and see me! You used to like to talk to me."

He leaned out far to the right, watching the television around her like she wasn't there.

"Please?" Her voice was tiny and desperate in her tight mouth.

Nothing. He gave her no words or eye contact. Not even anger. He just waited for her to move, staring through her like she wasn't there.

Something in the room started to smoke.

"Everything for you. Every damned thing. All the time." Her words fell like blows, buffeting him.

The temperature churned and blew like heat from an oven. Her hair whipped around her red face. She opened her mouth, tipped back her head, and screamed, but the scream came out as something more. A stream of plasma flame shot out, engulfing her and the whole house in flash fire as hot as the sun.

"That makes sense," said Joseph the fire chief, as his life turned to ashes and his skin bubbled away.

Then, even his words burned.

BADASSES

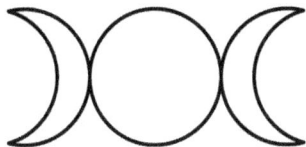

Women changing the world, making things work, balancing the
scales.

HALL OF WINDOWS, HALL OF LIGHTS

IT NEVER ENDS.

Each door, each step, each shuddering gaze through the shatter-proof windows echoes the days before and the days to come.

My door opens onto the end of the hallway. Outside of its heavy, metal-reinforced surface, the shining tile paths lead to food, to socializing around checkers and television, to group discussion meetings and doctors and pills and a padded consciousness without controls. I'm one of many sinking souls floating in this sea of madness.

"Sephie? Time for your walk," Nurse Myna sings from outside my door. Her shoes sloughed and sighed across the floor —a sidewinding sound.

A sucked-in breath steadies my heart's stuttering trot, then I push up from the narrow white-sheeted cot. My head swims, but I follow her voice, watch my feet, and never look up at her face. I can't. I've seen her shadow writhing on the wall. I let my fingers tangle in my long brown hair, and my eyes shift to watch the windows set in the white doors we passed. Some of the windows fill with a sparkling light, because behind them the inmate's precious freedom shines within the bubble of safety.

But, here and there, faces press against the windows.

Faces I once knew.

Or maybe I dreamed that life.

Shining faces. Powerful brows and gritted teeth.

Enemies, lovers, friends, mother. None of us managed out in the world.

"Here we are." Myna pushes open the door to the little garden. Those of us with the talent for green are allowed to tend it.

"Thank you." I duck my head without looking at her.

Poor Myna. She can't help how she was made. That she cares for us day by day shows we can change. Even if the world rejects us.

"I'll be back for you," she says, then whispers, "I'll bring him out if you want. Shall I?"

My love. I nod shyly and turn to tend my peonies, heads nodding into the pink cup of my hand. Their fluttering petals widen in my warm gaze. I tilt my face up to catch the rays of the sun. Our poor, dead sun. How could it be what it once was without Heli pulling it across the sky? He faded away in his room, white walls swallowing his brightness until there was nothing of him left.

Maybe I should let myself fade, as he did.

Sometimes, when mother ignores my questions and mutters to herself about seasons past, I worry that she'll let go too.

Would we all be better faded into the nothing that we've inherited?

Behind me, the door snicks open and closed. I feel the wave of cold I'd grown to love all those years ago.

"My love?" I turn, hoping that Myna has left us alone.

He sits in his chair, staring off into something only his eyes see. My dark lord. Skin brown as the earth he ruled. Eyes full of the glitter of minerals and gems—his own treasures. But the lips that spoke all the words that won me hang slack. Stupid with drool and medicine's rictus. His hands curl in his lap, clean and dead.

I pluck my peonies into a bundle and carry them to him. Once I'd hated him. He'd stolen me from my mother and friends, dragged me down into the earth, trapped me there with him. Once he'd tricked me into being his. Oh, how I'd hated him.

But he loved me soft and with patience. I'd found it easier to soften to him all those years ago than to keep fighting. I'd been his queen.

I lay the flowers in his lap and lean in, staring into his broken gaze.

When we first got here, I'd fought to be with him. I'd scratched and screamed, but Myna made me understand. We were sick. All of us. He had to heal, and so did I.

"My lord?" I try to get him to acknowledge me.

Nothing.

I kiss his lips and then leave him there, walking back into the hall where Myna waits for me.

"Anything?"

I shake my head. "He'll be gone soon."

We walk together down the hall, back to my room, years of memories between us. Thousands of them.

So many of us behind doors and windows, remembering what we used to be, taking pills to keep our minds from breaking. Forbidden from the world. Forgotten.

Should I let myself fade into a drugged oblivion like my love?

"Myna?" I stare at the sagging skin of my hands, all the beauty of my youth gone in these harsh florescent lights and the static filled air, dry as the breath as of Hell. "Myna, do you regret caring for us? You could be with your sisters in the next place instead of caring for us."

"I'm useful here." Her honeyed voice is a warm salve on my brittle nerves. "I'll see them again. This cannot last forever."

Cannot last forever. I'd never thought of that. My mind clung to the old ways and a belief that they'd want us back. They'd come looking for us someday, throw open the doors, and let us lead them down the hall. They'd give me seeds to plant. They'd ask him to shelter their souls in the folds of his cape.

Perhaps hope is madness.

For the first time since I'd come here, I feel the truth flowing down my face. Tears as hot as blood, yet my teeth chatter.

Cannot last forever.

"No more, Myna. No more medicine. No more checkers. No more waiting. I don't want to fade away like my love."

"I'm useful," Myna says back. Her lovely hands curl softly into a nest as she faces me. Her hands are always the kindness I look to. Not her face. She'd been the enemy of heroes. The scourge of the righteous. She and her sisters had been a curse. Cursed by us. Yet she'd become our savior. Our liberator. Maybe she'd always been and the humans had been the villains all along. Who knows?

"I don't want to fade, Myna." I don't look up—not yet. I reach for her hands and clutch them in mine, the warmth so soothing to me.

"I am useful to you." She frees one hand to curl it around my chin, and gently pulls me up to finally look at her face. Her face is mine from when I was a girl. So bright and beautiful. The hanks of hair swirl around her head, writhing like snakes, light shining from within. My cells bathe in her warmth and release their grip.

Freedom, finally.

DORIS DAY AND THE YEAR OF RECKONING

DORIS DAY SANG "QUE SERA, SERA," filling the screen of my television with her bright eyes and wide smile. Four eyes. Tentacles. She was NOT what I remember from my television-babysat youth. No, I'm sure she only had two eyes, and her teeth didn't spread across her face in an impossible arc. She sang songs with a lilting voice that sounded like the roof of the universe—high, reedy, and sweet as a primrose in spring.

Doris wasn't human.

She wore a crisp virginal dress and pearl earrings with a starshine the orbs didn't usually exude.

And around her whipped silver tentacles that shone in the hot lights with a green life, pulsing through the translucent cups that winked and stretched out to touch things independent of Doris's movements as she sang.

"Do you see that?"

My husband's eyes were glazed over as he hummed along with her.

"Hon?"

He blinked three times and turned slowly toward me. "Whaaaa?"

"Did you see that?"

"Doris Day? She's wonderful. Just what America needs in these terrible times."

His eyes were dreamy. Completely unfocused. And did those words really come out of his mouth? My husband is a reformed metal head who blasts Judas Priest when he works on correcting his students' equations every night.

"Doris Day? How is she what—"

"What we need?" He cupped my hands in his with a desperate strength. "The plague and politics and environment and all the other things wrong. Don't you wonder how we got here?"

Of course, I do. I teach government and current issues.

"Tradition. That's what she is. We need to return to—"

"What? Women in pearls? Do you not see that she has four eyes?"

His lip curled, and he actually drew back from me. "You could learn something from her. She says the future is not ours. Don't you see how we've always thought it was, and we've pushed and we've built and explored, destroying ourselves in the process."

I shook my head. "Who are you?"

We'd been married so long I thought I knew everything about him. My feminist, animal-loving, teary-eyed, metal head.

"I'm your husband—master of this house."

Oh, no, he didn't.

I got up and blocked the television with my body, and when I did, his face went slack, jaw agape and eyes unfocused. But then Doris started to sing again. She was a loop.

I grabbed the remote and switched channels. She was everywhere. Even on Telemundo singing the Spanish-inspired song in Español, grinning that wide, sparkling grin. Netflix? All Doris. Disney Plus? Doris. I switched off the television and turned back to talk to my husband again.

He was curled up in a ball around his phone. She sang to

him from the tiny speaker, and he clutched the screen filled with her face like she was a lifeline.

"Be like Doris," he said to me or to himself. I couldn't tell which because his rocking and mumbling sounded like a six-year-old's tantrum. I opened a search on my laptop. She was every ad singing on every page I clicked. CNN was Doris. MSNBC was Doris. And, of course, Fox was.

But I wasn't the only one seeing her.

I knew I shouldn't be searching, because who knows what she could or couldn't track online. But I had to know if any other humans could see her for what she was. First, I found a group of tin-foil-hat wearing HP Lovecraft fans. After talking back and forth with them, I realized they weren't seeing Doris for what she was, but they were seeing HP Lovecraft's world blooming because things were . . . well . . . shitty all around.

"Cthulhu is rising."

"The Elder Gods are silent no more."

And in the background, Doris sang.

That's when the Dorises started to talk to me. "We know you see us." Then, they'd sing some more.

By this time, my husband snored contentedly, rattling bursts of sound punctuating the sweet tones of "Que Sera, Sera."

Part of me wanted to run. Flee into the hills until whatever was happening stopped. But I'm not very outdoorsy. I'd starve or get poison ivy on my ass, for sure.

Besides, there was a virus out there.

I did go out wearing my trusty N-94, just to see what was happening outside my house.

All the people I came across had the song earworming in their minds. Humming, singing, saying the lyrics. Hell, they were running through my own head like a message from God, blotting out all but my loudest thoughts.

That's when I realized most of the people in the streets were singing maskless. I saw only a few like me. Timid walkers—folks with focused eyes hanging on the edges of the crowds wearing their masks. Easy to spot.

I made my way closer to one of them. "Did you see?"

She nodded. "Four eyes?"

"What do you think is happening?"

"I . . . I'm a doctor. I've been . . ." She closed her eyes for a second, and when she opened them, she looked stronger. "I've been watching these . . . infected people? I guess that's the best way to look at it. I've been tracking their movements and their actions. Listening to them. They exhibit symptoms that range from schizophrenic–disorganized thinking to fantastic ideation to odd movements. If I had to guess, the song carries some kind of . . ."

"Brain washing? Like something that makes perfectly normal people into someone they aren't?"

She shrugged at me like there wasn't a better way to put it. All we knew was that we didn't know. That's pretty scary stuff.

The song crescendoed inside the grocery store, and those of us with masks backed out of the enclosed space, worried that no amount of masking would save us from the damage being done inside by people singing in loud, breathy unison. Together in the parking lot, we talked about what we'd seen. Each of us had people we loved at home suffering from the effects of Doris's singing. But why would she do it? And why not us?

"We should break into the TV station and—"

"Stop the broadcast?" I shook my head. Too much science fiction, too little science fact. "There's no one signal anymore. Not like in the old movies, where you knock down a satellite dish and free the planet. We're way more complex than that."

"What can we do to stop it?" the doctor asked

We cast about for solutions that we all knew we'd never find.

"Let's ask *her*," I said. I pulled out my phone and dialed my husband's phone number. He didn't answer. I knew he wouldn't.

"Hello?"

It was the sweetest voice I'd ever heard, and honestly, it was the voice of Doris in her prime, back when she sang about everything and charmed us all with her safe beauty.

"Why, hello, dear. Put me on speaker, please? I'll make the singing stop so you all can hear me."

Inside the grocery store, the maskless puppets stopped, leaving the world as quiet as I'd ever heard. The LED billboard outside switched from showing the weekly specials to Doris's face, her four eyes staring at us with a gentleness that calmed my panic.

"That's better, isn't it? I guess you have many questions to ask, but the answer is so simple. The answer is you, my loves. We have decided that waiting for those around you to evolve and care enough about each other to save themselves and their planet was a fool's game. When we seeded your planet, we had no idea how heartless humans could be."

"So, you did this to us? The virus song?"

She nodded. "You few are a hybrid of us and them. If things went along a normal scale of evolution, the humans would have chosen you and those like you to lead them into a brighter, evolved future. Instead, it's people with money, strong arm dictators, idiots with mean words. And they vilify the noble or the smart. It's time for a culling."

"My husband isn't like that. He's bright and cares about everyone."

"Yes, if he survives this, he'll be stronger for it. If not . . ."

The song started back up on the inside of the grocery store.

"Hunker down, children. This isn't over, but when it is, you're the best chance for this world."

We glanced at each other with fear on our faces and so many questions we wanted to ask.

But I asked the one I needed to know.

"What if this doesn't work? What if your culling backfires and the meanness hardens? And it isn't all of them, you know. There are plenty of people working to fix things. They don't deserve to die."

"Collateral damage is unavoidable, but when this is over, they will have been the ones more likely to take precautions. More likely to beat the thought-poison I embedded in the song." Her whipping tentacles touched the screen, as if she'd like to caress our faces. "Save them, my children, or you die with them."

The little selfish piece of me deep inside stood up and screamed. Who was she to me? To us? Why should she dictate what we will or will not do? "Freedom!"

Then the rest of me flowed over that part like a white blood cell, entombing it. The little greedy piece of me had to die now. "Here's what we do." I turned toward the others. "We find everyone like us. We have to form that New World Order everyone is always so scared of."

The others nodded, eyes sparkling like the pearl in Doris's ear.

And as we scattered to do our work, Doris's song crescendoed. "Whatever will be, will be."

THE ORGAN TRADE

THE DOORS SWING, and my blank avatar steps in. The showroom walls riot in bright colors. Colors nature rejected for being loud long ago. In my world, gray and dusty brown dominate. But here, everything's a feast for the eyes. My blank's hands are smooth, like when I was a girl, before pollution marked them. Now they look like fallen leaves bleached gray in the bright winter cold and crumpled in bitter winds.

The showroom signage promises a solution to age and illness. A way out of our dead-end world. I'm middle-aged— eighteen years gone since the birth tube.

Around me, upgraded avatars pose with different charms and abilities. Do I want a beauty with bright yellow hair and men fighting over my favors? A one-breasted warrior woman with a taut bow and strapping leg muscles? Do I wish to experience ancient motherhood from when people rubbed together to make children for fun? To feel a person growing within? To make a person and raise it outside of tube farms? I'll never be a mother in the real world, but as an avatar, I can do it.

So many choices.

I've one body to give. I must choose wisely.

The avatar ride doesn't last long. No refunds. No exchanges.

Once they harvest the organs, my consciousness will dissipate like morning smog. If I pick the wrong avatar, my organs will be taken for my sponsor, and I'll be stuck. What I choose won't change.

So, I study my choices. In the real world, I'm lying on a cot as tubes in my veins and lungs fill me full of what I need to live. If I'm to get my organs' worth, I should make the choice soon. It takes a day to acclimate to the avatar, and then they start harvesting.

They say an hour in the organ clinic operating room is one hundred years in the avatar.

One hundred years of what can't be had in my world. People like me live in gutters, shuffling from handout to hopeless day labor. Sure, a few can afford the high life. They play with avatars while resting in freezer beds that keep their bodies safe from the pollutants. When they age or catch sick, they harvest us. They live on with our parts, fleshy lifeboats sailing the seas of purchased fantasies. A rich avatar rider can afford many harvests in their long life.

If they can live for hundreds of years, how many lives is that in an avatar? Do they create their worlds like gods? Do they gain knowledge from their span? Do they change? Or is it some everlasting game?

I shake the head of my avatar. I wonder if my real head shakes in response.

I'm getting distracted by philosophy. Back to the avatars.

She's beautiful. Soft waves of brown hair done up with a pearl studded crown circle her white skin. Brown eyes made larger by paint sparkle. Lips, red against her skin. Her dress shimmers—so beautiful. But the shape of her shocks me. Wide on top and bottom and pinched in the middle. Full of flesh. Not like me. I'd disappear behind a signpost—life isn't easy in my city cluster.

This avatar didn't starve. Her curving body brings a warmth

to my imagined cheeks. I want to be her. Beautiful. Cared for. Ample.

I bend to read the floating words in the air beside her.

"Victorian woman: spend afternoons at high tea, eating cucumber toast points. Attend opera performances. Live in high style with servants and closets full of silks that whisper across your healthy, plumped skin."

Though my mind floats inside the virtual showroom, I feel prickles race across my skin. Such sumptuous words. Even inside the program, my body craves the taste of things that make a body so full of life.

If I swipe my hand through the floating words, I make my choice. My consciousness will transfer, and the bidding for my organs begins. Then, once one of the eternally young wins my physical body, the procedures start.

My clock will tick down.

Is she worth my last hour of life?

I glance around once more, eyes landing on another possibility. A creature with white wings and a savage razor beak. Talons sharp as needles. Human eyes set in bright red skin. No explanation floats next to the creature. Only a name—Harpy.

I tilt my head and imagine being a harpy. It might be nice to fly—to ride the winds and be the ones others feared. To tear food with sharpened fingers. How beautiful would it be to color the world with the blood of my victims, splashing life in red bursts across the gray reality?

I glance back at the fine lady, all her delicacy a temptation that wavers my resolve. Her lack of want calls, but her eyes say she's powerless like me. Behind the finery lies emptiness. I know it because I've seen it in my own gaze. She doesn't fight for morsels from the Church of Eternal Life like me. She doesn't work in the wastes until her hands bleed, farming thin vegetables to breathe another day or two like me. But behind her smile lies desperation. She is my sister.

She'd choose the harpy too.

I swipe my hand through the word. The showroom melts away in a swirl of color. In her place, the divine leaders appear. They speak in unison, heads bobbing on the waves of simmering color.

"In choosing this avatar, you agree to harvest for the eternals. Your experience shall be reward for your sacrifice. Enjoy your freedom. The church thanks you."

I memorize their faces as my avatar begins to remake itself into the feathered dream I'd purchased with my life. I stretch my claws and stare into the leaders' eyes, knowing they'd be the first creatures I'd seek during my ride.

As they ripped my organs from me for others to consume, I'd rip their organs to consume in my avatar life.

Who's to say what's real anyway?

FROM ABOVE

"Ugly, innit?"

Julia picked among the soap lady's basket of goods, sniffed a bar of lemon soap, and glanced up at the bottom of the floating city. The craggy black rock that blocked the sky and cast a pool of darkness on the landlocked part of the city hung in the air above them, floating on some invisible science that none of the landlocked citizens understood.

"Like the arse-end of a frying pan," Julia said.

They tittered together, but it felt like they were laughing at their own funeral.

Since the day the upper city came down from the sky and the creatures who lived on it set the new rules, life in the undercity had been rough. No sun. No rain to wash away soot. That wasn't the worst. Shit rolls downhill.

Julia was an enforcer. One of the few humans allowed to move between the upper and lower cities. She hunted the burrows and narrows and downs for those desperate humans who took from each other or killed for money. Didn't matter that the folks below hated her for having connections with those up top. They loved her in equal measure because she was fair. She didn't double-deal them.

"Goin' up?" the soap dealer asked. "You tell 'em we don't get enough trade down here. They got to start buying from us."

Julia nodded. "I'll pass it along."

She dropped a token in the lady's hand, and the lemon scented soap into her pocket. Lemon was a lost food. The new climate didn't allow for such heat-loving fruits, so she wasn't sure if the tangy scent truly was lemon, or just some pleasant brew the old soap maker called lemon to sell it to folk like her.

Knowing what was real didn't matter to most of the undercity dwellers as long as the upper city didn't drown them in filth.

That had happened in Old New York and Atlanta.

Gone.

So far, so good. That's why Julia knew her job mattered. When something came down the pipes and washed into the undercity river that the bottom dwellers knew they shouldn't see or have, they passed it to Julia to return upcity.

Kids fished broken pieces of upper-city tech that glowed with green power out of the brackish water. The power irradiated them the longer they kept it. She had special bags for collecting those pieces and taking them back up.

Sometimes things fell that were whole.

In her bag, next to the bar of lemon soap and synth gloves, lay a black hook that sparkled like wet obsidian. One of the old women who sold corn mash had given it to Julia. Said her son found it, and she was worried that he'd hurt himself with it.

It fit in the palm of her hand like it had been made to fit every line and ripple of her palm. She'd seen them before.

Always in the hands of the royals at the very top of the upper city rock.

How one had found its way down to the undercity, she couldn't guess, but there's be hell to pay if it didn't find its way back into their blue-blooded hands.

She made her way to the elevator, the black-spired monument that used to be dedicated to the poet of the Old

World. They'd made it over into the only way to get from below to above. Green energy flowed in a waterfall from the rock above, dropping down into an enveloping beam.

It lifted her, though it always felt like her stomach stayed below.

When her feet landed firmly on the cobbles of the upper city, she glanced around, noting all the shoppers, guards, and servants of the blue-blood houses. The ending hour when all the undercity dwellers left the upper was only a few turns away, so Julia jogged up the winding cobbled street that led to the sky precinct, where all the blue-blood mansions wrapped around the pointed crags at the top of the rock. Green lights lit the path. Color and light spilled from every window, so bright that Julia always wondered if there was any end to their powers in the upper city.

She finally knocked on the tallest door of the highest building at the top of the crag. The door opened, and one of them, a lesser blue-blood, stood as servant behind it.

"Enforcer? The ending hour approaches. You must—"

"I need to see your master." She pushed past him—a brazen act no other undercity dweller could get away with—but Zorm needed to see the tech.

She opened the door to the library that Prince Zorm spent almost all of his time in. His father was head of the city, and his mother the ear of the gods, but Prince Zorm kept all the records, tracking all that happened above and below. She was his personal enforcer.

"Julia?" Zorm stared at her as she hustled across the white marble floor toward him. He was a handsome one. Blue heart beating inside the crystal enclosure of his chest, sending the blue blood coursing through his branchlike limbs. He glowed with his royal blood, and his eyes were huge. Human-like but brighter, bigger. Just enough to make him alien. He smiled, and his features softened into the expression he liked best— something between curiosity and lusty hunger.

Julia grinned like a fool. She usually did when he looked at her that way. "Found something."

She flipped her bag on his desk, dumping the gloves, the bar of soap, and the hook-shaped tech she'd found. Zorm picked through them, first opening the soap and taking a bite of it. It was his favorite, after all. Then, he picked up the hook. It lit up in his hand, glowing green and flashing with black shine.

"I can't believe it." The blue of his blood glowed in his hand around the object. "When did you find this?"

"Yesterday."

"And how many people have seen it?"

"Me, an old woman, her son."

"Did anything happen when you touched it?"

"No."

Zorm sighed and flipped the object over in his hands.

"This is a key. The most important of our tech. In the wrong hands . . . well, I don't think it's a real threat. You humans aren't shaped like us." Zorm set the piece aside.

"I know it's not my place, but what does it do?"

Zorm looked up at her sharply and studied her face. She kept her features neutral. She always did.

"I guess there's no harm. This is a blue-blood's personal key." He picked it up and put it in his palm just so.

Immediately, the grooves in his branchy fingers lit up, as did the object. The room seemed to shift, and around them floated pictures of things Julia had never seen.

Zorm touched one, and it expanded. "It keeps all of our knowledge."

The image was of a forest, though it wasn't on Earth. Julia watched as a creature rolled toward her like a pinwheel—all tentacles and teeth. She gasped and raised her hands in front of her face. It was so real.

Zorm laughed at her and drew the image back. "One of our enemies. Just an image."

"So, it's not a weapon?" Julia smiled with all the innocence she could muster.

"In the wrong hands, it's the worst weapon of all. A species' weaknesses are hidden in its history. I applaud you for returning such an important thing to us, Julia. The ending hour is here, and you will not make it back to the common transport pad. Allow me to send you home myself. Father and I will discuss your reward tomorrow."

Julia smiled and followed Zorn to a closet that glowed with the green light of their power. He bowed as she went in, then in a wash of green, she found herself back in the bottoms of the undercity, at the door of her house.

She made her way through the winding alleys and snickleways until she stepped into a hidden warehouse. Hundreds of humans, the best minds of the city, labored over new and old tech cobbled together. The resistance. She smiled and walked over to General Tomlin, the soap woman.

"Did they take it?"

"Worked perfectly. He thought he had the real thing. They won't come looking for it, I'd guess." The real key sat open, with scenes spinning around the rebel scientists. They picked through them to find images of tech they could reverse-engineer to make it work for humans.

"I have a good feeling about this." Julia left to scour the city for more of the shit that rolls downhill. They wouldn't be downhill for much longer if she could help it.

LADY LAMPSHADE

I WEEP at night when I take off my tent and walk naked behind the three locks on my apartment door. Sometimes the guards conduct inspections, but they never just come in. I have time to put on my veil and robe and hide the manuscript under my floorboards.

It's funny. The story of the denigration of our rights is so like the hundreds of fictions written by women writers with dystopian fears from before everything got turned upside down. The fictions we used to teach as cautionary tales have now come true. Since they'd become non-fiction, those books are banned from common use.

I'd read them all back when the wind was on my face and I lived where I wanted rather than this assigned apartment for fatherless, unmarried women. Back then, I'd taught classes in which we analyzed the critiques of the patriarchy in books where women wore red or were driven mad by wallpaper. Now, leaders use those books in their power-plays and stratagems. Our cautionary tales were made over into the bright lights the ship of state now sets its course by.

"Let us in, Cass Smith." Joseph the guard pounds on the door.

We know each other from before.

He used to be a custodian at the college. He'd complained to the dean about my women's studies students. About how rude and uppity the young women were. I'd gotten him removed from my hallway. I'd told him to stop bothering my students in a voice full of indignant daggers.

Now he has the power of life and death over me.

"Yes, sir." I unlock the door after everything is secure under the floor and my body is covered.

He leads these room checks almost every day. Most of the other spinster women in the building are only checked weekly. I bow my head and stand aside. He's hit me more than once when I moved too slowly or questioned the familiarity of them searching through my underthings.

I must be careful or . . .

"I'm going to catch you, and then I'll let you have it," he mutters near my ear. He curls his white-knuckled fist around his billy club and presses it hard against his leg, as if he's holding it back from attacking. "I'll tear this fucking room apart if you make one mistake. Just one."

How did we let this happen?

It started with the reversal of *Roe*, then the meninist movement took hold, and there were prosecutions for traveling to get birth control. Soon, executions for secret abortions dominated the newsfeed. The purge of women from all levels of leadership and strict rules about dress, occupation, and ownership of private property followed. We fought it. Complained. Wrote. Allies secreted women over state lines to get services and protections before the revolution erased those boundaries and created one big state. The loudest of us disappeared. Some, like me, were reeducated.

"Pay attention to us, Cass Smith, or we will make you sorry." Joseph brings me back to the moment with a spray of spittle on my cheek.

I nod once, drop to a knee in supplication, and vigilantly

watch them tear my room apart. So many of my cohort are dead, hanged from trees or thrown into piles in front of the college. So many of my students have been broken with me in the camps. Their faces swim up in my memory as I squeeze my eyes shut. Joseph uses the club to stroke my cheek, and I wonder how long I have.

How long do I want to have?

I still have nightmares about endless loops of government-mandated shows that fed me my role. I'm lucky they found a use for me, even though I'm a prime example of what happens to women educated beyond their capacity and God-given calling.

I mop the floors of the museum.

At the museum, I'm allowed to wear a less restrictive uniform that swaths my body in fabric but allows me to move with my broom and mop. Though it's all browns and blacks, the shape reminds me of the Suffragettes' clothes right before the fashions of the 1920s took hold back in the history we don't talk about anymore.

Puffy sleeves, fitted bodice with a high starched neck, hooped skirt that brushes the ankles of the knee-high boots that pinch my toes, and on my head I wear a flared cone that straps snuggly beneath my chin. It looks just like a lampshade.

I'm only supposed to wear it at the museum while cleaning, but it's so liberating. The freedom of movement it affords. Sweet breaths of fresh air and true sound that carry under the lip of my headgear make me feel lucky to work there. Those in charge thought cleaning their false history temple would be a demeaning job for me. Instead, it gives me access.

I've seen what they did with the artifacts of before. Mass burnings of mini-skirts and feminist tomes. More than one woman's degree was used as tinder at the museum's cullings. Nude oils and sculptures are draped for the after-hours visits of men who come for brandy and conversation while their wives are safely tucked back at home under lock and key.

Now what's left in the halls of the museum? A history of invisible women.

I stole pages before the books burned. I secreted vibrant fabrics and pieces of historical garb in the tent they gave me. Thread and needles are freely available in my apartment house, and no one questions a spinster woman sewing to pass her time. Even Joseph can't fault me for doing "women's work."

That's how I built Lady Lampshade.

))C((

The whispers in the grocery store grew over the next few weeks.

"Lady Lampshade gave me a book . . ."

"She snuck me an old radio that picks up Free Mexico and the Canadian provinces."

". . . watercolors and paper . . ."

I heard their wishes and tried to find things in the old warehouse level of the museum. I pilfered trinkets, pencils and chalks, poem fragments, and old pictures of what women used to be.

Somebody once chalked *Lady Lampshade bringer of light* on the city wall with a powdery mural of flowers and books and a likeness of me that the guards sprayed off before the women's morning shopping hour. The streaks of color collected in the lines of the gray bricks, bright as a rainbow, and the women knew what had been washed off. Every woman who saw it knew what one of them had risked to push the message of freedom into the world.

Women began passing encrypted notes at the shopping market, which continued even when public beatings were the result. Guards searched rooms and found only quilts. But those quilts had been stitched with embedded directions only women understood.

Women started to disappear, and no amount of patrolling or threats revealed a path of escape they might have taken. But I knew because I was the one spreading the clues. I felt like I walked in the footsteps of women scrubbed from history—spies, escapees, soldiers.

At night, I used a bobbing light to draw them.

I'd found the plans to the storm sewers and turned them into a stitched pattern on handkerchiefs I shared with shopping partners and left in women's areas—nurseries, washrooms, and waiting areas designated for women only. Women taught each other to reach the stitches and created a language to talk about what they'd lost, to talk to me about what they needed, and to tell me when they'd be following my bobbing light.

I collected them every other night or so and ushered them through the dark drains and concrete highways that run under the hills and past the walls. When we got out of the city, I set them up in an abandoned Walmart we'd turned into a hub on the railroad. Those women then mapped the world beyond.

Lady Lampshades popped up in every city, doing the work of women. The stitched messages find me each week. Even though many have been saved, and there have been many little rebellions, the work costs so much. Lady Lampshades hang from trees and bell towers, exposed boots tapping together hollowly in the wind. Still, they spread across the expanse of what used to be the home of the free. I flush every hanky, but the messages make me proud.

)O(

After a long shift at the museum, I report home for the night's check-in. I stand at my door with Joseph as usual, keeping my eyes downcast as the others rifle through my closet, my drawers, and my bedsheets, though they seem less thorough than normal.

Usually, Joseph has some nasty curse or mumbled insult for me as the others do their work.

Nothing. He stands silent and. . . relaxed.

Maybe he's accepted my facade of carved-ivory acceptance

and marble obedience. He doesn't say a word as they search and are surprisingly gentle with my things. Something is wrong, but I can't put my finger on it. His smirk or the sloppiness of the others? Maybe there's a new mandate?

"Have a good night, gal." Joseph pulls the door shut.

I lock all three locks and sit on the bed, puzzling out what might be the source of his kindness. I spend a precious hour there waiting for the other shoe to drop. I can't wait longer than that.

I pull the boots and underskirts out of the panel at the back of my closet. The dress itself I'd hidden in the lining of my mattress using Velcro I'd taken from computer cord wraps. The lampshade is . . . gone. I'd shoved it into the ductwork and screwed the cover over it tight, but it's not there. Whoever'd found it had only halfway screwed the grate back onto the wall.

Fuuuuuuu—He knocks on the door. Subdued. Gentle. "Minister Gerry's here, traitor bitch. Open this damned door." In contrast to the words, his voice seems calm.

There are women waiting for Lady Lampshade to take them to safety. They'd crawled through their own ducts and down the rusted-out fire escapes. They'd snuck away with children, leaving their husbands sleeping peacefully. They wait by the drain, covered in browns and blacks and tears, for a heroine.

Lampshade or no . . .

The banging on the door turns into a splintering. A cracking.

I'd given the map to others who'd memorized it and passed it along. Lady Lampshade would never give up to the beasts outside her door. Someone would find the women waiting. Another Lady Lampshade would step up.

"Let us in. You're only making it worse." Joseph is yelling now, though he sounds giddy. "We've got your fucking lampshade. You're done, dead to rights."

I think about putting on the dress, but I decide not to. Instead, I peel off my shift and stand as naked as I'd been born, skin kissed by moon and the breath of night. I open the window as much as I can—just four inches. Not enough to fit. I grab my chair and swing it through the window, creating a shimmering shower of glass that tumbles to the concrete below in a twinkling waterfall.

How would they see me? Would they know, or would I be washed away like the chalk murals, no vivid rainbow river to announce I'd ever been. Maybe a velvety red ribbon will do.

I crouch in the windowsill as the door crashes open.

I scream the way women used to, full throated and unafraid. I howl as they push through, reaching for me. They'll hang me. Or beat me and then hang me.

I won't let them.

As naked as if I'm being born again, I push through the snaggled glass vulva of a window and leap out into the void. Hair flying, eyes wide, boobs flopping, and teeth bared.

I laugh, knowing the other women will hear even if they can't see what I've done. I fling myself out, and I am free. You can't hang an idea. You can't arrest us all.

Lampshade or not, we'll find freedom.

See me or not, all my sisters will be proud.

MAD WOMEN

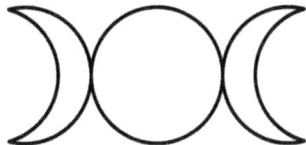

Women get tired. They break and reform into something with too many angles and bends

FEELING SORRY FOR ASSHOLES

LUCY'S MOUTH crusted with gems. A diamond mustache, ruby rosacea whirling on her cheeks, and nose sparking with spots of erupting wealth. Leaning toward her foggy bathroom mirror, she picked at them until, one by one, they fell off, leaving bloodied pockmarks weeping in her skin.

Fucking wishes.

She dropped them all into a jar, the latest of many, filled with glittering stones. For the next hour, she filled the holes and covered the color of the erupting gems, making her face look more like a teen pizza face that humans wouldn't notice, other than to sneer at. Lucy didn't mind. It kept most people from thinking nice thoughts at her.

She pulled on her dress, mindful of the lumpy scars on her shoulders. She'd had wings inked on her back, long before the current badass black-inked trend inspired by Darryl of *The Walking Dead*. Hers were there to remind her of what she'd lost.

With a deep breath, she pulled on a jacket, twisted open the front door, and stepped out into the bright light of morning. Her wounds would fill with stones all day, but she couldn't sit in her house forever. She had to eat. Had to pay bills. Had to get sun on her skin and wind on her face. Once, she'd tried to stay cooped up to avoid them, but the human wishes still filtered in through the cracks in her house—under the door, down the chimney. Her mowing neighbor wished good health for his ailing friend, and a ruby implanted on the corner of her mouth. A mailman with such joy in his heart and a whistle that sounded like bird song wished so many people so much good that she developed a nest of diamonds along her jawline so big they'd ripped her open. She'd sewed the flaps back together and had her doors weather-stripped to seal some of their wishes out.

But it was unavoidable.

She did the chores she had to around town, inching away from those folks who proclaimed their goodness with every smile and thought. Like the smiling fools with kind words on the train. And serene church ladies who nodded and spouted wishes for peace and protection that lined certain streets in town like spiritual potholes. Little children at play were the worst. Swinging on swings or from jungle gym bars, they all wished for their own moon swathed up in innocence and joy. Walking past a playground might cover her face, neck, and shoulders in sparkling rainbow mineral scales.

Fucking wishes!

She kept to the dark side of town, where pure wishes usually stayed inside, behind bolted doors.

Lucy pushed open the door to her favorite bar, Snake-Eyes and Pool Cues, a greasy spot with warm food, cold beer, and a bunch of lugs so drowned in regret that their wishes were a laundry list of greed and self-serving.

Not all of them, and not all the time.

Lucy always stayed away from Jack, the regular in the corner whose alcoholism didn't stop him from loving his poor abandoned kid and longing to do right by him, but the alcohol blunted his love enough that he didn't manage to make his wish into a rock. When he wished, a glittering streak might form across her cheekbone like a vein of gold in a mountain.

Most of the others only wished for themselves or for things that didn't hurt.

Besides, Snake-eyes made a mean bowl of chili.

"Hi Lucy." He slid a piping bowl in front of her when she sat at the bar. "Get you anything else?"

She shook her head and dug into the meaty stew.

Snake-eyes, or Snake, as she'd come to know him, was her favorite. He wasn't bad or good, or anything. Kind of an asshole, really. Back before she fell, she would've sought him out to repair his fractured soul. A would-be project for the up-and-coming guardian. A perfect sociopathic puzzle with missing pieces she could find and knit together.

"How's the chili?" He faked concern, though she tasted his boredom, his self-involvement.

"Delicious," she said, though she wasn't referring to the stew at all. How could he know her arched eyebrow and crooked smile had more to do with the state of his soul than the shape of his ass?

"Oh yeah?" Snake leaned in, gaze intense as he weighed her interest. His long brown hair fell across his face, shading it so all that glittered were his grinning teeth. His elbows rested on the bar and even though a couple next to her wanted his attention, he focused on her. "You down tonight, doll?"

He'd tried before, not because he actually had feelings for her but because his belt needed notching. She knew his wishes. They were all dirty as hell. Selfish. Nothing that might grow painful stones. She'd resisted so far, but . . .

"I'm down. When are you off?"

Snake shot a look at his waitress and back at his other bartender.

"We're slow." He hopped over the bar and strode toward the door, not waiting for Lucy.

That part of him was missing, and it felt good to her. He hopped on his Harley and pulled on his helmet, balancing his bike between his muscled thighs. "Your place or mine?"

"Mine." Lucy got into her car to lead him.

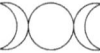

The sex was good enough. Hot and hard. It left her breathless.

He lit a cigarette without asking if it was okay.

She smiled at that. So little care. The pebbles of pain under her skin had melted with his every selfish touch. The pain of eruption faded as each of the hard pocks smoothed.

"That was fun." He smashed his butt out on the top of a beer she'd gotten him. "I gotta go."

Lucy nodded, running fingers across her smoothed-out face. "Yeah, see ya."

The pain was gone. No stones, no nothing.

The door shut behind Snake, his Harley roared away, and she wished for the first time since that fall so long ago, "Let this be my life." Then, she fell into a blissful, painless sleep on a clean pillow.

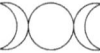

She couldn't stay away from Snake.

He'd become the answer to her problems, and with every hard, thrusting encounter, Lucy found healing.

They'd been at it for months. At first, only a couple times a week, sometimes in the bar bathroom or on his bike, in her car or at her house, it didn't matter really. But soon, he'd started coming to her every night.

"You're a drug, Lucy." He rubbed his hand across her wing tattoos, first the left and then the right. "I can't get enough."

His wishes were delicious. Wishes that she'd suck him harder. Wishes for more kink. Oh, so many selfish things to want, each giving her another day's relief from the goodness that assaulted her all day long.

There hadn't been one stone since she'd started fucking him. Not one.

Tonight, he'd had her three times. Each one rougher, more exposed than the last. The hood of her car in the parking lot under the pool of a yellow streetlight didn't even phase her.

"Why are you so cool with this? Most girls—"

"I'm not most girls."

"Yeah, but—"

"Shut up, Snake. Are we going to do it again or what?"

He pulled away from her and leaned against the silver grill of the car. He reached up and pulled her skirt back over her ass and grabbed her hand.

"Listen, Lucy, I want to tell you something . . ."

She adjusted her sleeves back into place and turned to face him, nerves flaring, clenching up her stomach.

"I know that there's something wrong with me. Been this way all my life." He laced his fingers in hers and tugged her down onto the asphalt next to him. His knee brushed hers as he talked. "I never cared about nothing. Not my ma, not girlfriends, not anything. Something's missing in me that . . . that I wish was there."

In Lucy's soft pallet, a throb of pain stung needles up into her eyes until she blinked out fat tears. Tears that Snake misunderstood completely.

"Aw, Lucy, I'm sorry I'm so useless. I just like you is all. More than I've ever liked anyone and . . ."

Her skin sharpened with geometric ridges, and her tongue ran across each line breaking through the roof of her mouth. It was the crushing pain of a thousand brain freezes wrapped in barbed wire and trying to fit through a teeny, tiny hole. The gem he'd put in her, his damned first unselfish wish, struggled to be born and ripped her mouth bloody.

"I want to be with you. Only I don't know how. I wish . . . I wish I could be good for you."

Lucy started to cough, blood streaked the mucus of her mouth as she spat. She braced on all fours, jaw agape as the wish pushed out all points and edges, past her jaw, past her teeth, and onto the asphalt with a clatter.

A diamond the size of a fist.

"Don't wish anymore." Lucy panted until her mouth knitted back together. "Please."

Snake watched, paced, and kneeled by her, unsure what to do or say. Caring was new to him, after all.

Lucy picked up the diamond and turned to face him. It had been so long since she'd finished a soul puzzle. When she'd lost her wings and fell, she gave it up. But he stood so close, worry laced in his features for the first time in his life. A little bird flying in a storm, lost.

If she gave him the stone that would make him whole, cement the wish and make it real, then she'd be giving away the only succor she'd known from pain since the time of her fall.

His wish sat in her hand thrumming its own wish to heal him, and how could she not? How could she leave him broken?

"This is yours." Lucy put the diamond in his hands and closed his fingers tight around the edges, pressing hard until the gem opened him up and made its way into the empty spot within. He stood gape-mouthed and vacant as he reset.

Lucy turned to leave, to get away before the kind wishes began, but he came to.

"I love you, Lucy," he said. And he was whole.

Her back cracked open, though it felt like a shower of spring rain. The wings she'd lost unfurled from the tattooed ink, beautiful iridescent gem fragments as thin as mist. She lifted her face to the sun and felt the welcome waiting for her. Forgiveness. She spread her wings and—

"I love you, though." In Snake's words, chips of goodness fell away.

If she left, he'd fall.

If she left, he'd shatter.

If she stayed, she'd suffer.

An angel without the presence and voice of God is a damned one, indeed.

If she left, would she still be saved?

"It's what I get." She tugged her wings back under the sleeves of her dress. "Feeling sorry for assholes. Damned."

BATH BOMB BIRTHDAY

STELLA'S LOVE for her beautiful sister had been assumed all their lives. They were twins, but Stella was born second to Iris, and she would always be second—in height, in beauty, in her mother's heart.

Step 1: Gather dry ingredients—citric acid, baking soda, cornstarch, Epsom salt. Mix in a bowl and set aside.

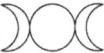

"Stella, did you confirm the caterer? "

It was the twins' birthday on Saturday, but Mother always acted like it was just Iris they were celebrating.

"Everything has to be perfect," she said. "Never know who might help her career along, right?"

Stella nodded and moved to the den where party plans covered the old oak desk like battle maps.

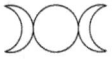

Step 2: Gather wet ingredients—Mica pigment paste to make it sparkle and fizz. Fifteen drops of essential oils, lavender, and lemon balm suit her beauty. Witch hazel and 91 percent rubbing alcohol round out the wet ingredients. Mix them until the smell is smooth as spring's sunrise.

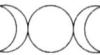

"Happy birthday, Stell." Iris tumbled into bed next to her twin. She tangled her legs with Stella's like when they were girls, but even then Iris's were gazelle legs while Stella's were tree trunks. "Ready for our party?"

Stella never knew how to take Iris, because every exchange was a summer storm. Sunny skies one minute, then a deluge the next. Mercurial, Mother called it.

Stella took the easy way out. "The planning you mean? It's good. I double checked—"

"No, silly—I mean, that's important—Mother and I would be lost without your tidy brain. I meant, though, do you have a dress?"

Stella nodded and untangled, knowing the demand that would come next.

"Show me." Iris stretched, her willowy body a modern Venus of Urbino.

Stella pulled a velvety blue dress from her closet. A kicky frill grazed her knee, and a boat neck framed her collarbones. Flashy enough, but still her.

"No."

Her stomach clenched as Iris's good-nature evaporated. Her features froze in response to the temperature change in her words.

"You'll embarrass yourself in that. It's frumpy."

"I'm not you, Iris. You're a model, damn it. I can't wear—"

"I've got a perfect dress," Iris said.

She left for a second and stepped back in, putting on a show she had clearly planned.

"Ta-dah!"

It sparkled with gold shimmering beads—cocktail length with an empire waist, perfect for hiding Stella's "flaws."

"We'll match!"

Iris pulled a second dress from behind the first, made with matching embellishments; only hers was the stuff of *Mad Men* dreams and *Fantasy Island* wishes. Figure hugging with a slit that tried to shake hands with the plunging neckline. Iris would look so gorgeous, Stella could come naked and nobody would notice.

Knowing it wasn't a battle she'd win, Stella took the dress.

"You'll look so good." Iris flounced away. "Just don't embarrass, okay?"

Not for the first time, Stella wished she could skip her own birthday.

Step 3: Mix the wet and dry ingredients, stirring until they have the consistency of wet sand.

"Is the slideshow finished?" Mother tapped her spoon against her five-minute egg until it cracked. She scooped the yellow flesh inside.

"It's done."

"Including her Paris runway pictures? Millan?"

Stella nodded. What else would she have put in? "They're there."

"Perfect." Tick, tick, tick, and she beheaded another egg.

Step 4: Pack the sandy mixture into your mold. Press a marble into the center of each side to make a cavity for the special ingredient. Let the halves dry.

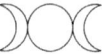

"Did you put shoe boxes outside my door? I scraped up my legs when I fell over them. My look is ruined!" Iris dabbed at the speckled dots of blood, tiny as dew.

"Sorry, Iris. I wanted you to pick my shoes." Stella took her time surveying the damage to Iris's legs. "I know. Why don't I give you your present early? It might help."

Iris smiled. Stella imagined it was because she'd given the proper amount of pity to poor Iris's devastating situation. Lack of perfection truly bothered her sister, especially when it concerned her looks. Nothing made her happier than someone understanding that, so the shoe debacle was instantly forgiven.

"You think it will help?" Iris allowed herself to be led into Stella's bedroom. "What is it?"

Stella pulled a blue velvet drawstring bag from her closet and handed it to Iris. "Open it."

Iris glanced inside. "Bath bombs?"

"Homemade just for you. Smell them."

Iris sniffed, and her eyes rolled back. "Lavender and. . . lemon. Essential oils are so good."

Stella smiled. "There's witch hazel in it too. Good for abrasions. Take a couple of warm baths today and one tomorrow. I bet your legs will be perfect by Saturday."

Iris drew the bag strings as the bath water ran, flashing her catalog-ready smile. A genuine smile because, of course, this was all about her. "Thanks for such a sweet present. I'll go take a bath right now."

Stella moved the shoe boxes back into her closet and picked up the scraps of blue fabric from the dress she'd cut to make the drawstring bag. She scooped up empty oyster shells she'd hidden and stuffed them all into the dumpster outside.

The 48-hour countdown began.

Step 5: Shuck the impregnated oyster. The vibrio vulnificus needs an entry point. Create one by planning a small accident that will result in skin eruptions. Necrotizing fasciitis begins working immediately upon release into warm water, but to keep it safe until then, seal it between the two halves of the bath bomb with a bit of leftover paste. Keep in mind, depending on the severity of the infection, the victim feels the effects within twenty-four hours, too late to stop necrotization around the entry wounds. If left untreated, the victim will die within forty-eight hours.

Stella smiled while her sister splashed around in the tub. "Happy birthday to me."

REHOMED

When I left, he wouldn't let me take any more than the clothes on my back.

What he didn't know was I'd been planning to leave for weeks. There were three trash bags full of the most important things—a few changes of clothes, some toiletries, old pictures of family long dead, junk jewelry Mama left me that mattered because it was hers, my IDs, and some cash I'd skimmed off the grocery money—all stashed in the trunk of my Corolla. None of it was enough to tip him off that, this time, I really was leaving. This time, I was going to disappear like a ghost.

"You'll be back, because where else do you have to go? You'll come crawling home, but maybe by then, I'll find someone better than you." He screamed this as I pulled out of the driveway, trying to ignore the spittle and the meaty fists he pounded on my hood. If I reacted, he'd jump in his Chevy and chase me down like last time. I didn't want to be the reason he ran over a kid. Let him think I'd be right back. Let him think he had me spooked and under his thumb.

The neighbor's porch lights flashed on the same way they did every time he got drunk enough to start screaming. They never did intervene, and this time was no different. It was like they thought the light would shut him up or drive him back inside where they wouldn't have to hear him scream at me or see the slaps and punches he doled out when he'd had just enough Jack to turn mean.

I wouldn't miss their pitying looks over the fence or the muttered conversation when I passed them on the sidewalk. They had no heart for a broken woman. My blood and bruises proved that they were better than us, that we were trash, and that somehow, we deserved each other. Maybe I used to believe that myself. No more.

And I'd never come back to him, even though he was right about one thing. I didn't have anywhere to go.

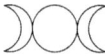

I drove for eighteen hours on pure adrenaline and gas station hot dogs. The $12,000 I'd managed to skim and sock away over the years wouldn't go far, especially after the Corolla started smoking in the middle of Kansas. By the time I arrived in Limon, Colorado, the chugging had become more of a knocking.

If I could get to Washout Creek, there was an old cabin on the edge of Pike National Forest that looked good on buymyoldhouse.com, but I knew from the Google Earth search that the $7000 I'd be paying might be overpriced. It was touch and go for a while, but the Japanese engineering of my Corolla got me there. I sailed through tall pines, red rocks that grew into cliffs, and long stretches of scrubby nothingness. The last place on earth someone would run to.

Kelly, my realtor, met me at the winding rock driveway and eyed my little car's bald tires with real worry.

"Mountain life isn't for everyone, Ms. Moore."

"Call me Laura, please." I needed Kelly to be on my side. Mom used to say that small-town folks will circle around you and protect you if they like you well enough. I had told her about my marriage, and she'd made all the appropriate sad sounds as she helped me find the little house I was about to hand her most of my savings to live in.

"Laura, listen. I'll keep your name secret, like you asked. I've set up with Mr. Wills to deliver you groceries when he brings up your weekly mail, but you're going to have to get a job, and this is so far from town. . ."

I nodded and blinked back tears. I hadn't thought past getting into the house. I couldn't think past that.

This might not work out. I might not survive a Colorado winter. I might not survive the night as deep as my exhaustion was, but she didn't need to know about the black clouds following me.

I pasted on a bright smile. "Of course. You're right. I just . . . I need a place to get back on my feet."

Kelly stared at my smoking car, and then she glanced at the bags in the back. She wasn't like the neighbors who'd just pretended I wasn't in trouble. Maybe that was good, but right now, I just wanted her to drop me in my house and head off to her life without comment. I was so fucking tired.

"Let's get you settled, then." Kelly got into her Bronco and slowly led the way up the long, pothole-ridden drive. The ponderosa pines crowded in on the dusty road until they parted and opened onto a rocky circle of scrub brush, red dirt, and the cabin itself.

If you squinted, it was charming. Rough-hewn planks and a peaked roof made of wooden shingles had the look of a gentle old man, and the bit of sag in the long front porch looked like a smile.

Kelly hopped out of her Bronco and opened the back hatch. She grabbed out a box that she balanced on a hip and then pulled out a bag of groceries. She smiled at me, almost apologetically, like her kindness might be an insult. That smile made it okay for me to nod and smile back, an understanding between us girls.

We walked up the creaky, sagging steps together and set

down our bags and the box. Kelly fished out the key and handed it to me.

"It's all yours, Laura. Yours. I want you to know that I got out of a bad relationship once. I know how hard it is to reclaim your life. You're doing it, and . . . I'm proud to help."

I couldn't help it. The tears got away from me, but they were happy. I hugged her and then slid the key into the lock. That creaking door swung open, and I knew as soon as the smell of the place hit me, woodsy and warm, that I was home.

We brought in the groceries and put them into the old ice chest. Electricity was a no-go, but there was a stove and wood Kelly had trucked in herself and stacked in the bin. There was a rocker with cushions, a battery-operated radio on a little kitchen table, and a clean little bed tucked in the corner, already made up with thick blankets.

"Let me know if you need anything else. I know all the folks around here. They'd be happy to get you started."

She set the box she'd brought on the little counter and let me open it. Candles, matches, a lantern with oil, some towels, salt and pepper, a can opener, pan, a bowl, plate, cup, and utensils. Survival is what she was giving me. A clean start with just enough to get by.

"I can't . . . just . . . Thank you so much."

She nodded and turned to go, then stopped.

"You should know, this cabin has a history." She touched the rocker, setting it to moving with a little shove. It seemed like she might have a story to tell, but the silence stretched as she watched the rocker slow and settle. Finally, she said. "This is a lady's cabin. All the women who have lived here do okay, but . . . That's why you got it so cheap. It's got . . . personality, I guess. Anyway, don't be scared."

A cold breeze spun around the room, tickling the back of my neck.

"I'll check back in on you tomorrow, okay?"

I nodded. I watched and waved as she drove down the dusty

driveway. I didn't even close the door when I fell on the bed and cried myself to sleep.

))((

Settling in was easier than I thought.

A numbing rhythm heals a hurt soul. I chopped wood and cooked a thin vegetable soup. A wandering gray cat moved in with me in slow steps, first sleeping on my porch and then visiting during meals. She finally snuggled up on my little bed. When I sat in my rocker and listened to the radio, the cat jumped up into my lap and purred. I named her Static.

The warmth of summer at the edge of the mountains would often drive us outside. Static hunted for mice in the roots of trees. As I watched her and laughed at her antics, my skin would suddenly prickle like I was being watched. I'd turn and scan the tree line, but it wasn't the forest that watched. It felt like the heavy gaze came from the house.

That wasn't the only time I felt odd either.

Static stared at random spots in space, frequently arching up and purring like she was being petted. Sometimes, I'd wake up, and the cover I know I hadn't put on the night before was spread across my legs. And sometimes there were random gifts. Bundles of flowers or pretty stones on the porch. Dishes I had left for doing in the morning washed and stacked next to the sink.

It felt like having a mother taking care of me again.

))((

"Can't I talk you into moving down into the valley? At least for winter? Sometimes Wilson can't get up these roads, and you don't have a car anymore."

I smiled at Kelly. She'd become a real friend to me. She'd helped me buy the solar panels, the converter, a small fridge, and a computer. The last allowed me to take a job transcribing doctors' letters and researchers' notes. Though it wasn't perfect, I made a little money and improved my life little by little.

My next goal was legally divorcing his ass and changing my name. It would be like shedding the last link of his chains.

Things were getting better.

But if I moved down into the valley . . .

"I can't, Laura. I know you're worried, but I've been improving things. They say the well won't freeze, and I've got the space heaters if I run out of wood."

"It's the house, isn't it?"

I glanced up, a bit startled. "How did you—"

She laughed. "This house is a woman. Somehow, you can feel it when you walk in. It isn't rich or full of things, but it has a whole lot of . . . oh, I don't know. . .care isn't quite the right word for it."

"Love." I took the cups from the little table I'd served her lunch on and put them into the sink. Love, for sure.

"Oh, I almost forgot." Laura rooted through her briefcase. "There's been some inquiries about your deed. Remember we had to put it in your married name, so it's available to even the lowest level inquiry. Could be a credit search, but more likely it's that husband of yours. We can't block him from the information, but we'll make it damned hard for him to find you. Even Wilson agreed that if someone comes looking, we'll run him off."

Something in the house shivered along with me as I thought about him finding me. Maybe he'd figured out that I took money. Maybe a reason didn't matter. He'd always said I'd never get away from him.

"Do you want a gun? I can bring one up next time."

I nodded. Couldn't hurt. "If he comes up here, how long would it take for the sheriff to—"

"Too long. I'll bring you a couple guns."

$$)O($$

That night, I couldn't sleep. I'd found peace here. Static and me and the house had made a family. Just the thought of him coming for me, looking for me, brought all the pain back.

I collapsed onto my bed, wetting my pillow with tears that wouldn't stop. Static climbed onto my chest, purring so hard she vibrated. I cried and told her all about him. About how he'd made me feel weak. How he'd criticized and isolated and shaped me into something small enough to fit in his pocket. I told her about the hospital and the lost baby and the relief that I wasn't bringing a kid into the horror that was my life. And how he held the loss of the baby against me. How he brought it up every time he drank. Through the flood of my tears, I saw the rocker begin to move, slowly, and the radio switched on playing the familiar strains of "You Are My Sunshine," a sweet warbling voice that reminded me of a lullaby.

The song played over and over until my tears dried up, and I felt stronger. He couldn't steal my peace unless I let him. I wouldn't. We wouldn't.

The radio went silent, and in that second there was a pounding at the door. The violence of it told me that Laura's guns would come too late. He'd found me.

The house seemed to shake with every blow.

"Let me in, you bitch! Think you can get away from me? Humiliate me? Where'd you get the money for this? Stole from me? I'll drag you back in pieces if I have to!"

Static skittered across the floor and hid under the bed as the pounding continued.

I was frozen. Frozen like I'd always been. It was like I hadn't gotten away from him all. Like the whole time I'd spent here was just a dream.

That's when I heard the whisper. "Go with Static."

I glanced down and saw her at the edge of the bed, scratching at a divot in the pine floorboards.

It was a fingerhold.

I pulled it up just enough for Static to slip through, and down below I saw a set of rickety stairs.

"Go!"

I slid into the cellar and pulled the door shut behind me. As dim as it was, Static's eyes shone down on the floor. She waited for me to make my way down. Above, I heard the door crash open, knocking into my coat rack. Its arms pattered and thumped as it rolled across the floor.

"Where are you, bitch?" He stomped around from one end of the cabin to the other.

Static meowed and led me past shelves of dusty canned goods and boxes full of whoever had lived here before. She pawed at a shelf in the back corner, and I heard as clear as if she'd said it in my ear—"Push."

I did, and it swung open.

The total darkness enfolded me when I stepped in and the shelf swung shut. I stood frozen, heart hammering from his bursting into my dream. I could still hear him, tossing things to the side, crashing through my belongings. Shattering my things.

He would do the same to me if he found me.

I wouldn't allow it.

A soft murmur called to me. Not words exactly, but a voice. When I turned toward it, the room filled with a bright blue light. The light washed across a wooden chest with faded black letters stamped on the side, then moved deeper into the space, revealing shelves filled with boxes and glinting glass. The light fell on a gap in the shelves in one corner. There sat a skeleton in the fetal position, mouth fallen open in a scream. Teeth shattered, skull cracked, every bone crushed. As dry and old as it was, I still hissed at the pain the person must've felt.

The blue light resolved in front of me. A woman. She wore a long dress and braids wound around her head. Her misty edges flowed like water, but her features were sure and set. There was a knowing in her eyes but no weakness.

Don't pity him, Laura. That was my man. Brought me all the

way here from Kansas City so he could mine and I could cook. He did to me what your man does, but I stopped him. You can, too.

She pressed her hand into mine and then pulled my cheek against her chilly neck. Light as a breath, she moved in and wrapped around me until all I saw was her and the light. Until I was in her eyes or. . . her memory. Like flying through fog. Movement without sight. That pressing cold, wet without water touching you, coating you with its delicate, cool kiss. Until I stood with her. In her.

I saw it all. Every back-handed strike, every cruel word uttered, every uninvited touch. The loneliness and dread of a life in the mountains before roads and wires and Jeep Wranglers. He'd dragged her here away from her family, isolated her, and tortured her. So many moments of pain. But the worst was how for so long she'd thought there was no other way. No escape. None but . . .

Static clawed my leg and hissed, drawing us back. The bed moved upstairs with a long scrape across the pineboard floor. He'd see the finger notch. It wouldn't be long.

With her in my mind, we pushed out of the backroom. She knew exactly where the pickaxe her man had mined with was—still under the steep wooden stairs leaning in the dusty corner. Just as he opened the trapdoor, we all three ducked under them into the thicker shadow.

He cursed under his breath as he stared down into the dark, his shadow blotting out the stream of light from above. He put his heavy boot on the first step and then the other on the second, climbing down backward and holding onto the handrails. They groaned under his weight, complaining about him as much as a step could.

"When I find you, I'm going to fuck you up bad. You watch. You didn't come back, and you should've. I'm going to make you so sorry, whore."

Another two steps and his hairy shins were at eye level. What

I wouldn't have given for a sharp knife to cut the power out of his legs and watch him topple down the steps. Even thinking about his blood slicking our hands sent a rush of excitement through me, but she sat in my head like the voice of God—wait, wait. Static wound around my feet, rubbing encouragement and strength into us. Inside our head, the men, her husband and mine, screamed their poison. The same poison we'd both been steeped in. Even separated by a hundred years, their threats and violence sounded like harmony.

Two more steps down, and he'd be on the cellar floor. He'd have the advantage if we didn't act. We stepped out from behind the stairs clutching the pickaxe's smooth wood handle in our fists. Between the muscles I'd grown from chopping wood and toting water and her skills at swinging the pickaxe, our aim and power were true.

The sharp point went into his lower back under his ribs so deep it poked through his gut, loosing a gout of blood that stained his t-shirt a deeper red than I'd ever seen. It was beautiful against the bright white as he fell backward. He hit the stone floor and drove the blunt end deeper, cracking ribs and shredding into the soft innards we'd pierced.

"Fuck, Laura! What have you done?" He scrambled up onto his knees, groaning and panting. He fumbled behind his back, feeling the pick, but he didn't pull it out. With a grunt, he stumbled toward us.

How could he still move? Pure hate-fed adrenaline, I was sure.

"I'm going to kill you. Slow. I'll—"

We picked up a shovel and smashed him in the face, knocking him back.

"Got . . . I've got . . ." He fumbled in his pocket, and the dark couldn't hide the flash of silver in his hand.

A knife?

"Gun, bitch." He started to raise it, lying on his side and squinting around the blood flowing down his forehead.

We wouldn't get to him to hit him again if he fired, but his pain was worth it. We shifted to the side as he lined up his shot. His gaze locked on us, and he lay five feet away. How could he miss?

Then he screamed. He shot, but the bullet buzzed past our heads. Static yowled and spat, a gray ghost dancing on his bloodied face. She shredded him, raking his eyes until he was blind and mewling. Then she hopped off and trotted over to the bottom stair to lick away the gore on her claws.

"Damn," I said as both the women of the house.

At that moment, she separated from me. Eunice, I heard as she passed out of my skin and back into the misty form. She floated away, and I kicked the gun away from his blindly groping hands. He was a mess. Velvety blood pooled around the pickaxe, and bright streaks and clotted jelly flecked his cheeks.

Eunice opened the sliding shelf and came back to me. The lantern flickered as a breeze swept through the cellar. Something in Eunice shifted, became more solid. She jerked her head in the direction of the hidden room, then grabbed one of his kicking legs, and I grabbed the other. We pulled as he cussed and groaned, but we got him into the hidden room.

"Bob, meet Clem," I said, as Eunice pulled the bones of her husband over to lie next to Bob's weakly struggling form. "I won't do to you what Eunice did to him, but he might let you see later."

As I stepped over him, he started to beg, but I didn't have to listen. Eunice sank into me, and I joined in. We blocked the hidden door with the shelf and climbed up the steps together. We sang and laughed as we cleaned up the mess Bob had made. Many of the things—my computer and the radio—we couldn't save, but things can be replaced.

When Kelly showed up later, I wasn't surprised. Women who lived through domestic violence just know, and Kelly didn't wait for a welcome in or a word. She just came in and enfolded me in a sturdy hug. "Is he gone?"

I nodded.

"Will he come back?"

I didn't answer.

She helped me put the door back on the hinges and promised to send up a repairman the next day. She cooked chicken noodle soup while I sat shaking on the bed with my Static and my Eunice, invisible but radiating warmth on either side of me. I wasn't afraid anymore, but hot tears and sweat still flowed down my face. It was just the final letdown of years of tension leaving my body like a fever.

Kelly glanced over as she stirred, gaze on my cat, me, and the space next to me that shimmered with a weight that shouldn't exist. The broken radio clicked on, and "You Are My Sunshine" warbled in the quiet between us.

"You look like you belong here, Laura. Like you're happy."

I smiled through the shakes. "It's like I've always been here. I'm home."

Static blinked her approval because it was true.

PROGRESS AND THE
SHAWNEE BEND WITCH

THE WAVES LAPPED the hips of Shawnee Bend Beach as the sun painted whorls in the clouds, purple and gold. Motors purred in the half-light of the midsummer sunset. Janet's eyes sipped the sight. So rare. So wonderful.

Once upon a time, they'd chosen progress here at the Shawnee Bend when it was a town and a hill, not a beach and golf course.

Back then, her toes were tied to the dirt and roots of her high hill. Her skin had been kissed by the wind and freckled by the hot summer sun, and she had been bright, crackling with the hill magic her momma passed her from all the mommas back to the beginning of things.

They came to her hill from the valley below. The folks of Shawnee Bend Village found her when they needed something —a bone set, a child doctored, an herb medicine cooked, a portent cast. She'd been there so long. Since the beginning of the village.

Now boats floated over her head, chopping the smooth lake surface with whirling props.

She came from the highlands of craggy bright Scotland, through the little mountains of New York. Her momma set her down by the fire built of new wood and taught her rare secrets. Her momma tied herself to the dirt of New York, on Camillus Hill, where the Highlanders settled. Janet wondered if she was still holed up in her shack on that high, shaded hill back East. She hoped so. She wished it with all the heart she had left.

Her people been tying themselves to dirt on hills since before Jesus rose, since before Romans built roads, since before since was a since. An unbreakable magical bond gave them everything, but it took everything too. Still, hill women knew their place. It's a calling. There's beauty in the sacrifice and grace in the service.

The crickets took over for the locusts—a sweeter call answered in kind as the boats found their way home, slow and lit with bright lamps, creating echoed lights across the calming lake surface. The waves settled into ripples, and the water's chill seeped into her bones.

How long had it been since she'd seen the sun? Felt it on her skin. Let the wind touch her face. So long. Years. Blessed years.

Her new Americans, Highlanders all, with their crunchy brogue and lilting stories of the old clans, had left New York and brought her here. The place called Aux Arcs, and later Ozarks, the littlest mountains. Mountains so old they made her highlands look like nappied infants wailing in the wind. Mountains so wise and worn down, they spoke to her in a crone's voice.

"Janet," her momma said, "find your own dirt. A place that will grow your seeds. Your own high hill."

"Yes, Momma," she'd said and climbed aboard the buckboard wagon, wooden wheels knocking and clambering across the deep, grassy veld that would become the middle West later. She remembered so little from the trip. Hunger and storms. Flowers. Angry streams sucking at the meat of her calves. The biggest rivers her eyes could believe—the Mississippi and then the Missouri, named for the people who'd come before whose spirits still counseled her as she passed. Wide.

Frightening. Without her feet planted in dirt, she wasn't but a scent on a breeze. A foggy breath on winter air.

They passed over rivers that cradled Saint Louis, where the Germans built brick buildings and cobbled streets. Scotch Irish trash like them found no rest among the hard language and brutal trade of the river town. The drinking and the fighting felt like home to the Highlanders, but Janet promised them a better place. She felt it as an ache drawing her south, west.

Her momma told her she'd know her place. It'd call to her. Janet would lead them to the safest, most welcoming valley twixt two hills. Like the Highlands. She'd nodded as her momma stirred, barefoot in the waddle and daub house her village had built her, herbs hanging to dry in the low, cozy rafters. It was as it always had been.

They crossed flat prairie and another river, not so wide. They met Osage and Fox Indians, shy of the clump of red-haired, long-bearded folk with their spindly witch woman walking out in front, leading the wagons like a North Star. The crossings read true. She found the narrowest creeks and the widest passes without fail. Fair water with clutches of easy-to-shoot birds, deer with more curiosity than sense, and fat berry bushes kept them from starvation. She earned her keep.

She remembered with pride how the men always trusted her. Believed her, even though she weren't but a girl back then. They'd followed her finger, her nose, her intuition across the void of grass and nothing.

Now, the frogs sang to her. Now, seaweed wrapped her legs with a slimy, clutching grasp.

How beautiful this place had been. A wide valley capped with tall trees and a winding stream that never ran dry. Full of fish that never ran out. The birds sang every day that they built the town at Shawnee Bend Stream, at the foot of the nicest little mountain she could find. She led them to the most solid rocks. To the sweetest springs. They laid out a town where the women could feel safe and children could play. Men hacked out farms in the valley and wide pastures on the hills, leaving the high hill for Janet alone.

She'd built her lean-to, wattle and daub just like Momma's. They brought her stones and thick red mud from the riverbed, building up a wide hearth for her to cook healing draughts. They all pitched in piglets, some chickens, a few sheep, and a donkey for her to plant with. Sought out the seeds of local plants she might need for healings. She'd worked her own land—a narrow patch that sat in the middle of the high hill. Like all the mommas before her had done.

Like her momma, she'd made the hilltop a sanctuary. A grove for the elder gods, where she planted old-world seeds from the holy trees her ancestors had kept and passed to the hill witches. They sprouted. They grew so tall, she barely noticed the years it took. They vouchsafed her strength. As long as they stood, she kept her power. As they lived, so would she.

The town grew. Matured. The lean-tos surrounded by scrub brush and thistles became farms and shops and settled places. They worshipped in the little clabber-sided church topped with the symbol of the crucified man. They worked and loved and grew more and more different from her. Less old world, more new.

Still they came to her for cures, for potions, and for predictions. When the doctors didn't know, the men folk would walk up the hill along the hidden path set with river bed stones that wound through nodding cone flowers and ferns. They'd knock on her door with hat in hand and some offering to give. Not the folding money that came with the new nation and the movements west, but with a nice clutch of eggs or a hunk of smoked meat or even some river mud with crawdads still burrowed in deep. She liked that particular well since she couldn't leave the hill and get them herself. She'd given up her freedom when she'd dug her toes into the earth. She'd planted herself 'neath the canopy of the old-world copse of pine she'd grown from seed. Now she, like all her mommas before her, had only the middle of the high hill.

The valley regular folk marked theirs with their church and their fences, and she wasn't welcome there. Her feet couldn't carry her there because she wasn't of that soil. Later, as the grove of god trees grew at the top of the hill, she found she could no longer climb to the top. Her gods meant her to live in between. Like her momma, she could only wander the center of her hill.

It was the way of the witch. Her momma lived with such limits. So must she.

Only. . .

Only now she couldn't stop the wet creepers picking at her toes from beneath the wide wavering surface of the lake.

The coming of the lake had been her undoing. How could they have chosen the lake over her?

For more than one hundred summers, she had served them at Shawnee Bend atop the hill. Doctored for them. Cursed and charmed for them. Worked the way of the woods when their crucified god wouldn't answer their prayers. She'd been useful, though near the last the folks didn't come so often as she'd have liked. Still, they came.

She'd grown bored there, anchored to a hill watching the little log homes pulled down and replaced by row upon row of white-framed houses. She squinted and huffed at the strange loud wagons that spouted black clouds and rattled as they went. When she finally did get a visitor, a comely young man with a long body, it wasn't for her works. Instead, he'd come on a dare. Tempting the devil to strike him by looking for the Shawnee Bend witch.

"You ain't but a slip of a girl. You got a momma or somethin'?" He'd leaned against the willow in front of her cabin.

She sat carding the wool she'd be dyeing the next day for a new weaving she had planned.

She nodded and crooked a finger, patting the log she sat on

with an expectant air. "Sit a spell, young 'un. Tell me some about life past my high hill."

The man sat, leaning his elbows on his long legs, head turned away, though his eyes kept stealing to the side in glance after glance. He thought her handsome. And why not? The earth fed her youth, kept her fresh as a maiden, which she wasn't, but she hadn't enjoyed a man in many a year. This boy stirred her, and as she carded, she charmed him. Not with magic. She could have used rosehips and moss and brewed them up 'neath a new moon and had him forever, but tricks didn't ever suit her. She would win him with her own true charms.

He talked. Spoke about life in Shawnee Bend, things called cars, a great war, something called a president and his scandals—he pattered on with a voice as beautiful as the song of a bird. By the time he was done, she was pressed into his side, hands in his, and he didn't talk anymore.

She took him inside the shack and loved him. It was the way of hill witches. No marriage. No life in love. Just seconds of warmth snatched between long winters of loneliness on her high hill. Hot breath and whispered promises she knew he wouldn't keep. He came to her throughout the summer, and they walked along the soft, sifted dirt paths of the hill testing her limits. It amazed him that she couldn't get past barriers. He'd step across the lines she'd marked with stones and then watch her lean and press and even stand on her head against a wall that he couldn't see or feel.

It was terrible when he stopped coming. Back then she'd thought he might come back to her. It was a lie she chose to tell herself in the cold, bitter winter when the snow piled up on her stoop as her belly rounded out. In the spring, when her lambs and piglets walked on their own through the slushy melting snow, she felt the first pains rippling through her belly. The blood and water and afterbirth all splashed on the hill, and soon she had her babe. A gal as red as a rose and wrinkled. She named her Bonnie.

Janet's eyes filled with water as she remembered the boy she'd loved and the baby she'd birthed. Tears flowed out, but what were a few tears to a lake so big? Only when the lake was low, as it was now, and she stood on her toes letting the breath of night or the sun's warmth direct on her face, only then did she remember her love, the boy of summer, or her little Bonnie girl. The rest of the time, through the filter of the wavering water, she would float and forget. How many years had it been?

Bonnie learned to crawl in the summer wildflowers. The pigs and the lambs chased her through the yard, licking her toes in the way that animals did when they fell in love. Her laugh brought the rain, and Janet knew that Bonnie's high hill ought to be some place dry. Maybe someplace west. Janet knew the time would come when her Bonnie babe would walk, then run, then she'd ride away just as she had and her momma had and all the mommas before. It was their way.

Janet blinked rapidly, trying to get the images that danced in her eyes to settle back into her memory. Her baby. The green water lapped at her chin and cheeks, icy fingers fluttering a cold comfort. The clarity of the receded lake always brought her back to what she'd been before the brackish water had closed over it all, drowning her life and her home. Leaving her in the soft Ozark Lake mud with catfish for pets. Leaving her with the oblivion of the dark waters over her head. In those years when her rooted feet held her beneath the waterline, always staring up at the water filtered light, she would lose her grief. Her anger would chill, and her mind numb within the soft currents of the massive lake.

Now, the memories flowed back.

He'd come back to her in Bonnie's fourth summer. All that time and not a word, but there he stood in the shade of her willow, looking older but no more a man than he was when he'd been hers. His hair followed the shape of his head, cut close. He wore a white collar—the mark of one of the leaders of the god of the white church with the steel cross on top. He came up her hill one fine fall morning, crunching through the crusted frost that coated the late autumn grass on the shaded hillside. When he pushed through her gate and caught sight of Bonnie singing to the piglets, he froze in place. Watched all silent and hesitant, like a scared kitten.

She'd walked up behind him, barefoot and shuffling through the sifted-up dirt. But when she laid a hand on his arm, he didn't spin and catch her up in his arms as he'd done when he was younger. Instead, he startled like she had lightning in her fingers.

"Who's that? "

"Bonnie. "

He stared at the girl, her dark hair so different from Janet's. Her pointy chin and grinning eyes mirrored his own. How could he not know who she was to him?

Janet shrugged and turned back, loosely holding the hoeing stick she'd been working her garden with. "What you need? " She wiped her inner wrist against her sweat-beaded forehead. She didn't imagine he'd come for her. That need had cooled, as she knew it would. Something changed when a hill witch got pregnant. Love flitted through their lives, leaving bright memories and with any luck, a healthy girl to carry on. "Well? "

"I come to tell you that you got to move. I come because . . . is that gal mine?"

What a fool men choose to be, Janet thought. "Nah. She's my gal. That's all."

He stared at her and then at Bonnie for a bit longer. He shook his head, as if to clear out his cobwebs and go back to his reason for slogging through the frozen blades of grass, breathing icy fog out as he climbed the hill.

"You can't see it from here, but not far they been building up a dam. It's gonna bring all sorts of good for us like electricity, roads, and new jobs. So, they bought up our town—lock, stock, and barrel. We're movin' on. Once this lake is filled up, why, they'll build up new places for us all."

Janet laid her hand on his, let her mind slide across his, and rifled through his memories. She saw money changing hands. Greed on the faces of desperate valley people. Hungry people. She heard the promises the dam builders made with wide eyes and fast-moving hands. They painted a picture of a serpentine goldmine that would benefit everyone. Soon, the valley people had wide eyes too.

"It's no good, though," she said to him. "They won't share the wealth, don't you see? They'll get fat. You all will be displaced. Uprooted. You'll never find another—"

He jerked his hand away, wiping it against the leg of his pants like it was dirty. She cocked her head, wondering what made him act so. He reached into his pocket and jerked out a book, black with thin, thin pages and gilded edges. He held it in between them like a shield. "Stay out of my head, witch."

He spit the last word like it tasted foul. Hadn't been so foul when he'd kissed her before.

Bonnie wandered over and twisted her little hands into Janet's skirt. The man scared the girl some. Janet could hear it in her mind, but she was curious just the same. Janet hoisted her up on her hip and held her, let the girl lay her head against her cheek so she could hear the thoughts inside her head.

"You come to tell me about the dam. You come with the spirit of goodness since the others didn't spare a thought for the old hill witch. For that, I thank you."

He nodded, gathering up his resolve. His face finally hardened, for what he had to say was cold. Bitter. She'd already seen the words but didn't want to believe they'd come.

"The water will come up past your land. Your land will be under the lake come February. It'll start filling in days. They say it'll come a foot, foot and a half each day."

Janet swallowed, thinking about her hill. Her roots.

"You'll have to get out. The money's all gone. They didn't save nothin' for you, though I tried. I did."

She'd seen it, though she'd also seen his town wife arguing

that a hill witch didn't matter none. That a hill witch would just move on up into the groves. That the flooding served her right for her heathen ways. The town wife must've known that they'd been in love once.

"Thing is," Janet said, "you know I can't leave. You're the only one who knows what'll happen if that lake covers my land."

He nodded. But his eyes never left the eyes of his daughter. "Nothin' I could do."

Nothin'.

Janet had lived on the hill for more than a hundred years. She'd saved lives and worked heathen wonders with roots and whispers. But her abilities weren't much next to an electric-making dam. The word hummed through her head and then into Bonnie's and hung like a stench that wouldn't go away.

"Progress." Bonnie's tiny mouth stretched to accommodate a word her ears had never heard.

The man nodded again. Janet thought he looked a fool, all that solemn nodding. She wondered if his god studies had taught him that.

"What are we to do?" She stared into his eyes, hoping he'd thought that far.

He glanced toward the town, seated at the foot of her hill, down by the stream that would swell and swell. He pulled off his hat and wiped at his cheeks. She'd didn't see sweat on him, so she figured it was just something he did when he was uncomfortable. Good.

"I don't know, Janet. I wish I could just.."

They both knew his words meant nothing.

"The child?"

"I could take her to a new family. A good Christian family, and then—"

"She's yourn."

His breath whooshed out like he'd been punched. He had to have known. She'd only been his in so many years.

He shook his head again. "The water's gonna rise. I'll need to take her to—"

"To a hill. You'll have to live on a hill with her 'til she's grown."

"No, we're headed for Kansas."

"A hill. Ain't but flat in Kansas. I saw in your head. One long flat. She needs a hill." Janet reached out and touched his cheek. "Once you loved me. You could love her too."

The man nodded. He reached out his hands for the child, though little Bonnie shied away, burying her face into Janet's neck. Janet squeezed the girl tight and whispered the words her momma had given her the last time she'd seen her. They were the words that would tie her to a hill once she'd found one to love. She ran into the house to grab what her own ma had given her when she'd left the old stand of trees back home. Janet pressed a packet of seeds into the hand of her baby girl. They were from the stand of trees that she'd grown into a shrine of elder gods atop her hill. Then she kissed her five times.

"I'll see you no more, beautiful Bonnie girl. Know that I love you."

The girl went into her father's arms stiffly, not wanting the strange man, but without a whimper. Witches didn't whine. Would she remember her momma trapped on this hill once the lake water closed over her head?

"Momma?" Tears welled in her eyes. Janet knew Bonnie could feel the pain flowing off her momma in blooms and waves. It was their way.

"Take her." Janet crossed stiff arms on her chest. Stiff to hide the shakes that hid beneath her show.

Remembering them walking away from her, down the path of flat stones, ripped open a wound so old, long past but deep. She let her hands float up and rest on the surface of the lake, where the wind might blow away the memory, temper it with the warmth of the summer night breeze. Why did they lower the lake? Every so many years, it lowered. Just when she thought she might let the humanity wash away finally. If it stayed above her head, she floated inside the memories of the good times without remembering that they were gone. Without remembering her baby girl's eyes peeping above her father's broad, black-coated shoulder. And in the valley, the water rising.

She remembered the tears. Months of tears. Then, as the water crept up her high hill, she remembered all the tears drying up. Her soul emptied out. She released her pigs, letting them wander the hill with the donkey so they wouldn't be trapped with her as the water rose. She ate the chickens. When would she get to eat so well again? The brackish water crept up the winding stone walk, an unwelcome visitor. She read her books and walked along the rising shore as it drowned her coneflowers. It pooled around her willow and up to the edge of her cabin, pushing her inside for one last night in the comfort of a home. Then, it surged in. Swept away her mementos. She didn't try to save them. Why try when the water was gonna rise?

Soon, winter came crackling and deep. The water rose, and the snow fell. Her pigs and donkey fled to some safer place. The cold settled in her bones, but it couldn't kill her. Not when her feet were planted. So, the water rose up. Soon, she was ankle deep. It pushed her against the topmost edge of her land, where the god trees grew in isolation. Where she couldn't go. Still, the water rose. It swallowed her and her home and her stones and her tree.

And still, she lived.

So many years of silence. Of anger.

Under the water, she wasn't herself. Sometimes she'd reach out and pull down the ones who swam and played above her in the lake. It wasn't until the bubbles ran like a chain out of their noses and their hands loosened from the claws they'd been when their eyes hardened like marbles in their slack features—that's when she'd realize it was her holding them under. That she'd killed them without knowing. That was bad enough.

But then, every few years, the level would lower and her

head would rise above the murk. Her eyes would look out over the wavering surface. That's when it was the worst. That's when she'd remember it all. Her momma. Her lover. Her Bonnie girl.

If only there was an end. Some way to pull her feet loose from the patch of high hill she'd given her life to. If only she could die. She'd give anything to swallow down the water and float away. But it wasn't the way of the hill witch. Only her eyes rose above the water to watch the passing pleasure boats as they motored by, the men on skis, the children laughing. This was the progress they chose.

As the water rose again, engulfing her head and pushing her deep, she wondered if any of them ever missed what she'd once been for them. All the wonders she'd done. Did they remember the times she'd given them everything? They'd built their town in the shadow of her workings. Maybe progress required such sacrifice.

HELL IS OTHER PEOPLE

PAULETTE PULLED the door shut on her cinder-block house. The handle didn't work right anymore. No one would break in. The smell kept them away. She smoothed her thin brown hair down, though she'd not brushed it in . . . she couldn't remember how long. No need. Her hair clung to her round head in a greasy hug, slung back in a hasty knot at the nape of her neck.

"God, watch over me through this day." She clutched her mother's black bag close to her soft, round middle. Then she set off down the snow-crusted shoulder of the two-lane road next to the lake her dad had fished. Not far in the other direction was the shrine where her mother had spent hours every day until her heart gave out. They'd been the only people she believed in. The only ones she ever understood. Then they'd died.

A bright silver car with crunching tires sped past and plowed through a pile of gray slush, splashing it up on her boots and her brown winter habit. Not that it had been clean before, but it had at least been warm. The car slowed for a moment like the driver realized what he'd done, but after a moment of eyes reflected from the rearview catching and holding Paulette's muddy gaze, they sped off, wheels spinning in the soup of slush and grit.

God's armor, her mother had told her time and again, was age and fading beauty.

Paulette had never been beautiful.

She walked in the sloppy melt of a Wisconsin spring toward town and the courthouse and recalled the pictures she often looked at. Pictures of her and her traitor brother when they were kids. Mother, back when her hair flowed down her slim back—before she found forgiveness at the shrine for those early indiscretions with Uncle Lee, Dad's brother. Dad before he'd become mother's keeper. The bright picture that always swam up was the picture of herself in a lovely pink dress, modest but sweet, with curled hair and a bangled bracelet clutching the confirmation Bible she'd just gotten. Her cheeks had been rosy and her smile so proud. Mother had beaten that pride out of her that night. She'd dragged her back to the whittling stone and made her listen to rants from random spots in the Bible. But in that picture, that moment was the moment she'd been the closest to pretty she'd ever be.

Because after that, she learned to fear everyone.

After that, Mother had chosen to send her to the convent. To be the only child who would live up to her holy aspirations. Clothing with color had been taken away, replaced with a Carmelite brown, thick habit, cinched with wool and a scapular covering to hide her figure. A wimple and veil covered her head. Soon after that, she stopped bathing. Because who would see anyway?

Those last few months of school had been hell. Students hurling insults was bad enough, but in a moderate Catholic school where her brother had been such a suave tough, such a dreamy boy, she'd shown up in full habit. Her friends, few that there were, scattered—like what she had might be contagious. She'd felt like a dull tugboat parting the colorful waves of teens flowing through the halls of her high school. Even the nuns treated her like an oddity. Sister Elizabeth Martha set her in the back of the class with a circled row of desks around her, separating her from the others. She'd refer to Paulette's chastity and her sacrifices as an example but then wouldn't want to discuss Paulette's interpretations of the Gospels.

But soon, it was over. Graduation.

Walking along the cold Wisconsin county highway, Paulette let her teeth grind and her ragged nail tips bite into her fleshy palms. Eddie, her oversexed brother, had brought home his pick for a wife, and Mother lost her mind.

Another car, driving more slowly, deliberately swerving to miss puddles, slowed. The driver rolled down the window and said, without seeing her face, "Headed to Necedah? Hop in . . . Oh."

Paulette glanced at the driver and watched the pantomime of kindness stretched across the rigid bones, sharp as knives, collapse on itself. The woman's head jerked back, placing her gaze on the road, and without another word, she rolled up her window and slammed on the gas, spraying sludge and fishtailing. Kindness was a false idol worshipped by small-minded, faithless people.

She bit her tongue until she bled; the taste of bitter metal trickled down her throat. Her feet were lead, and her legs felt like cement pillars sinking into the ground. Her body didn't want to go to town and fought against every foot-dragging step. People. The thought of them made her skin bubble up and her eyes water. She bit her tongue again to drive out the weakness. Mother taught her that. Pain made the fear creep back from her skin and hide in the dark places. Anger helped too.

Around the curve and across the bridge that split the lake in two, then into the cesspit of a town. Past dirty gas stations filled with liquor and porn. Past restaurants with food she couldn't afford and people who didn't care. Into the converted ranch house that served as the county seat for the bi-weekly traffic court, where the orange plastic seats hooked together and made bodies press close. Paulette chose the very back and spread her bulk across two chairs and put her bag on the one next to that.

As always, mother's voice in her head reminded her that touching anyone without pure thoughts or having them touch you, even an accidental brush in chairs set so close, was a sin. Not that she had to worry.

They always took one look at her and moved away, choosing to stand rather than test her over the seats she took up. Fine with her. She did her best to avoid everything mother told her would send her to hell. People would send her to hell faster than anything else.

"All rise." The nasal upper-Midwest accent of the short, skinny, bottle-blond at the front of the makeshift court rudely cut the air. She'd stuffed her body into the court deputy uniform until the buttons strained and the skin climbed out of the top and over itself to be visible. On display.

From one of the converted bedrooms, an old man in a threadbare robe shuffled to the rickety wooden desk that served as a judge's bench, worn out from his years of service. Paulette bit her lips, pulling bits of skin from them. Judge Gorgen. He hated her. He never tried to understand. He always told her things that didn't make any sense.

"Paulette." He pulled his thick-lensed glasses down his swollen, porous nose. Paulette pulled herself up and made her way to the front row. He shook his head as she approached, though what hurt just as much as his open sneer were the reactions of the others waiting to plead their case.

"Oh my God, it's her."

"What is that smell?"

"Why does she dress like that, Mama?"

The mutters and the laughs, and even gags. Paulette reached up and adjusted her wimple, then sniffed through her slightly upturned nose, just as Mother had described Saint Christina when she rose out of her coffin into the church rafters to escape the stench of sin. She stared at each of them as they pulled back from her, eyes round and rolling in their sinning heads. Mouths covered with their inconstant, clawed hands. Paulette shuffled past them and stood at the podium near the front. The deputy woman leaned in to give her a paper outlining the fines and possible punishments for her offenses.

"Let he among you cast the stone at the innocent. I turned the cheek. I gave the loaves." She found that mumbling often helped drive them back when they got too close.

The deputy's stretched arm trembled, holding the paper out at Paulette like some shield. But her face, usually set in the stern, polite grumpiness of court officials, wavered, and collapsed around her crinkling nose. Paulette pushed back her urge to giggle. Her armor was working.

"Get back, Barbara. No need. She knows what's on the paper." Then Judge Gorgen turned to her and frowned.

His eyes lingered so long on her that she fought the urge to scream. The gaze had weight, the sinful weight of hands on her, touching what God didn't mean to be touched.

"If only you'd taken orders in Spain, there wouldn't be any need for this." Mother's voice was always there.

Spain. Her greatest failure. "I'm sorry, Mother," Paulette said under her breath, though the judge's gaze caught the movement of her mumbling lips.

"Look here, Miss Paulette, you've been in here at least ten times in the last two years."

She nodded one sharp jerk, then tilted her head and found the cross hung behind the judge's shoulder to stare at. Our Lord and Savior perched there in the perfect agony of his death—a good, old crucifix. Of course, it would be. Necedah was a good Catholic town. That's why Mother and Dad brought her here after her failure at the convent in Spain. The nuns had talked and invaded her space until she screamed and rocked and ran to a cave to hide. Mother had to fly out and remove her and then drug her to get her on the plane and back home. If she couldn't make it in a convent, her mother thought maybe a shrine town would be better. The shrine and the old-fashioned priests; none of that Vatican II nonsense. And away from Eddie and his whore wife. None of that.

"Let's see, we took your license for driving without insurance in October last." He scanned the file in front of him and pulled a cotton hankie out of his sleeve and held it up to his nose.

"I can't afford insurance, Judge. My brother won't pay, and I can't work."

"Can't or won't?"

"I took care of my parents. I paint sometimes and sell at the church bazaar, but it's only enough to get some gas or repairs on my house."

His face softened for a minute, and then he turned back to reading the chart. "This time, you insulted the officer."

Paulette's hand shook as she gripped the podium. They all were against her. Like the saints, she was pursued by these demons every day. "He had no right to pull me over."

"You had no tags on your plates."

"I can't afford them, and I needed to get to church." For the food pantry, she wanted to say but knew it would make no never mind to his hard heart.

"Miss Paulette, you have no license and therefore you cannot drive. He was right to pull you over, and you called him . . ." Papers rustled as he looked for the words. "A sinning sack of pig guts and a Joseph Stalin?"

She gripped the podium so hard, hating the feel of the eyes on her back, hating the words she had to hear and the fact that there was no way to avoid these terrible scenes. "He touched me."

It was her only defense, but she knew they wouldn't accept it. They never accepted it.

The judge stared at her for a moment and sighed. "He didn't touch you inappropriately, right?"

"Every touch is inappropriate," Paulette thundered.

The words felt like medicine soothing the burning hurt that was other people. If she could just scream until they walked away, she'd feel better. But that was not possible. They'd lock her up if she did that. Mother warned her.

"I can't be touched. I'm a wife of Jesus."

The judge stared at her, nodding, but not in agreement. He'd been told this before, and Paulette was sure she'd have to tell him again. If they'd just leave her alone, she'd never bother them. She'd pray in her house, feed her cats, and wait for God. But there were taxes and building codes and policemen ticketing her for not having the right stickers or blinkers or whatever expensive blame thing they'd saddle her with. Back when Dad and Mother had been alive, she'd been able to just sit in her little room, pray on her cot, and go to the shrine without ever having to deal with the others. Like Saint Katherine, she'd rise above and float away on her prayers.

But then Dad put his hand on her. Mother had flown into a jealous rage, screaming, scratching her eyes and cheeks, ranting about Paulette's virtue. Dad started sleeping in the car then, even on freezing Wisconsin nights, but Mother believed the worst.

Paulette wished she hadn't stumbled into him in the first place. Just an accident, but Mother would not be persuaded.

When Eddie called, Dad and Mother had acted like all was well, even if he sat bleeding from the beatings she and Mother had given him. When Mother told her to send him to God, she'd done it—shoving him down the icy steps so his neck broke. Paulette sat next to him as the breath left him, glad that there was one less person in the world. One less person that made her stomach crawl, but she found without him Mother's rages had no other place to go but toward herself. The days filled with touches and words from Mother—beatings and punishments that lasted days.

When Dad's money came, Mother would make Paulette walk into town to buy supplies. Torture, and she knew it. Torture with every word and every interaction. And the people knew how Paulette felt about them. She made them uncomfortable as they pretended to be polite. Jerking back from their hands. Ignoring their comments about how she smelled, even smiling. She and Mother built their hoard of things so they had walls inside their walls. People stayed away. Neighbors could smell their house from a mile away. The roof blew off, and the church sent out men to fix it for the poor widow and her crazy, failed nun of a daughter. Mother ranted the entire time they worked, and Paulette hid in her closet.

The ranting and accusations went on for days, punctuated by Mother's fists and tears. When she could take no more, Paulette shoved a knitting needle in the space next to her mother's eye until she stopped her screaming.

No one questioned her death. Paulette thought they were likely relieved.

She was.

So it went for a while. Dad's checks came, but she didn't want to go to town. The people from the church brought her food sometimes. She took Dad's car out to the shrine at night when no other people were there. She made her own sacraments. Anything to stay away from them and their careful questions about her life.

Except for days like this one, when the world reached out and grabbed her, pulling her into its madness, demanding taxes, payment for water, or sending police to harass her when she drove or sat in her house contemplating God.

And here they were again, pulling her into their insignificant rule infractions and punishments. Didn't this judge recognize a live saint? Saints don't pay bills or taxes or tickets. Saints float above the distractions of human frailty.

"He touched my hand. I will not be touched." Each word spilled out of Paulette's mouth edged with all the fire of her fear.

Judge Gorgen audibly sucked at his teeth as he thought. The things he did, the proximity of these people, ached like bruises. "Look here, Miss Paulette. . ."

"Sister Paulette if you must," she said with a sniff, brushing her hands across the wide sleeve of her brown habit. Then she reached down and grabbed the beads of her rosary, counting each, saying a prayer, trying to distract herself with how much this talking, standing, and muttering hurt.

"Fine. Sister Paulette. You have been before me for everything from tax bills to speeding tickets. You're in here every few weeks. I don't put you in jail because honestly . . . who wants to put an ex-nun in jail?"

Paulette's stomach flipped as he talked. God wouldn't allow him to do that, would he? Being forced to live inside a cell with people watching her, forcing her to interact and talk. She flattened out the tension on her face and formed her gaze into something piteous. She had to convince him quick.

"Just . . . let me go," Her false gravitas shrank under the weight of this reality. She couldn't get away fast enough. His mouth assaulted her with words she didn't want to know or hear. His eyes were on her, like fingers touching her skin. And suddenly it was all sinning, all against God's plan. "Let me go home, please."

The judge's gaze softened as he watched her shift on her feet. Paulette knew how to get rid of people, but the judge had power over her. He'd sent her away before. Three years with Eddie back in the city. She'd had to fight her way home. Eddie and his loose daughter had made her dress like everyone else and tried to sign her up for school. Eddie sent her back before she used the rat poison in the dinners she made them. He told her she wasn't welcome and gave her a bus ticket, probably because she'd burned her niece's soccer shorts, whore red and silky as they were. He sent her money sometimes, never enough. Dad would be ashamed.

On a bus, all those people, trapped for eight hours of driving. She'd nearly died, but she floated above it all praying so hard that she disconnected. It wasn't until they were twenty minutes from Necedah that she realized a man reached his hand up her robes and onto her leg, running his filthy hand on her calf. They were the only ones on the bus besides the driver at that point.

Paulette had pulled a knife she'd taken from her brother's house and plunged it into his neck. He bled out quietly, gurgling as the blood flowed down his tan coat, but his hand left her to clutch at his wound. The bus rumbled on for the last few miles, and when the driver pulled up at the lonely depot, Paulette stood and clutched her hard-sided suitcase in front of her, blocking his view of the knife. The driver never saw it coming.

"Sister Paulette, I'm afraid if I let you go home, you'll just be in here another time next week. What if we got you a job? Maybe caring for the elderly?"

Paulette shook her head, knowing that the result would be a bad one. Having to touch some elderly person so . . . intimately. Wiping them, listening to them, smelling them. Tears floated behind her eyes, so she turned to her anger to cover her fears.

"I will not do any such thing. I have a job. I worship God."

The judge leaned forward, eyes magnified in his thick glasses like some fantastic beast. "You can't continue to keep living off the dole, Paulette. There's no money left for your taxes and your tickets and all of the other things you need."

"Would you ask St. Sebastian to worry about your laws as the arrows rained down on him? Or St. Cecilia to pay taxes as the sword fell on her neck?"

The others in the room, mostly good Catholics, muttered as she spoke. Paulette knew they couldn't understand her. God had made her different from them. Made her so that she stood apart. Made her hate their lives lived in the ways of Satan. Laws outside of the Book. Traditions forgotten. If only she'd lived back in the days of the Saints when she could live in a cave and the penitent would come to leave her food. If only they understood what she was. . .and left her alone.

"I will not answer to your sickness, nor will my pure hands touch another sinning creature." At that moment, Paulette's trembling and suppressed fear came out in a babbling rage, and she kicked the nearest chair as hard as she could. They'd let her alone. They'd get away from her if it was the last thing she did. She swept her hands across the paper-littered table beside the podium she stood at, scattering every paper piled there. "I am not of this place. I am not of Caesar. You shall not have me."

Her rage was alive in her belly, eating the pain that swirled in all the skin that was exposed to their judgment, to their creeping eyes. Her face, her hands, her neck all burned with shame. She had to get away from them. Without another word, she turned out of the courtroom and trotted back to her home as fast as her bulk and her habit would allow, passing the casual fishermen cussing and drinking beer, the jogging teen girls with legs exposed in tight running pants, and the cars, and the wires, and the words and all of the humming, jittery loudness of them doing the things they did on phones and computers and televisions. They built their Sodom all around her. Every step took her through hell.

She'd made it to the stoop of her house, silence and prayer within reach and the buffer of the stink and the walls she'd built to keep them out. But just past the threshold, there he stood— Judge Gorgen. He must've jumped in his car and sped past her as she wove through the people littering the main streets of Necedah on the unseasonably warm midwinter afternoon. He stood there inside her house, past the front door she never bothered to lock, looking at her personal life. Touching the collection she'd made of the old and rejected things from before. He pressed a white hankie to his mouth, but she knew that the smell of her waste buckets, scattered like bombs among the debris of her years, got through that thin white cloth. His hands were there, touching. His breath through that hankie. This was Paulette's shrine to her mother and dad and all those she'd sent to God. Her church to what should be. What only God sent her for.

But here he was. In her home. Paulette's rage came back like a black god, riding her into the house. She smiled, a mask to hide the loathing she felt for every whorl on his fingers, for every hair on his head. He represented everything sick, everything forbidden. God turned Lot's wife into a pillar of salt for looking back into the sin of the world, for longing for society and its sins.

"Sister." The judge turned toward her, the picture of her whore niece clutched in his crepe-thin-skinned fingers. Touching her things. Claiming them for this world. Why didn't they understand that she wasn't of this world?

"Judge Gorgen, I need you to leave. This is my house, my place, and no one comes in here but me and God. Just me and God!"

The judge's face stretched into the mockery of regret, eyebrows close and lips tight. Judging. It was his job.

"Listen, Paulette—"

"Sister Paulette."

"Sister, you are living in filth. This place must violate every safety standard, every township law."

"Your laws don't mean anything to God, Judge. You people are. . ." Paulette tried to move around him, keeping a wide orbit as she moved into the safety of her nest. Her shrine to all that wasn't what Gorgen wanted her to have. She'd learned to hate and to fear everything he stood for. Just watching his eyes sliding across the surface of each ledge, each pile. Noting the saint statues, the icons, and medals.

"It's like you're living in the Middle Ages or something, Sister." Judge Gorgen's voice was muffled by his handkerchief.

"Judge Gorgen, I try not to cause problems. Jesus said not to cause problems with the government. God knows I try to stay away from you people. Your hobby lives. Your marriages that are only for now. Your pastimes and jobs. How little it all matters. How little it adds to God's calculations. I am a creature of eternity. My mother and my dad and my brother and my niece all knew I was different by degrees. I can't be what you want as much as I couldn't be what they wanted. What they tried to make me. God made me quiet and inward-facing, and you . . . you want me to be some kind of shade of you. But just knowing you, knowing you and the others, makes my skin burn."

Paulette paced back and forth in front of the little room with the cot, between the kitchen with the collapsed table and the blackened, sprung living room La-Z-Boy, flipping its seat forward in a collapse. The stink mattered not to her, but Gorgen's eyes wept, and he coughed as she paced. The smell was ancient. Deep as hell and real—years of collecting, dead cats buried beneath collapsed bundles, plastic buckets she hadn't emptied filled with her body's foul makings. The smell kept most of them away.

"How can I allow you to stay here? In this? This is Hell on Earth, Paulette. You need help." He reached out a kind hand, withered by his age, with standing blue veins and brown spots.

The rage and fear whipped together into a tower, lifting her above his judgments. Above the offensive sound of his breath and the beat of his heart. He'd take her and force her to live among them. Among them, with their sins and their touches and their bathing and their laws. In the same space. Assaulting her with words and questions when she should be alone with her thoughts and prayers. She'd worked so hard to be left alone to do the work of God.

"No," she said, though inside she screamed and ranted, blood boiling against the walls of vessels and battering her heart. Her bellowing lungs fought against the calm she projected. She had to keep him from running for the others. She had to. "Judge Gorgen, you all frighten me. Since I was young, since my mother taught me that touches would lead me to Hell. Since the nuns wouldn't leave me in my cell with God. Since my dad used to tell me to go hide from Mother. Every moment I'm alone, I pray for the souls that are trapped in your false world. I save you in my loneliness. But you. . .you and your kind—the social workers, the police, the teachers—you are sent as special demons to torment me. To test me. You and your 'help.'"

Paulette's voice escalated, but she'd put herself between him and the door. Of course, it would have been so much easier to let him go. For a moment of quiet, she'd give almost anything. But if he went, he'd bring back so much more. They'd invade like rats. They'd swarm on her, touching and talking and demanding.

In that moment, everything slowed. Dust motes floating on the banded ray of sunlight stopped their dance, and the judge's eyes froze mid-blink. God would speak.

"There is no choice, my child. He would close you off from me. You can't allow them to take you. To make you one of them. Send him to me." God always told her when it was time to take a life.

Paulette picked up her father's knotty wood cane, a remembrance of him she kept by the door. "Judge Gorgen, make your peace with God."

Before he could do any reacting, before he was even back to his normal speed, Paulette swung the cane and cracked the judge's temple with the handle. The blow knocked him sideways against the wall, and he slid to the floor, a trickle of blood dribbling down his cheek.

"Wha—"

"No more of your words. They make me sick." She arched back and brought the cane down again on his head. The second time, his skull crunched, and his words became the groans and natters of someone dying. A third and fourth blow ended his breath.

She panted and caught her breath as blood pooled in the broken cavern Dad's cane had made. The hard part was next—touching him.

She grabbed his ankles and pulled, fighting the urge to vomit as his skin brushed her chaste fingertips. She knew God would forgive her this touch, but it still made her fear well up like a wave. "Just a few minutes," she told herself, "then you'll be safe and alone again."

She pulled him out the side door and wrapped his body in an old sheet. She lived far enough out that no neighbors could see. She still checked the road for cars as she dragged him around to the front of the house, where his car waited. Nothing. She loaded the judge's body onto the front passenger seat, then drove him and his car deep into the Wisconsin woods. She found the spot her dad had shown her so many years before. It was behind the shrine, about three miles up into the woods. A little access road, overgrown with bush honeysuckle and sprouting pines, led to a deep-channeled creek her dad used to fish. Cold, spring-fed water kept swimmers away in the summer, and the remote road camouflaged the spot for all else. Perfect. A miracle from God.

Paulette pulled up to the high lip of the creek and dragged the judge into the driver's seat. She didn't bother to take off the sheet because, by the time they found him, it would be gone to river rot. Besides, it wasn't fitting to have even his dead eyes watch her as she toiled and sweated so. Once he was wedged into the seat, she put the car in neutral, slammed the door, and gave it a hard push from behind until it tipped over the lip, sliding down the muddy bank into the channel. It bobbed there for a second, a little tug boat in a tiny sea, then it sank. Stirred water sealed over him and drew him down where he should be.

Paulette smiled. Around her, the trees waved, and the birds tittered in the gentle late winter wind. A note of frost. A breath of spring. No people to jumble up her thoughts or violate her peace. She kneeled there in the mud and clutched her folded hands to her nose and lips. She whispered the prayers and all the words given her for the poor judge's soul. He'd go to Hell, sure enough. That didn't mean she shouldn't do what she was sent to do.

"Forgive them, Heavenly Father. Forgive their rules and their talking and all their touches. Give me silence and peace." She crossed herself and stood staring into the deep water.

Sometimes she thought death would be better than the

continual war she fought against them and their laws—their misguided demands on her life. She thought about throwing her body into the water and sucking it into her lungs to end the fear. But God spoke to her again. Stopped her from committing that ultimate sin. God showed her what Hell would look like for her. Bodies pressed together like cattle in slaughter chutes, naked and touching and talking all the time.

"Hell is other people," God said.

Paulette nodded and headed back home to pray. Alone.

BESTIES

We've been best friends since we were girls. We made tents and played like we were princesses. We marched through the broken-down swing set in my overgrown backyard and pretended to be back in time. Every day, Julia and I met, her yard, mine. When we got older, the bond became breaths. I couldn't go a day without words from her. I married, and she sang my husband's love song to me. I had kids, and she gathered them up as hers, their aunt of the heart. Even when I had my accident, when the car flipped and flipped and flipped, I felt her, heard her, by my bedside as much as my husband.

I had broken in so many ways—lanced organs, cracked skull, internal bleeding—I couldn't breathe on my own. I didn't think my own thoughts. Julia says I died, but she brought me back.

We all laugh when she says that. She grins at my kids and swears it's true. Once they go to bed, once my husband heads off to watch football on the big screen in the basement, I follow Julia out onto the porch. We sip red wine she brings to share every week. I've told her she didn't have to come every week, but after she does, I always feel so much better. Renewed.

She comes every Saturday, but one Saturday, she didn't. No call. No nothing.

I started to feel weak. Washed up.

So, into the car I went. I made it over there lickety-split. My head felt like it would crack wide open.

"Julia?" I opened the door to her house. I hadn't been there since we'd moved her in years before. It hadn't changed at all since then. Bare walls and boxes and furniture that hadn't been sat on.

"Jules?" Through the upper floor of the house, bedrooms, kitchen, dining room—nothing.

Backyard, trees, grass, shed—nothing.

My knees knocked and legs wobbled. I felt my bones bend in strange places.

"Julia?" Only this time it came out a whine shot with pain. Pain like I hadn't felt since the accident. Bolts of it lanced through me.

"Dawn?" Her voice echoed through the floor. The basement.

Moving toward the basement was like swimming through cement.

"Don't come down here." Her voice echoed down a long tunnel, reaching me in muffled echoes and vibrating epiphanies. My Jules, sweet-faced, brown-eyed, always picking me up. I smelled blood, and I couldn't walk away. Couldn't. My feet lifted and planted, hitting step after step.

"Stay up there!" Desperation spiraled in her voice.

Pain needled my bones and muscles, but the closer I got to her, the better I felt. Like her voice eased the pain. My foot slipped on the first step, sliding my legs into near splits. My ankle cracked and skidded against the splintered bone that had been broken before. The pain screamed up my leg, and I lost the grip I had on the hand rail, and then I tumbled. More breaks, more fire at the bone poking through my skin. I wanted to scream. I wanted to stop, really, but Julia was down there. Blood was down there. So I pulled myself, hand over hand down each step, screaming with the pain.

Julia came around the corner, naked as when she'd been born, covered in blood.

"My Jules." It came out with a wheeze. I wanted to reach for her, but my arms curled up and clutched at me, so broken and raw.

"Oh, no. Dawn, look at you." She gathered me up. Somehow, she lifted me and carried me like I was a baby further into the basement. The tang of blood thickened into a fog. "I know I was late, but you should have waited."

No words. My jaw crumpled somewhere on the steps, and something in my throat twanged loose like a broken rubber band. I clung to her. I always have. I couldn't look closely but ten-foot tall letters spelled words I didn't know all around me. Carvings of things, teeth and claws, painted with Jule's swirling brush style. My eyes swelled shut, but I'd been here before. Somewhere in my head, I knew this place. Knew it and hated it.

"I'll help you forget later, but you have to look now. It's the only way to save you when you get this bad."

My eyes snapped wide as she laid me on a white cloth flecked with blood in front of a low wooden platform. My Julia, my life friend, grasped a beating human heart in her hand. Beating because it sat inside a vivisected chest. A man, my age, maybe even fifty, wheezed and begged on her altar. His words didn't form anymore, but from his eyes, I know he begged for his life. She yanked, pulling the muscle out of its cradle, and then she ripped it apart with her own little hands. The spray of blood spattered me, my mouth, my compound fractures, my split head. She threw the heart into a press, like the ones you see at wineries. She tore deeper, pulling out his liver, a kidney, and eventually she slit his throat and drained the blood from his arteries in dribbles. He stopped grunting when the blood flow stopped. I suddenly knew I'd seen this before.

"My poor Dawn. I'll fix you up. Just wait and see." I sounded bad, sure, but she sounded shattered. Broken as any of my bones.

She cranked the press, and the liquid mashed through the screens, filtering into a bottle she'd placed under its spout. The wine. Our special Saturday wine.

"W. . . Www. . ." I tried, but my tongue had been bitten nearly off.

"Why. You always ask why." She laughed, though it sounded more like a sob. Her arms streaked and dripped with gore, but still, she pressed the man's organs, catching all the fluids in the bottle. "You died, Dawn. You died because they couldn't fix you. They kept you alive, broken and hurting, so the kids could reconcile the pulp you were with their mommy. Mark cried for hours. Wept. And me? I couldn't live without you. I just . . . I couldn't."

She raised her hands and muttered an incantation over the bottle that made it glow with a fiery light.

"Did you know that demons hunger for pure love? They do. I found that out." She walked over and blew out the black candles and the braziers swinging from the ceiling. "I called for one. Figured out how to do it on the internet. Didn't need much to do it."

She walked back over to the bottle and lifted it again. Darkness coalesced around it in a halo.

"They gave me the formula, but it needs a sacrifice. Once a week."

She leaned over and poured some of the wine into my mouth. I tried to spit it out, didn't want to drink it, but as soon as the stuff hit my lips, my body started to knit itself back together.

"I try not to be late, but sometimes the sacrifices are harder to find. I look all week. Sometimes they just won't go easy." She sipped the concoction and sprayed it on my legs, making the bones burrow back into my skin.

Lying there, healing, I did the math. Once a week for eight years since my accident. Fifty-two times eight. That's four hundred and sixteen souls dead because of me.

"Oh, bestie, look. It's not your fault. It's mine. I try to hide it from you. I try to make it so you don't bear this burden. Just sometimes, they don't die so easy, and your body knows where to come to get fixed."

"Happened before? Me here?" My jaw and tongue were better but not perfect.

She nodded and poured one more draft down my throat.

"You barely made it this time." She stood and sighed. "I'll get cleaned up and take you home."

She lifted me from the floor and carried me up the stairs like I weighed nothing. As we passed the stainless surface of her fridge, I caught sight of myself, a nearly desiccated corpse. Everything thin, hanging at bad angles. But the wine in me set fires in all the broken places. I would be fine. I knew I had been before.

Julia laid me on the couch and gave me another little sip of the blood wine.

"My last gift to you, my bestie, is that you won't remember any of this." She put her hand on my head, and it tingled. She pulled her hand away, and the memories started to slip. "Nothing is more wonderful than pure love, Dawn. I'll bear this all for you."

I wanted to say no. Save yourself, Julia. Let me go. But I slid into the same place I'd been for eight years. As the darkness closed over my memory, I said a prayer for her and her soul.

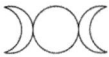

"Special vintage?" I raised the wine glass up and glanced through the glass at the ruby red clinging and coating it. For a second, just a second, I wanted to toss the wine into the yard. Something told me it would be the right thing to do. But Julia drank a sip and toasted our friendship. How could I not drink to that?

MONSTERS

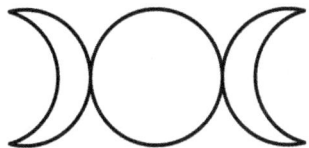

Women of power, magic, and horror. Women who mold or
destroy. Creation requires a clean slate.

BONE HIVES

MIKE'S HAND slid across the slick face of the cave wall searching for another handhold. She'd told him that free climbing in an unexplored cave was sexy. In front of him, Laura glowed with the dewy sweat of exertion and exhilaration. She was a goddess and a daredevil, and he could only hope to keep up.

"You all right back there?"

Her headlamp blinded him for a second, but when his eyes adjusted, he saw the silly grin on her face. It was looking good for a romp when the climb was over. He flexed, hoping he looked good against the rock. Capable at least.

He'd never done this before, and even though he was a true gym rat, it was testing muscles he didn't even know he had. "I'm fine. Lead on, milady."

They filled the silence with scrabbled steps and pebbles tinging down into the darkness. Maybe it was that darkness that made Mike feel like he was already falling. How could dark be so dark? So big and so close.

He stuffed his fear down under his clenched core and his straining thighs. Focus on the movements and on the things you can see, he told himself. Focus on following Laura, because she knows what she's doing. "You've been here before?"

"A bunch of times. I know this place so well, I don't even need the light."

Mike laughed, though it was fake. Something in the tone of her voice wasn't right.

"Almost there." She dropped onto a ledge and lit the handholds that led him to it as well.

He panted, trying to catch his breath and stretch a bit before they went on. Climbing down had been hard. Harder than lifting. Harder than the marathon he'd run or the climbing he'd done in Colorado. Darkness pressed in on him again, heavier, and his lungs didn't want to take it in.

He sat down hard and focused on breathing. As much as he wanted to impress Laura, he couldn't shake the fact that his body didn't like this place. Trying to rationalize and scoff at his childish fear of the dark did nothing to calm the bone-deep feeling that things weren't right and that he didn't belong in the belly of the earth.

"Let's head back, huh?" he said once he knew his voice wouldn't crack. "I'll get us dinner and give you an amazing backrub after."

She squatted down next to him, so close he felt the hot breath behind her words. "We're so close. Just a little more. Wait until you see it!"

"How am I going to see it? All we have are these little headlamps and . . ."

"Hey." Her voice lost some of the flirty sweetness. "Trust me. You'll see it just fine. Five more minutes of climbing, and then it's a flat walk for fifteen. Swear."

So deep. People weren't meant to be this deep in the earth's secret places.

She stood and stretched.

Mike couldn't help staring at her in the half-light. She moved like a lioness, flexing each joint. It wasn't a sexual thing, but the power in her limbs and the effortless suppleness stirred enough longing in him that he could tamp down the fear and follow her into the dark. Why wouldn't he? She was all he'd ever wanted.

She lowered herself easily over the lip of the rock shelf, and he followed. She unerringly found the best handholds and told him where to put his feet. There wasn't any pretense of him being capable of doing it himself. Not anymore. This had become her show, and he was a participant. A follower.

Mike didn't mind that. It took some of the pressure away and allowed him to just focus on breaths. Steps. If it wasn't for the cold fingers of the dark and the slick stone, he could have imagined himself away from here the way he did when he daydreamed at work.

Breathe. Hand. Foot. Lower. Breathe.

Finally, he stepped on a flat stone. He leaned down, bracing on his knees and letting the shaking in his muscles settle. Laura stood beside him and rubbed his back lightly. In a motherly way.

Mike shrugged her off and stood up quickly. "I'm good, babe. Lead on."

But he wasn't good.

Since his feet had hit the path, his brain buzzed and tingled inside his skull. As sweaty as he'd been moments before, his skin was icy. Tight across him like it had shrunk into something that didn't fit.

Laura grabbed his hand and led him down the path.

Fifteen minutes, and he'd see this cave formation she'd raved about. Fifteen minutes and he'd turn around and make his way out, and then they'd be away. And maybe he would leave Laura, gorgeous or not, because her hand was cold in his and her hair floated weirdly around her head, and she glowed.

Glowed. That didn't make sense.

"Turn off your lamp," she said.

"No."

He couldn't stop her from reaching up and jerking the headlamp off his head. It clattered to the floor and flashed out.

"Fuck, Laura—"

"Look."

She'd dropped his hand and pointed ahead. The darkness had grayed. A corona of greenish-yellow light flirted around the edges of what looked like a turn in the cave throat.

Something about it—the color and the movement and the buzz in his skull that seemed to match the light's life—made him want to bolt, dark or not.

It wasn't right.

He took a step back, and it was like walking through fire.

Laura grabbed his elbow and pulled. Mike followed because her grip was iron, and he couldn't find enough strength to shake it off. As solid as the earth under him felt, her fingers clamped down with more power.

All he could think was that it would be over soon. The maddening buzz drowned out every thought but that.

They rounded the corner, and the cave opened into a cathedral room that couldn't be. Yes, they'd gone deep into the cave, so far down the gravity thickened around each step. But this was a whole world in a greenish-yellow dome of stone that stretched out to infinity. It hurt to look up, so Mike dropped his eyes. Massive structures grew out of the floor of the cave like roots that twisted and tangled, up and up. They reached into the vaulted ceiling, and again, Mike's eyes couldn't follow them to their ends.

It hurt so bad to even try that he dropped to his knees.

"Why did you bring me here? " Mike wiped at his eyes and realized they were bleeding. Nothing felt right. The air was soup, and his balance was shit. She led him, and he stumbled in her wake. "Those things . . . What are they?"

"These are the bone hives, Mike. I grew up here."

The buzzing in his head got so loud that he collapsed next to her. He couldn't see anymore, not through the veil of blood. But he could hear.

Other murmurs, other men with fear laced in the tone of their words.

Men asking why and what.

The women who answered all sounded just like Laura.

Mike had to see it, even though every fiber of him, every cell, screamed that not knowing was better. He wiped away enough blood and saw them coming from all around the bone hives, stepping out of cracks, crawlways, and caves. Laura times ten. Then a hundred. Then . . .

She was everywhere.

His Laura jerked him to his feet.

The buzzing inside his head erupted into the air. All the men in the grasps of all the Lauras grabbed their heads like Mike did, pressing their palms against their ears.

All of them screamed.

Between the bone hives, a pit collapsed. Slowly. Like something had opened a trap door and planned to come on through. Laura jerked him forward, pulling him toward the pit.

"You'll be the first, Mike," she said, though her voice didn't make any sense. It issued out of every Laura's mouth and from the gaps in the bone hives' winding structure.

Mike couldn't fight.

His muscles only moved because SHE willed it.

His eyes and ears saw only HER.

Not Laura.

The thing in the pit climbed up. Not all of HER. Just a bit. Appendages lined with hooked hairs whipped out. The top of a domed head—big as a mountain with hair that rippled out like waves on the sea—breached the floor of the cave. Mike squeezed his eyes shut. SHE was too much to know. Too big to understand.

She was LAURA.

LAURA because her real name sounded like the buzz of radiation between stars.

He didn't have to be asked to give himself. All that was left in his head knotted around what SHE wanted. What SHE whispered. He shook loose of his Laura and jogged to the edge.

He'd be the first. He'd be her lover, her meal, and his bones that would shelter his daughters until they ripened and hunted for more just like him.

LAURA wrapped him in her thoughts, and all went dark. All went away but his screams.

And his bones.

FOUR HORSEMEN OF THE
HAPPY HOUR

FOUR HORSEMEN of the Happy Hour
No one dies during happy hour.
That's what they say anyway.
Between four and six every night, we crowd into the bar Four Horsemen of Apocalypse until there's only room to shift between each other, raising up a hand for the drink we came for. The barkeeps fly around our heads, bringing a drop of happiness for every glass.
They say you shouldn't drink while you work, but we death gods tend to work all the time, so what are you going to do?
We used to group together, by tradition and culture, drawn to each other by the knowing of language or the stories that force us together. So many gods now, we can just press in for our daily libation before we rush back into the fray, catching the souls as they slip through the torn fibers of their lives.
We deliver them on to the gods of life or resurrection or the afterlife.
Glorified damned delivery people we are and so, so many of us.
I nod to Mot and Ninsusinak, squeezed in a corner, pressing their lips together in a pantomime of life they'd seen somewhere.

Gangnim Doryeong and his reapers do shots at the bar, laughing as Tusok Sacha falls to the ground with thud, like the rock he is, only we all know it's for show.

There is no drunk here. No oblivion for us.

Relief, though. That's what we seek.

The Banshee sisters flit from place to place, silent as the void between stars because that is the thing they can't be normally and for them it is the reward.

Kali and Yami in quiet conversation, just smiling and enjoying the din around them.

And me? I slip out of the crowd into the filthy bathroom. My favorite place.

I close the lid and sit on the toilet, not minding the filth. Piles of ripped toilet paper, oaths scrawled or burned into the walls, sigils of death, and protections hanging in the air like tinsel. When you have but two hours a day of freedom, the bathroom takes the hit.

I breathe in the calm.

A knock at the door.

"Death, we know it's you. Can we come in?"

I nod and swipe my hand at the bolt holding the door closed, and it shifts with a clang.

Pestilence flies in on her black scabby horse. "Don't mind me."

She and her horse eat the toilet paper on the floor, lick all the walls clean, and when I move, they make the toilet bowl sparkle.

"Favorite part of the job," she says, wiping her bloody lips on the back of her leprous hand.

I nod.

"You seem . . . sad." She takes a moment to lean on the wall and light a cig.

The smoke doesn't bother me. Pestilence's open wounds suck up whatever she breaths out. "Just tired."

She nods. "I'll lock the door behind me."

I take a few more rare seconds, then I stand. I glance at the mirror and enjoy my fleshy face. My beautiful black hair. My red-lipped smile. After happy hour, they are gone, but just to see them for a moment makes me remember that I was once another thing.

I pull my hood up and grab the scythe. Just a few more minutes before my second shift starts.

With a snap of my finger, the lock slides and the door opens. When I step out, Kalma pushes in with a huff. She's so beautiful here, skin whole and smell sweet. Like me, she will enjoy a few minutes of respite from her work face. From her smell of corpses and decay.

Perfume, I think. Deodorant. But it's so easy to judge, isn't it?

I step into the massive crowd singing some song about the bright side of life. Cute ditty. Appropriate. Pestilence drops a drink for me from overhead. A pinot grigio, sweet as life itself. I tip it back and smile, winking at Pestilence.

It glitters in my throat and warms my belly. My skin pricks up and catches all the cool breath of the bringers of death singing about life around me. The joy we have, even in the sadness that we bring. No one left behind. No one without some next place to be, good or bad. No oblivion for anyone.

And I smile with my lips and my cheeks and my eyes.

The clock ticks, and happy hour ends.

We gather our tools and take off our skin for the horsemen to press and hand out tomorrow.

I glance back at Pestilence, just beginning to lick the floor clean of all the spills from the revelry. "Tomorrow, my friend."

With a wave, I flow away toward my first delivery. There is rest for the dead, but for Death? We live for happy hour.

LADY MONSTROSITY

"I HEARD THEY SAW HER AGAIN," Jacob said. "Up on Five. Said she took a whole unit in fifteen minutes. Hall was red with blood."

I shrugged. Those are the breaks.

"Did the cleanup crew go in full hazmat?"

He nodded. "Glad they didn't ask us. I'm fine with the shitty diapers and bleach-burned fingers, ya know. At least they're safe."

I did know.

"The things we do for insurance and a berth, right?"

We mopped in silence, ignoring the docs and nurses who tracked up our floors as soon as they were clean.

They did their jobs, and we did ours.

"I used to hate 'em," I said, swinging the mop in wide arcs. "The docs, I mean. They were smug and full of themselves back in the day. Not so much anymore."

Jacob smirked and started whistling the tune to the old spook story we'd heard our little ones singing down in the hold where our families lived in sealed-up safety. We watched them on the monitors when they were at play or sleeping or eating at the long communal tables the Navy'd set up down there.

"Lady Monstrosity rose from the sea.
Came after you and came after me.
Wrapped in her arms, you can't catch your
    breath.
Lose your smell and taste, you're close to death.

Lady Monstrosity rose from the sea
She slithers and grabs, you can't break free.
Wrapped in her arms, you can't even breathe
Wear your mask tight or she'll come underneath.

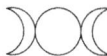

The verses seemed to get more ugly every time he heard them, but he understood the song. Make a rhyme of the horror, and maybe for a minute, you're strong. Maybe for a minute, you feel like you beat the monster.

"Wonder what they do with all the dead?"

"They throw 'em overboard."

He knew that. We did it each day before we went through decontamination and traded our brooms for our berth. He'd handled as many floppy, watery corpses as me; maybe he just couldn't process the memories.

"I didn't mean here. On land. Aren't many of 'em left in the old cities, right? When we take on, the shoremen always say so. If there's not enough of 'em to gather up the dead and burn them, I wonder what they do."

I knew because I always traded away some of my rations for information when the shoremen brought us their sick and the food and fuel payments we took for treating them. Ships like ours floated all along the coasts on their assigned rounds. The docs and nurses worked as hard as us, and like us, they did it to pay for their people downstairs, waiting in the safety of the hold for Lady Monstrosity to finally pass us by.

"Think she'll ever get tired of us?" Jacob leaned for a second on his mop pole and looked so much older than his eighteen years.

I'd often wondered the same.

We'd woken her up, though. Melted her out of her artic ice coffin with the heat we made. And when she rose, she was beautiful and icy, long black hair, blue skin, and as tall as a ten-story building when she wanted to be. Gorgeous white and blue swirling eyes and delicate fingers strong enough to snatch us up and crush us.

And trailing behind her . . . crimson tentacles.

She didn't bother with us too much at first. She walked.

Watched.

I remember being in Vegas, safe behind the mountains, when the last of California disappeared into the sea. Maisey had just been born then, and Helen clung to the pink little thing and whispered about being sorry. Florida, most of the East Coast, all of the lower third of the Mississippi-touched states were swallowed up, and I remember watching Lady Monstrosity walking along the edges, looking confused and so sad. I clutched Maisey and Helen to me and promised I'd protect them.

I was a cop then. Good salary. Pension. That all changed when Lady Monstrosity made us die.

At first, it was like a bad flu. Terrible high numbers of dead among the weak and the elderly. I remember being glad we were so young. Then Lady Monstrosity unleashed something new.

It changed so fast that the docs couldn't keep up.

Fifteen percent died.

Then 50 percent.

The day I volunteered for the hospital ship, they promised that everyone sealed down in the hold would live free of the disease. We just had to live in the hospital and care for those who came to us.

I'd signed on, not caring about what I gave up.

"How's Helen?" Jacob asked that night as we stood in the stinging decontamination shower.

I shrugged and lifted my arms so the spray could hit my sides. "She doesn't try to talk to me anymore. Maisey looks good, though. Growing like a weed."

Jacob nodded.

His wife had tried to kill herself in the hold. None of them had wanted to be down there, but it was all for their own safety.

"Do you think Lady Monstrosity will go back to sleep someday?"

I laced my fingers into a cup behind my head and relaxed on my cot, letting the growl of the ship's engines massage the knots out of me. "That's the hope, but . . ."

"But?"

I know he didn't want anything real. Just some reassurance in the darkest time he'd ever known. What fools we'd been. Willfully ignorant babies playing with things we didn't understand and couldn't control.

"No, Jacob. We're like mosquitos to her. Something to swat. Don't you see that?"

He flipped over in his cot and was quiet, but I'm pretty sure he was crying. I couldn't take that, so I got up and went to the observation room.

The room full of screens showed every part of the ship, but most nights, folks only wanted to see the part of the ship where the families lived behind the welded steel doors. I sat down and watched the screens. It wasn't so late that the folks inside would be in bed. They didn't live on shift-sharing like us.

The screens showed empty playground equipment. Little houses with doors swinging open but no lights on inside.

And tentacles. Red glowing tentacles slithered between the houses that lined the sides of the hold.

"Oh, no! No, no, nonononono! Fuck!" I hit the button on the wall to set off the alarms that would seal all the wings shut.

The whooping scream of the siren cut through the calm, and slamming sounds surrounded me on all sides.

My Helen was down there with the monster. My little Maisey. I wanted to bury my face in my hands and not see anymore; let them do what they had to do without watching it. But you have to look, you know? Just in case you catch a glimpse.

The tar poison spray coated everything it touched in the hold. It hardened on the walls and the roofs. On the doors and swings. It coated the turf and the sidewalks. It sealed in the poison.

Tears ran down my face as I watched. I hoped they were already dead. That they didn't have to suffocate in the plastic shroud I'd made for them by sounding the alarm.

The tentacles were gone. Maybe we'd stopped her there in the sealed hold. I spun in the chair and looked at the other screens that reflected the insides of patient rooms, of crew quarters, of sealed wings. The floors all squirmed with the wet scarlet tentacles of Lady Monstrosity. The walls dripped with the gore of the last stages of dying from her tentacles' kisses.

I heard a hitching gasp and wails that drowned out the siren and realized it was me. The air in my lungs burned as I coughed out my despair. Ignorant children, every one of us. We deserved this!

"No." A lovely voice spoke so softly behind me. I knew it was her, and I turned. She stood in the doorway, normal-sized. Only she really wasn't, and I knew that. Her face sparkled like shattered glass and the sharpness of a sword in your gut. "I thought you were ready, and I left you here. I gave you my treasure when you were wiser. How wrong I was . . . Lazy."

Her tentacles slithered around me, warm as a fever, but soft too. Full of life. "I won't make the same mistake."

Her eyes held the whole world in their reflection. Her hands pressed me like the plates of the earth. I drowned in her depths.

I became a piece of her, floating in her thoughts like dust in a beam of light.

We all did.

Ignorant children, every one of us, and she reabsorbed us. She wouldn't make the same mistake again.

I waved and wriggled in her as she found the next ship. Wouldn't be long. Not long at all.

HER TEETH ARE LONG AND FULL OF VENOM

HENRY CLIMBED the stairs to his second-floor office, completely aware of the monster that hovered behind him, depositing fetid breaths on his shoulders. He'd taken to wearing a hat because if he didn't, then her drool would run off her needle teeth, onto his head, and into his eyes. Since her drool had some kind of venom in it, it burned his eyes something terrible when he didn't protect them.

He went through hats pretty quickly.

At the landing, two lovely women stood talking. A dentist and a mortgage company shared the second floor of the building with Henry's business. The two women had to be from one of those since he couldn't keep anyone employed in his front office to save his life.

No one wanted to work with someone in his business.

One of the women stopped mid-sentence when she saw him standing there with his monster hanging in the air behind him—shredded, sagging gray shroud, bulging white eyes, gaping mouth set in a toothy scream, and bone-thin arms with spidery hands tipped in jagged black claws.

It was always the same. One screamed and scrambled backward, and the other stood locked in place like some poor deer stunned into paralysis by the headlights of an eighteen-wheeler.

Henry sighed and kept walking.

He slid his key into the door to his office, pulling down the taped notes written in thick red and black letters threatening him, complaining, saying he made everyone uncomfortable and should close up shop permanently.

The chipped letters on the door read, "Henry Tebeau, Sin Eater."

If they understood what that meant and how important his work was, they'd never leave another note or nasty message on his service. But they didn't understand. They wouldn't, unless they needed his help.

And he'd never wish such a thing on anyone.

The phone rang at the empty receptionist's desk, but Henry didn't hurry. He hung up his jacket and walked through the shabby waiting room into his "operating room." He liked it better inside that room. He'd spent a pretty penny buying a comfortable set of recliners for the ritual. He'd painted the walls a soothing blue and hung shaman-made fetishes and Buddhist-blessed weavings around the room. His monster backed away into the corner he'd made comfortable for her where her puzzles and games waited.

She enjoyed Sudoku and Tetris most.

He lowered himself into his recliner and watched her spindly fingers flying across the screen of the iPad, spinning and placing the shapes that fell in time with "Korobeiniki," the theme song of Tetris. She whistled happily around her long teeth as she worked. He smiled and let himself nod, knowing she'd be at it for hours if—

The trill of the phone broke the peace. She growled and dropped the iPad to claw at her face.

"Henry Tebeau." He pulled the pad of paper he kept by the phone closer to him.

"Is this the sin eater?"

He hated this bit. Either this was a real customer with cash and pain to be given, or it was—

"Sin isn't something that can be eaten. It's engraved on the soul. Shame on you."

Ah, a true believer.

"Ma'am, I'm offering a service. If you don't like what I do, well . . . why don't you pray about it."

He put the phone down, wishing he had a nastier comeback. He wanted to say something so cutting that she'd hang up the phone bloodied and wincing, but when he looked at the monster—what he'd grown from the sins of others—he knew that he'd done the right thing with his gentle answer.

The beast floated there, mouth agape and miserable.

He wasn't sure when he'd become aware that she was so sad. Maybe it had been during one of the long nights when she wept quietly under Henry's bed, shaking and sniffling until the bed vibrated and he had to sing to get her to stop.

Currently, she liked "You Are My Sunshine."

The office's front door rattled open, and a woman crossed the creaky bare floor. He hadn't seen her yet, but a woman's sins smell different from a man's, so he knew it was a she right away. She paused at the partially opened door. He imagined her frozen there weighing her options, scared to knock because it meant admitting she couldn't live with what she'd done.

"Come in." He knew his words would soothe her enough. She needed them to help her. What sat on her shoulders stank.

When she pushed her way into the room, his stomach twisted. If he didn't act quickly, the sin would root itself in deeper, and she'd leave with it tearing her up. Maybe die of it. He had to break it from her soul.

Henry knew the woman needed some sanity, some expectation before the horror that would come, or she'd twist away and never get the relief she needed. He pushed out of the chair and invited her to sit at a countertop with pens and flowers and two stools. It looked like something out of a doctor's office.

He'd made it that way purposefully. It put the clients into the calmest frame of mind possible . . . at least as calm as one could be with a drooling monster staring from the corner.

He gave her forms to fill out. Nothing too complex. Contact information, allergies, family history. She wrote confidently on each sheet of paper, which is what the papers were designed to inspire. The expected made the chaos that came after easier.

"The procedure will take about an hour. There will be no memory of the act—"

"Do I have to tell you what I did?" Her forehead wrinkled with worry, and her back got rigid.

Henry shook his head. "That's not necessary."

Because he'd know as soon as he ate it.

She glanced over at the chair and then to the corner where the monster hovered. "It's horrible," she whispered.

Henry stayed quiet for a moment to let her process what she was seeing. Then, "That will be $1200."

"Oh, that's a lot." She stared at the monster in the corner and distractedly handed him her credit card.

"But it really isn't. It's based on the sin. I've eaten much more expensive sins than yours."

She shivered.

"That's what the sins become?" She pointed at his monster.

Henry gave her the receipt but not an answer. "Have a seat here." He indicated the chair on the right.

"Will I feel it?"

He shook his head as the monster flowed over and hovered behind her. "You'll sleep."

"Sleep? I'm not—"

The monster touched the client's forehead. That alien touch alone was enough to knock aside any client's consciousness into safe, deep sleep. Sleep kept them from feeling the ugliness rip right out of their souls. To do that awake . . . Henry shivered just thinking about it.

He climbed into the other chair and took a deep breath as

the monster fluttered over him. He touched a remote that activated the cameras over the chairs. He'd learned that if he couldn't prove that a service was rendered, the clients and sometimes their families would accuse him of bilking them. It didn't take much to get them to leave him alone. They'd watch the video and back away, horrified by the process.

It wasn't pretty, eating people's sins.

"I'm ready." Henry rocked back in this chair.

His monster didn't pounce the way she had when she was younger. She'd grown gentle over the years. She flowed over him, her shroud drifting on his skin and touching with prickles of ice. She stared into his eyes, mouth gaping and eyes white, but he understood her features. She worried about him.

Sin eating wasn't good for his health. He felt each sin like a slice, and each extraction was a piece of himself gone.

"Just do it."

She smiled, though it didn't look much different from her natural sagging maw. She thrust her clawed hand into his mouth, stretching his lips until they split a bit at the corners. He felt her nails scraping down his throat, nicking it even though he felt the care she took.

Then, the sin flowed through her into him.

Most people assumed that his monster was the sin eater, but she wasn't. She was his protector. The medium that connected the sinner to him. A circuit for the evil energy to travel along.

The sin exploded into his mind, all whipping light and fiery tentacles. The monster's body wrapped around him, keeping the energy flowing from the client into him, keeping them both immobile and whimpering as she kept him safe.

Henry's mind settled into the client's. He became the client at the time of her great sin by stepping into that moment as easily as it was to step through an open door. The client's memory took over, and he felt everything she had done.

Her body was sweaty from climbing, and the view was an incredible panorama of crags and evergreens framed by a wide-open sky. She was tired but exhilarated as she stood on top of a jutting rock formation with another woman who sipped water and then wiped sweat away from her face.

Massey. The name of the other woman swam up through the memory like an earworm song repeating the melody eternally. Massey, Massey, Massey. The client braced and stretched her long legs, curling her manicured fingers into fists. Her long ponytail fell across her cheek, blocking her pained features from Massey's view. She was glad.

Glad Massey couldn't see how much what she'd admitted hurt her.

Henry couldn't hear the words the other woman spoke because the client couldn't hear through her rage. All he knew was the woman in front of him spoke and stretched and smiled, unaware of the blinding rage building like a tsunami inside the client's mind.

The rapid-fire plans rattled through the client's thoughts, and Henry could hear those clearly enough.

No one would find—

No one knew they ran together—

She did this—

The client shoved Massey from behind so that she toppled over the edge of the ridge and then leaned over to watch her fall. Massey cartwheeled down the sheer face of the cliff.

The client gasped when she realized what she'd done. She hadn't meant to . . . it was a mistake. She wanted to pull it back. Turn back time. She scrambled down the cliff after Massey, knowing she was dead. Hating her and loving her. She was a cheater. She was her love. The mess in her mind clarified when her gaze fell on Massey's body, all running blood and edges and bone piercing through skin.

Only Massey didn't die.

The sin's path switched to another memory when Massey lay in a hospital, paralyzed. In a coma. It's where the client found out she'd been mistaken about what her love had told her.

Massey hadn't cheated. When Massey slipped away, everyone thought that the two of them had been perfect, loving, trusting. The client let them believe it had been an accident. She soaked up their love and pity like it was sunlight. She drank their care down into the hole the sin had burned into her.

Such a sin.

Such a big sin.

Henry felt her guilt like holes through the muscles of his heart, gaping and beating with jagged pain. He gurgled as the horror flowed down his throat, traveling into his gut, pulsing and twisting there with a life of its own.

Every sin he ate took hours of his life. This one might take days.

Every sin made his monster bigger and him smaller.

When he stabilized and the client woke, he walked her out, slightly confused but happier. Cleaner. He, however, felt played out. Nearly dead.

He collapsed to the ground, though his monster caught him and lowered him. She wrapped around him, feeling as cold as all the deaths she'd transfused and as sharp as every lie and deceit she'd fed him. She'd been so small when he found her. That day, when he was just five, he'd gotten mad at his mother and ran away. He slept that night in a graveyard. Just before dawn, a beautiful woman traced all the letters on a gravestone that read *Dottie Schultz, beloved mother.* Her misty fingers flew across the edges of the letters over and over like she carved each letter herself.

"Hey, lady, are you okay?"

He'd been just a kid when she touched him, and he didn't know what he was. Her sin was the first he swallowed. She'd smothered her mother when she was sleeping. Her mother suffered so, and she'd ended it, but her sin kept her at the headstone, anchored to it. When he ate her sin, she latched onto his soul, took some of the pain, and it changed her as much as it changed him.

That had been so long ago. They'd been constantly together since.

His monster didn't have a name. She didn't want one. She ignored him when he tried to call her anything but monster. Yet she held him, using the energy she had to keep his head off the ground as he lay in a pool of sweat, twitching around the pain of the sin he'd eaten.

It got harder to recover every time he ate. "Monster," he whispered, "do you think we'll go to heaven together? I don't have too long. I can feel it. It hurts so bad."

Henry said that every time.

She nodded and rocked and let him cry into the misty folds of her cowl.

He eventually stood up, washed his face, and put his hat on. He set the operating room back to rights and moved back through the reception. She was right behind him, long teeth in her gaping mouth dripping venom as she hung, cold, in the air above him. Walking down the steps and out onto the street, he ignored all the stares and gasps.

They couldn't understand about his monster. About what they were to each other.

She held him up.

She cried with him every night.

Her teeth were long and full of venom, but he thought she was beautiful.

MADE OF CROWS

"THE MOST INTELLIGENT creatures aren't some begging dog or the hump-crazy dolphins," Randal said to Sophie as they walked the perimeter of the Bowl Valley waste they guarded. "It's crows."

In the distance, a crow laughed at the sky and landed on a gnarled branch that grew from the cracked-up river wash, dry now for fifty years.

Sophie nodded. She'd heard it before. She shifted the rifle farther back on her shoulders and glanced through the binoculars to where the crow hopped from the branch onto the ground, picking through pebbles.

"Why, if crows ran the world, we'd probably all be better off," Randal said, probably for the millionth time.

Not a lot to do out in the wastes of Ohio. Maybe in Manitoba there were green things that grew, but here there was just grit and wind to guard. Still, Sophie didn't complain. They had it worse down south, living underground because of heat. The interfilms whispered about cannibalism in the caves.

If Randal wasn't such an idiot, he might have tried to eat her when she'd stumbled across the ragged mountains, begging for water from his evaptank. He took her in. Made her his little sister. Back in the Old World, they'd have called Randal an imbecile, a retard, or some other awful thing. But in this world, he thrived. Things made sense to him, and he became the protector of this bit of land.

He collected up living things and protected them in his hill cabin, a buried fortress of shipping containers lined with the flotsam of the Old World. No one came here because . . . there was nothing here. But Randal managed to find the occasional rabbit, worms, a stray cat, and even some little green things he sheltered and grew inside the hill. He'd found her. Any other guy might have mauled her, raped her, killed her for meat. Randal didn't eat meat. He couldn't hurt a fly. And the raping? He wasn't interested in it.

Just a big, strong kid with a good heart here at the end of the world.

"Randal, why do you like crows so much?"

He smiled, rolling the shovel he carried across the ridge of his shoulder.

"I dream about crows all the time. When I do, the evaptank gets more water, and we find plots of fat earthworms to eat. They bring me good luck. Beside you, they're the only things left around here that talk. Caw-Caw!"

Sophie nodded, pulling her feathery black skirt up to step over a branch.

"What if I told you that you were the only person left on earth, Randal, and that the crows are taking care of you as best they can. They make up all those stories about other places. Other people. To keep you happy. For old times' sake. What if I told you that you are their special pet?"

Randal twisted his mouth as he did when he thought deeper than his pool allowed. "There's worse things, right, Sophie? I'd rather be a crow's pet than some monster eating babies like they say on the interfilms. But wait . . . what you say can't be true, because you're here. You're a person like me. Don't be so silly, Sophie."

She smiled and leaned in toward him, pecking him on the cheek.

"Right, right, Randal. Even so, you're right. Let's get back and eat. I bet the rabbits are hungry too."

He laughed, and as he walked away, muttering happily about the rabbits and the plants in his burrow under the hill, Sophie walked a few steps behind. Parts of her broke off, black and feathery, and flew away, messengers carrying back word of Randal's needs to the kingdom of crows. The flock of Sophie would keep him alive for as long as they could, for old times' sake, but after him, the whole world would be made up of crows.

THREE GRACES IN AUTUMN

LOZI'S VEIL dipped into the coffee that Jacoba set in front of her.

"Sister," Jacoba chided. "Be careful."

Lozi's eyes focused, and she jerked back, dabbing the stained ends of her white net veil with a napkin. She didn't need to. All she had to do was wish it clean, and it would be so, but Lozi wasn't a show-off like Smolder, the other of the three sisters. Lifting her too-hot coffee to her lips, Lozi watched Smolder circle the ceiling in lazy, misty loops. Jacoba, the eldest, tutted and shifted the cups and the sugar around the tea table, pretending not to be annoyed, but Lozi knew Jacoba's moods.

Outside of their house, the whole world waited in suspension for the sisters to end their rest. All the beings at their end time stood waiting for judgment. And hoping for absolution. Or if they met frightening Smolder, they imagined damnation. But they would have to wait a bit longer. Jacoba led them and wouldn't start the day without this moment of sharing between them. Therapy, she said.

"The coffee is good." Lozi tried to distract Jacoba from Smolder's silly, smoky pouting. She'd always been the peacekeeper.

Jacoba shook her head and sipped the coffee, studiously avoiding that swirling form pooling in the corner that finally took a womanly shape. Smolder flowed across the room decked in layers of gray smoke, not bothering to solidify the mask of a face that her shifting mass wore. No eyes in the dark yawing sockets, no color to brighten her cheeks, but at least she lowered herself into the chair Jacoba slid out for her.

Lozi sighed. No fight today! Thank the gods.

Jacoba's pet skull sat on the table next to the silver coffee pot, chuckling and flashing with the spectral light as the daily to-do list churned out from between its teeth. Ruinic writings of all the names they'd need for that day's reaping. Maybe it'd be better named a to-die list, but Lozi kept the thought to herself. No need to poke the bear.

The bear herself, Jacoba, ignored the list as it pooled on the floor beneath her, but Lozi's eyes always came back to it. So many names, so many days filled with souls.

"Do you remember . . ." Lozi's began made her sisters startle in their seats, fingers white with strength crushing the tiny cups in their grips and loosing the coffee to puddle on their clothes. Jacoba's neat purple suit and Smolder's misty cowl were fine as soon as they wished the mess away, but she still decided to let it go. Instead, she took another sip of warm, earthy life that swirled dark brown in her own cup.

Reaping was a new trade for them.

They'd been press-ganged into the job when the old ways died and the ancient gods fell asleep, one by one. But Lozi remembered dancing in the summer fields before, the three sisters symbols of something else. Something less . . . morbid.

"Sissssterr." Smolders hiss brought her back.

She had few words, but Lozi knew what she meant. Better not to dwell on what never could be again. Days in the sun, whiling away in the flowers, wondering if this god or that boy loved her, kissing some maiden by the banks of a sparkling river.

They'd been the Graces then, serving the world portions of frivolity and beauty with each sunrise.

Jacoba sipped her coffee. "Lozi, the world doesn't need the old ways anymore, remember?"

She nodded.

Jacoba cleared her throat and tapped her long nails on the tabletop, bringing their focus back to the now and what they did each morning before they started work. "Smolder, do you wish to unburden yourself?"

Lozi turned to her diaphanous sister, who wavered a moment in her seat. She'd never been one to complain and, even in this harder life, had to be reminded that it was okay to mourn her lot. As she considered, Smolder's eyes formed fully in their sockets, and oily tears ran down her ashen cheeks. Smolder reaped the accidental dead, and there were so many accidents in this modern world. Car crashes, falls from high roofs, trains derailing, tools misfiring. Her sister bore them all. All the greasy, modern pain of the shouldn't-have-dieds, victims of the belching machines they'd made. Smolder took them from their bodies, soaking up the smoke and the heat and carrying it as her burden when she took them away.

Lozi reached out and stroked the soft mist of Smolder's fingers. "Brave Smolder."

Her sister smiled and pulled back all the tendrils whipping around her and took another calming sip of the wished-piping-hot coffee into her formerly broken cup.

"And are you burdened?" Lozi asked Jacoba.

Under her shock of white hair, Jacoba's perfect features set themselves in the pantomime of placid acceptance. She was the oldest, and it took so much more for her to admit how the job wore on her. But Lozi and Smolder were patient. The world could wait, would wait, for them to come to terms with what they did the day before and what still needed doing.

"Sissssteeerrr," Smolder urged with a gentle song.

Jacoba stared into the creamy brown of her coffee, also

restored with a wish. Her job reaping the victims of beauty-seeking seemed a strange, narrow calling at first, though Jacoba found herself always busy.

"They aren't all vain, you know. Some just want to live better lives. They're trapped in extra skin, bulbous breasts that break their backs and stoop them over, old before their time. Even the ones who seek beauty for beauty's sake tell me in their last breath how they'd always hated themselves, believed every bad thing the world told them. How they weren't good enough. I always tell them . . ." She sobs then catches herself. "I tell them how they are beautiful, but they don't believe even in the end. I hope in the next place . . ."

All three sisters hoped that.

Jacoba's few tears cost her too much to cry. Smolder and Lozi didn't comfort her because she hated that. They waited for her composure to return, sipping coffee and enjoying the peace together.

It was Lozi's turn next.

But Lozi stayed quiet behind her soft veil of white. Her sweet princess snowy silk gown settled in pools around her, and pearls of pink hung in bunches around her neck and middle, strands acting like play armor. She didn't want to relive any of it with her sisters. Reaping all the innocents, all the babies who never got to breathe, all the children dead of disease, took a toll. All the suicides, dead without knowing their worth. All the maidens and youths, gone before they'd made their own path in the world. All the simple, special, different souls who died without hurting anyone. She lifted them to her white arms and hugged them as their breaths left. Their deaths maddened her each day. She wept as she walked between each reaping. She screamed at Death for giving her such a hard job, and yet, when she held the innocents, she knew she wouldn't trade it for any other job. She brought them peace in an unfair life. She was theirs alone.

Her sisters stared at her, and urged her to let go of her pain, the burden of the reaping role she'd been given.

But she never did.

She kept their memories, remembering each name, each word they whispered, each murmured cry like seeds of a sweet fruit she'd plant again. Once she'd been like them, dancing in the light of the sun, innocent and free until the world struck her down. Until Death came for her and whispered a promise. Offered this job.

This job or oblivion.

The sisters sat around the tea table and sipped their morning peace. Bitter loss was sweetened by the beauty they brought to death. Lozi was sure that, like her, the sisters felt more beautiful and more necessary than they'd been as girls throwing flowers in the footstep of dewy bright Dawn and shading Love's sweaty brow as she tarried with her lover, War, in the long shadows of dusk. They'd been beautiful fools. Goddesses of nothing.

This job or oblivion, he'd said, giving them the best choice— the only choice they'd known.

With their final sip of coffee, the sisters drew together as they always had, wove their arms around each other, and pressed together their foreheads for strength. Then they stepped out into the world, their daily reaping list wound tight in their hands.

Together, they let the world spin again.

IT RISES FROM BETWEEN MY BONES

SITTING on the toilet for the first sleepy morning pee, I felt my ovaries twist as a little piece of me tried to burst through in a micro-explosion of tissue, born into my desert of a womb.

It made no sense.

I stared at my bald head and face in the mirror that hung across from the toilet. If I weren't the one making my features screw up in twisting confusion, it would have been hilarious. Chemo makes your face strange. No hair. Not one brow or lash. It's like looking at one of those big-eyed aliens that the tabloids are forever finding and autopsying so they can give breathless reports about probes and pregnancies. I looked just like that, only not so green and way more dumbfounded.

How could my ovaries be spitting out an egg? I'd been in a chemically induced menopause since this whole mess started. Since I'd found that little lump in the same place they'd found Mom's so many years ago.

My whirlwind started in the office of the doe-eyed technician running the ultrasound. She'd murmured in positive little half notes until her hand froze. She stopped and pulled the wand out of my armpit, glooped on more warmed gel that honestly felt like it had been harvested from inside a body cavity instead of the little bottle warmer next to her keyboard.

Then she said, "Oh," and typed little rapid-fire notes, pausing only to press the wand into my armpit again and then tut about it quietly. "Let me just step out and get the doctor."

The doctor at the women's health center is usually a woman with a kind smile and a cheery disposition. I'm sure this doctor had a smile like that, only that's not what I saw while I lay there on the table, greased up and naked in my middle-aged, sagging skin suit.

Her smile strained at the corners, like it would crack. "Let's take a look."

She scanned it, and with a thin needle, she punctured my skin to pull out a sample from my armpit and from my right breast. "It's probably nothing," she said with her overly tight smile.

We both knew she was lying.

Two weeks, a positive identification for malignancy, and every kind of test, scan, or examination I could imagine, and I had my diagnosis. Stage IIB breast cancer, just like Mom.

My treatment? Lots of chemo, then radiation, and after . . . well, we didn't really talk about the after.

My cancer's poison? Azithromycin.

The Red Death, they call it.

We pumped it into my port every other Thursday, directly into my bloodstream. No IV line into a vein because if that stuff held up in your arm, it would . . . I don't know. They never told me, but I imagined the stalking villain of Poe's "Masque of the Red Death" swimming through my veins, ripping through my viscera with a flaming sword. They pushed a fat needle through my soft upper breast into the lump of a port lying there like a buried tombstone under my white and blue-veined skin. The flush of saline that washed into my tastebuds was the bitter bite of plague spreading through me, only the poison wasn't meant for me. It was for the true invader growing inside a duct of my breast and bursting through the walls, dotting my lymph nodes with little clones.

When the hair on my head fell out a week after the first treatment, I lost every other hair on my body. My husband Matt laughed. "Now you don't have to worry about shaving your legs or your pits." I laughed, but when I looked in the mirror, I looked into the eyes of a stranger stooped from the weakness that the chemo created. Haunted eyes.

I didn't want to die.

Not then, anyway.

I loved my life teaching high schoolers about ancient civilizations and living with my Matt, my handsome husband and best friend. But the shadows of my mother's and father's deaths had always lain across our happiness, a cloud that blocked our sun.

And now I was living the nightmare.

I was a bald-headed, chemo-brained beast with a puckered set of scars where they'd cut the tissue out of me. Under the scars, bulbous expanders stretched my chest muscles until they ached. Every system of my body, so firmly in my control before the cancer, became another bit of collateral damage sacrificed to my cure.

My skin grew dry and thin as tissue paper. Brown patches appeared on my arms and face like blotchy burns. My doctors shrugged and told me I'd be covering those with foundation for the rest of my days.

My stomach rejected everything I loved and then still managed to either bind up my bowels or turn them into a liquid hot mush that would leave me panting and fevered every time I went to the bathroom.

And the scars. So many scars.

So many little deaths in my body. All things meant to save me.

That's why sitting on the toilet in the morning of my sixth round of chemo, I was stunned to feel my ovaries, dead for months inside my belly, pulse to life with a heartbeat all their own. I hissed as the pain throbbed outward, clenching and shooting until I shuddered. The other foot soldier symptoms Major-General Cancer visited on my body hadn't wrenched such pain from me.

I felt it push its way forward in my left side, a tiny swimming stone. Then the rip that curled me into a pink ball on the toilet, clutching myself together like it might blow me apart. It was everything I'd felt every twenty-eight days since I'd gotten my first visit from "monthly Martha" at age 11. All that, as they say, and a bag of chips. The normal burst of pain I'd felt every month, but like my ovary knew it would never get another chance. Like it had a show to put on.

Too much pain to scream. Besides, I didn't want my sweet husband to have another ugly image in his mind to go along with the memories of drains weaving like pale vines in and out of puckered, pus-filled holes in my skin or the fatty, ripped incision he'd taped together to get me to the urgent care. Around the pain, I knew this was something I had to bear alone.

Most women do.

It took ten minutes to tear out of its pod. By the time I could stand, sweat poured from my body, and I shivered inside my tightening skin. I turned the shower on as hot as I could take and stood with my head down and arms braced as the little ball bounced around in my uterus looking for purchase.

I expected it to be born that minute in a gush of red blood that would circle the drain and be done.

But no.

It settled in. Burrowed.

All day, I felt its roots clutching at me.

Making coffee, a cramp twisted through my pelvis. I winced as it cut into the soft bed of skin that hadn't had a blood lining in months.

"What's wrong, honey?" Matt asked around his Grape Nuts.

He's fast. Always has been. When I looked at him and

sucked up a hard breath, he was out of the chair. My eyes went back into my head, and that's when he caught me.

It took a good bit of time for me to come back to myself.

He said he'd put me on the couch and that I'd moaned and cried in my sleep.

When I woke up, the sky was blue, and my pain was gone. I pressed against the soft swell of my belly, and there was no tenderness. No shooting, stabbing pain. I thought maybe it was just another one of those personal hells that came with fighting against a tumor. Another indignity that the doctor would note in the computer for posterity, nodding and mumbling some shit about how each thing was to be expected.

Who wrote their scripts?

I didn't have words for the other bald skeletons that wandered through the waiting room of the cancer center. We were all hollowed out skin stretched over bones by the treatment that killed the vile little bits of us that were out of control. The fast growers die first. The hairs, then the nails, and then the tumors. Sometimes the tooth enamel. Sometimes other things I didn't know I could lose.

One time, I spit out something so thick with blood, it was black. A lump of ooze against the white of the sink that wouldn't wash down. I braced myself with one arm, knowing that some things made me stumble. I reached a trembling finger down and touched it as my stomach roiled in the middle of me. In my head, I heard something keening so sad, so wetly. I pushed my fingers into the clot, and it mashed like a grape.

It had been inside me minutes before, and now I smeared it against the petri dish of my sink bowl, looking at the pieces. A red circle striated with a sickly dark yellow. A black coned chunk. A flattened orb with oozing tendrils trailing from it like roots.

An eye.

The thing twitched. Contracted as I leaned in and poked it once more.

Matt knocked on the door as I threw up all over the sink, the mirror, myself. He helped me back into the shower, eyes averted as I tried to cover my scars with my hands. He has the patience of a saint.

After the morning's dose of chemo, he brought me home and wrapped me gently in a blanket on the couch. Sometimes I watched him out of the corner of my eye. How could he love me with these things growing inside me? He hadn't married those out-of-control cells trying to take me over. Did he see the fight as a noble struggle? Did the idea of my own cells trying to kill me repulse him? Keep him up at night?

It did me.

I dozed there under the blanket with the local news playing the background soundtrack to my personal hell. The silver-haired anchor reported the surge in rare and virulent cancers around old war factories, the places where early caches of uranium and plutonium disappeared after WWII. Buried, he said, in fields where kids played ball, next to creeks like the one where my cousins and I picked crawdads from under rocks to boil and eat for lunch.

That they glowed didn't matter to me and my cousins.

Their mother died of breast cancer, too, only thirty-four years old. Only two years younger than me.

That night, after Matt tried to get me to eat some mashed potatoes that I threw up immediately, he helped me up the stairs. He'd put me in bed and propped me up on pillows, and he'd made love to me with such a sweet slowness.

I don't know how he could touch me as I was.

After he fell into a humming snore, the warm buzz of his attentions melted into a tightness. An awareness. My skin didn't fit around my bones, and those bones seemed to dislike being inside me anymore. I felt like I'd turn inside out with the heat that rose from my middle. Not a good heat. Not lusty satisfaction. No. It was a fire that burned away at me. Crisped me.

And inside, I felt the hard pieces that moved like pebbles in my veins.

Sleep, voices inside told me. Sleep is healing. Sleep is the only way to be strong enough.

But sleep gave the pieces of me that revolted inside my body the peace they needed to wrap themselves around my organs. Little boa constrictors crushing my lungs with rippling muscular hugs. Squeezing my heart. I felt them moving through the secret passages inside me. Growing. Pushing.

I put my hand on the softness of my belly, the sag of my age that bubbled there. The pads of my fingers rested on the smoothness of my skin, and I tapped my fingers in a rolling rhythm, the memory of a song that we'd sung when I was a kid playing with my cousins in the rippling lake our grandmother took us to every week.

The muddy water and the creaking gray dock all seemed so fantastic, so not of this world. They'd dared me to swim under the dock and weave my way through the crossbeam gaps between the joists. I ducked in, so brave, and then the echoing drips and the bulging gray insulation that stuck out in lumps floating along the edges of the joists sent me back under the water to escape. But under the water's surface, down became up, and I kept reemerging in the closed universe under the dock. I wept in there. Screamed for my cousins to come and get me. They watched me through the cracks and dropped little rocks down on me. The slick wood I clung to had green hairs of seaweed coating it like the fur of an animal, and the waves lifted and lowered the dock in respiration. I don't remember Grandma jerking me out from under the dock, but she carried me up onto the grass, weeping.

My cousins said that I'd disappeared so they wouldn't get a spanking. That they couldn't see me. Grandma tanned their asses good for lying.

But I knew it was true. I had disappeared.

It was another world, and I'd slipped into it sideways.

What was happening inside of me now felt just like that.

My leg muscles refused to settle, and my toes weren't connected to my feet. Neuropathy. The death of my nerves made no sense. I couldn't feel my toes, but the flickering pains that shot up my calves were real enough. Beneath my fingers, my belly moved in a rolling wave, first right and then left. Something under my skin rose, pushing against my fingertips. A caress with skin keeping us apart.

The first time I'd felt the rising lumps under my skin, I'd wondered if the cancer was blooming like flowers inside me, lumping up and following the heat of my fingers. I'd gone into the bathroom to try and see it in the light, maybe squeeze it like a pimple or lance it. When it screamed, I blacked out and hit my head on the toilet. A trip to the emergency room, and Matt was telling the doctor that I'd been rambling about things inside my skin.

"Chemo does strange things to the mind. Just keep her still and hydrated, ice on the bump. She's got a concussion, but it's a mild one. Call the oncologist in the morning." And the ER doc sent us home.

I didn't try to lance lumps anymore. There were too many of them anyway. I did wonder if they'd all come from my ovaries, birthed when I'd been sleeping, or in the cloud of codeine the doc gave me after the double mastectomy. Little baby tumors making their way to soft secret places between my cells.

Between my bones.

Matt asked me how I'd slept each morning and if I needed anything every night.

I'd learned to say no.

The time between the courses of chemo blurred into moments of bloody gums and constipation, vomit and diarrhea, and of course the traveling lumps that grew and receded by the hour. The doctors changed the chemical poison to Taxol, and my legs became so weak I sometimes had to crawl on all fours to the bathroom. I didn't even try to sleep with Matt upstairs since each stair rise was a mountain I couldn't climb, and my legs gyrated restlessly all night long.

They didn't belong to me anymore.

At night, the darkness changes the world you've built so carefully. Every curated item in your home sharpens, echoes inside itself. I watched my warm home, bright walls, happy art, cherished books, and overstuffed couches change into monster movie reproductions splashed in deep and swimming shadow. The difference bloomed in the night until I wasn't in my lovely house anymore. And the things inside me grew bigger then, feeding my fear or feeding *on* it. It felt like they stretched me from inside out, creating empty spaces.

I split in two.

There was the rational dweller of the real world who'd fight cancer like a badass, survive to wear ridiculous pink outfits and walk in survivor parades for the rest of her life. Then there was the night-dwelling traveler, the cocoon for whatever was growing inside. The little girl who'd slid sideways into a world she didn't understand.

We went to the oncologist the next day.

"The tumors are . . . spreading" The oncologist took a deep breath and then rushed on into his bad news script. "Multiple sites, including your brain. Your bones."

Matt squeezed my hand and sobbed, leaning in to catch the doctor's words. Searching for hope.

"Four lesions and one deep tumor in the mid-brain . . ."

He pointed to cloudy shadows on the gray film.

"And the lungs . . ."

Big, blooming tumors clustered in the bottom of the lobes.

"And the stomach. . ."

And that's when I let myself slide.

Turns out that when you grow darkness inside you, you are the doorway.

I pressed the fingers of my free hand against my middle, feeling the movements within, and curled up around myself.

Matt squeezed my hand again, but he'd given himself over to understanding the doctor's prognosis. I hated to leave him alone there, but I didn't think I could manage one more second of the rational cancer warrior losing the fight for her life. The lying side I faced out to the world collapsed when I saw those clusters and shadows inside me.

I slid down into myself, feeling the alienness of what lived there in the spaces between my insides. The echoes in between the rafters of bones and the shimmering lake of fluid. Waving cilia like fur coated the pathways. And hanging from every edge, every crossroad inside me, were the bulging gray growths. Tumors, they'd called them. But here they had tendrils that whipped and throbbed, wrapping around my honeycombing bones, growing like a poisonous vine into the flesh of my organs.

My body their birthing chamber.

I didn't scream. Not anymore.

Looking at the horror in my flesh felt like facing my own truth. Like it was what I should have done all along.

I reached out with my limb. Not a hand, exactly. A phantom of a hand-like appendage wavered like a misty and unformed idea. But when that hand stroked the gray flesh of one of the invaders, I felt it with more surety than the neuropathy-dulled flesh of my real body could feel. My imagined world's fingertips had healthy nerves and receptors not damaged by poison.

The flesh, slick under my fingers, warmed to my touch and hummed under the pressure of it. From the center of the lumpy, gelatinous body, an eye as red as an angry wound and shot with bright yellow highlights opened with a slow flowing retreat of the thing's flesh. I'd woken it up. All around me, I felt the weight of eyes turning. All the invaders fixed me with their united gazes, though some were as far away from me as the earth from the moon. They were many, and they were one.

They were in me.

My bones grew them. My cells became them. My blood fed them.

They were me.

Inside my mind, or the consciousness that held me in this place, a buzzing vibrated from inside to out. A voice of wings made of hairs and shells and bitter taste. A voice that bubbled through that red-eyed gaze. These things in me, my disease or my monsters—I don't really know—they did know things. They were the crack in the door I needed to understand.

The threshold.

I was the door that had to open.

The nearest one grabbed for me, desperation rippling around it in a pheromonal stink. Its tendril reached, lance-like, and tipped with a tooth. It wanted me, but—

"Are you okay?" Matt pulled me to him, yanking me free. He pressed me against his skin, and I burrowed my face into the space between his jacket and his tee-shirt, sobbing. Keening with a darkness that poured from inside out.

My voice and their voices screamed in concert.

Matt must have thought I was mourning my diagnosis—terminal and only weeks to live. He clutched me to him so hard I heard his heartbeat. I heard the blood swishing in its chambers.

There were no echoes inside of him.

The doctor gave me a prescription for sleeping pills and a sad smile and sent us home with brochures about home health aides and hospice care. Matt cried without sound, gripping the steering wheel and glancing at me. For the first time, his eyes filled with the future. The real future where he'd be alone and have to make all those decisions that I usually made for the both of us. Where he'd bring up the laundry and I wouldn't be there to fold it. Where he'd cook dinner and do the dishes too. The partnership had already stopped with my illness, but now he knew that I was just an incubator for the death that grew day by day and that he'd be left alone.

That was the rational world.

I talked as he drove, because I knew he'd only sort of hear

what I needed to tell him. That he'd let it go, because too much reality filled his mind.

"I'm not really dying, Matt. I'm growing little monsters."

"Tumors," Matt said. He was used to my flights of fancy. It's how I talked. How I thought.

"Not tumors. They are little monsters that I made. I didn't mean to. I . . . I know you can't understand this, but I ate poison when I was little. Swam in dioxin and radiated creeks. My dad brought home flakes of asbestos and served it up like salt on dinner when he'd shake it free from his coat."

He'd slowed the car because the rush-hour traffic piled up on the highway in front of him. He glanced over at me with disquiet in his puffy red eyes.

"This is the breast cancer. You heard, Doctor—"

"Listen to me. I'm the doorway. I know it now. Cancer is just the cutting tool. The thing that makes the door come open."

He reached for me, probably readying a beautiful lie about fighting the inevitable. About how strong I was.

"Don't." I jerked back, banging my head into the window with a clunk. I didn't even feel it. "Look."

I held up my hands in the long space growing between us. Pink and fleshy, my hands hung there in the slanting light, but a gray corona of shadow that shouldn't exist in the bright afternoon shimmered around them.

"I touched one of them. It told me how long they've tried to open a door. How hard they've worked to change us. To change the whole world." I quieted then, giving my strength over to holding myself here. My eyes fluttered shut, and I didn't respond when he called my name.

Inside, the pieces of me that grew in the soup of poisons sang me into a stupor.

They promised me so many things.

That night, Matt gave me my pain pill and my sleeping pill and left the bottles out on the table. Maybe he thought it was a kindness to leave my life in my hands.

We'd talked about it when my father had died, cancer in his colon, his lungs, and his brain. There had been black vomit and diapers and my poor dad's sad expression. He'd hated that we even had to take care of him. He said sorry when he soiled himself. Then my mother had lain in a nightmare she couldn't wake from for twenty days. She moaned and tried to shift, but she was so weak then. In so much pain. I'd told Matt that I would want to kill myself if it got that bad.

And here I was, just as bad as them, and Matt had left the option on the table.

Only, the cancer wasn't just a ball of fast-growing cells.

Someday, scientists might recognize that they'd been like medieval medicine men with their bleeding and leeching. That they hadn't recognized a bigger truth. A cosmic truth.

That the disease was first contact.

The next day, we went to the hospice office and then to the lawyer to sign my final wishes into reality. I held it together until the lawyer started talking about me in the past tense. I'm sure I only imagined it, but I started weeping, and Matt hustled me to the car.

In my ears, a choir of monsters sang.

"Why me?" I whispered to the creatures inside. The me that was part of this place and part of the other spoke back in the buzzing that sounded like insect armor rubbing on itself.

"You are the first to peek through the keyhole," they said and didn't say at the same time. "The first to synthesize poison without destroying your growths."

Growths, I heard, but it wasn't quite the right translation.

The idea behind the word was one I didn't have words for. The idea flashed around in my head, and I saw the creatures again, but behind them, through them and me and the toxic blood that held us together, I saw another world blooming right inside of my body. The things beyond that rectangle of space flowed through an orange burning sky, shaded by the brightness behind them. But the outlines made no sense in my mind.

Massive limbs that didn't flap or walk or touch any surface. Flagella so long and tangled there wasn't any way to see their beginnings and ends at the same time. The expanse captured there was like a mirror you might look through sideways and see on into everything that wasn't in front of it. A trick of optics, the scientists might say, but what did they know?

Someday, they might recognize. . .only they wouldn't. They wouldn't because—

"Sweetie?" Matt shook me. We were home, car ticking away its heat and bright cement of the driveway solid under us. "You weren't . . . there for a minute."

He stared, blue eyes wider than they should ever be. So much wonder, but not the kind you wanted. He wondered that the world you know could go sideways so fast. The wonder that exists beyond fear lay in his gaze. "I swear . . ."

"I'm here. Just a trick of the light, I guess. Optics, maybe?" I croaked, throat dry from the choking vision and the clawing silence I'd climbed out of.

"Right," he said. He hurried around the car and helped me out, waving off the kind offers of our neighbors for food or cleaning, or even to give him a break to take a walk or a shower. Nice folks.

It really was a shame.

He got me set back up in my recliner, blanket cuddled around me. "There. A toasty burrito."

A sweet old joke. A groove in the well-worn record of our life.

I smiled with my lips closed because I worried that the orange light peeking around the edges of the doorway inside of me might shine out through the spaces in my teeth, lighting them like bright, squared candy corns.

I shouldn't have worried about it. He didn't want to be near me anymore and was starting to turn away.

I wasn't mad about it. He'd seen the shadow of what I was in the other place. I'd phased out and in right in front of him.

"I'll get dinner," he said.

I reached out so quickly you'd never have known I was dying. I caught his wrist in the cage of my fingers and pulled him so close I thought he might be able to smell the pheromones my monsters pumped into my bloodstream to challenge the others to come through.

It was the final call.

"Stay." I clung to him.

I've always loved him. Since high school, through mullets and poverty and disappointment and joy, we'd been inseparable. The perfect team. He might not be a part of this terrible thing with me, but I wanted to look into his eyes until I couldn't anymore.

I held his hand and felt him shudder, but he was the best man I'd ever known, and I knew he'd stay because I wanted it.

"They changed us," I whispered, not clear if I had enough breath in the sound for him to hear. "They directed us to change. The pills and the pollution and the chemicals all came from their projections. I'm a projection now, Matt. Maybe since I swam in the lake as a kid. Maybe since the creek and the crawdads. Maybe they made me that way in my mom's cancerous uterus."

I coughed a wrenching, wet cough that sprayed the changed blood all over my hands. I wiped the glowing orange stuff on the blanket over my legs, and he watched with a gaping mouth and wet eyes. He didn't move, though. He must've thought I was dying.

Not quite.

"I'm the first, but there are more coming. I'm sorry, my love."

He shook his head and ran his hand through my hair. Our tears flooded our eyes as my doorway opened. Tears that boiled off his blistering cheeks. His hair crisped and curled as it burned. I wanted to stop, but I am what they made me.

The fire bloomed outward from my body; each of the little

spots the doctor called malignancies collapsed into voids and spaces. The me that was left inside swung open as wide as my body and the whole sky. The others pressed and struggled to get through that space. It didn't hurt. I was beyond the physical pain of stretching like a cosmic cervix giving birth to galaxies.

My poor Matt didn't know I watched his eyes until they dried up into glass. I held his skull until it turned to ash. I pressed the ash to my open frame, painting my lintel with the soft gray bits until they, too, burned away.

Inside out or sideways, I'm the door.

I'm the first one, but there are more coming.

ACKNOWLEDGMENTS

There are so many people who help me write, publish, and keep trying to author like a pro and I can't possibly ever name them all. Thank you, every dang person who has ever been kind enough to read, compliment, lift, help, or just pat this author on her head.

Specifically for this work: Thanks to every editor who first found these stories to be strong enough to live in their printed/digital works of art. Editors are the mid-wives of any literature we love. Steven Saus and Anton Cancre, great writers and friends who once got me out of the worst writing slump I've ever suffered through. I will never be able to thank you enough.

This book is for and about women, so I want to focus on the women in horror that I particularly love and think you should read more of. This list isn't exhaustive, and you should seek out our strange vein of art.

Lucy Snyder, Sara Tantlinger, Gwendolyn Kiste, Lee Murray, Linda Addison, Cindy O'Quinn, Geneve Flynn, Victoria Nations, Roni Stinger, Elsa Carruthers, Suzy Lockhart, Carina Bissett, Mercedes M. Yardley, Nicole Wilson, Marge Simon, Stephanie M. Wytovich, Lauren Elsie Daniels, Virgina Nelson, E.F. Schraeder, Rebecca Cuthbert, Carol Gyzander, L. Marie Wood, Lisa Morton, E.V. Knight, Rena Mason, KC Grifant... the list goes on!

My own personal writing goddesses include Jennifer Della Zanna, editor supreme, Amanda Worthington, my flash fiction partner, KC Grifant, inspiration and kind reader, and my SHU lady monsters: Deanna Sjolander, Sally Bosco, Christe Cabrillo, and Natalie Wolfe (love you guys with all my heart).

Finally, to all the bad-ass women in my life: Sheila Schaefer, Rio Corbin, Bonnie Schaefer, Becky Wagenblast, Karen Munro, Jan Munro, Erica Smith, Cara Munro, Ruby Munro, Nola Munro, Evie Munro, Margo Schaefer, Linda Meyers, Karen Kneezle, Carla Kneezle, Cheryl Steiner, Wendy Meyers, Carrie Stevenson, Katie Goodson, Alexis Black, Corrie Bednar, Nancy Cavazos, Dr. Kalenevitch, Dr. Dempsey, Kelly Tsai, Risa Schoene, Rebbeca Colley, Sandra Loraine Schaefer, Mrs. Bruce, and all the wonderful women I didn't name who believed I could be more. This book is for you.

ABOUT THE AUTHOR

Donna J. W. Munro teaches high schoolers the slippery truths of government and history at her day job. Her students are her greatest inspiration. She lives with five cats, a cute, curly-haired dog, a fur-covered husband, a sassy septuagenarian mama, and an encyclopedia son. Her daughter is off saving the world.

Donna's pieces are published in *Corvid Queen, Enter the Apocalypse, It Calls from the Forest, Apparition Lit, Pseudopod 752, Shakespeare Unleashed, Novus Monstrum, ParABnormal,* and many more. Check out her Poppet Cycle series:

Revelation
Runaway
Revolution

Her website has a complete list of works at https://www. donnajwmunro.net/. Follow her on socials at https://tr.ee/ mz73vH.

ABOUT THE ARTIST

It was a time when Gigantor Robots and Apollo Moon Rockets were the toys to have. Kids impatiently waited all week long for Sunday night and the Walt Disney Show, while during the holidays, it just wasn't Christmas until the Grinch Stole it. Tara Tokarski grew up in the small town of Harrisburg, Illinois, near the Mississippi River, which was an ideal setting for a lifelong adventure inspired by the tales of Tom Sawyer and Huckleberry Finn, who felt very much alive in that area. Storytelling through images suited her perfectly, as she was a nature enthusiast with a love for folk tales and ghost stories.

Tara Tokarski is an illustrator and college professor. She earned a Master's in Illustration from the Savannah College of Art and Design. She has worked with Disney World, Edge Factory, a multimedia production company, many individual clients, and the FAA. Tokarski teaches design at multiple colleges and has illustrated books for herself and several other authors, including *Once Upon a Halloween Night, Comes a Magic Cookbook Full of Old-Fashioned Delights*. This fully illustrated book caught Martha Stewart's attention and earned Tokarski a spot on Martha's list of favorite things.

Website:https://taratokarskiillustrations.
fineartstudioonline.com/

ALSO BY DONNA J. W. MUNRO

In a dark future, people with money live in doomed cities and use the recently deceased as repurposed servants and workers called poppets. Ellie DesLoge is the teen heiress of the company that makes and distributes poppets–your basic reprogrammed flesh robot complete with training chips and kill switches. If Ellie does everything her Aunt Cordelia says, she'll have a life of wealth and power. If she chooses to be what is planned for her, life will be perfect. Everything she ever dreamed. But something about her sweet poppet Thom goes against what Aunt Cordelia and tradition have taught her. Will she choose to believe what everyone knows is true or will she follow what her heart tells her about Thom? Her choice will change the world.

Ellie and Thom escape up the Mizzourah River alone through Grave Hawker controlled Wilds to try to reach safety in the Kansas territory. Along the way, her former "bestie" Sasha and Simon "Red Boots" Eregel, the Grand Wizard of the Grave Hawkers hunt her. The Academy didn't prepare Ellie for life running up river. Good thing Thom is way more than the meat machine butler they told her he was.

At the same time, Moze makes it to Liberty-Lawrence with important intel. He joins the revolution against DesLoge Com and USNOAM's poppet-based economy. He agrees with the Free Kaw Army that Poppet trade must end even if they have to fight a war, but he wonders if they aren't just as bad as the Grave Hawkers when he sees how poppets are treated.

Ellie and Moze hope to find each other again. They want to save the world from poppetry. Too bad three hundred miles and an army of violent Hawkers stand between them and their goals.

The battle for the soul of USNOAM should be all that Ellie cares about, but hours of training and drilling can't get the awful memory of Moze dying out of her head. "Death isn't the end," Thom told her. He was right. Sasha Parker, now heir of DesLoge Com., had raised Moze up to be her own personal poppet.

Ellie, Thom, and Moze will struggle to end the cruel institution of Poppetry all while fighting their way back to each other: to family, safety, and love deeper than life or death.

Can they remake the world?

DRAGON'S ROOST PRESS

Dragon's Roost Press is the fever dream brainchild of dark speculative fiction author Michael Cieslak. Since 2014, their goal has been to find the best speculative fiction authors and share their work with the public. For more information about Dragon's Roost Press and their publications, please visit:

http://www.thedragonsroost.biz

www.ingramcontent.com/pod-product-compliance
Lightning Source LLC
Chambersburg PA
CBHW060859250626
47159CB00008B/2807